Ewing reached into his coat, produced a wallet and slipped a check out, handing it to Athearn, who examined it as the rancher spoke.

"You take that. It's more'n enough to give you a good fresh start somewhere else. Git someplace where you got a chance."

Frank shrugged. "You want me off the land, you better gun me right now, 'cause you won't get no better chance." He smiled, then moved the check to his lips, and gripping part of it with his teeth, tore the check in half with a swift jerk of his hand.

"Son, if I had wanted you dead, we wouldn't be having this conversation. Ella had no right to sell you that land. Won't bring you nothin' but grief in the long run. A man who has served his country deserves better." Ewing turned and started off, then looked back to Frank. "Seems I might be able to trust my back to you, Athearn."

"I was wonderin' exactly the same," said Frank quietly.

COMES
A
HORSEMAN

DENNIS LYNTON CLARK

A DELL BOOK

Published by
Dell Publishing Co., Inc.
1 Dag Hammarskjold Plaza
New York, New York 10017

Dell ® TM 681510, Dell Publishing Co., Inc.

ISBN: 0-440-11509-4

Printed in the United States of America
First printing—October 1978
Second printing—December 1978

COMES
A
HORSEMAN

I

NEW SEASON

There was no light, and the only sounds the cowboy could hear were the occasional grunts of coyotes nosing around the buildings, and once in a while the yip of a fox as she snared her prey, more than likely some rodent or other. Earlier, the horses had been restless, but he assumed that was because it was spring. He'd known it three days earlier when the light changed and the gramma appeared which had died back in the fall; it had spent its energy throughout the winter growing a tangle of roots that would disappear quickly when the cattle would tear at the grass with the fine blue tips.

He'd always liked the spring although he couldn't remember all of the reasons. The only ones that lingered were the ones fostered by the imagination of youth.

The cowboy had reached an age where most men have forgotten their youth, but he could remember things that others would never retrieve. He had total recall, or at least enough that would make most men happy, and comfortable. But in the case of Dodger, for that was the cowboy's name, the things he recalled brought him moments of great pain along with the pleasure. He'd always felt that you didn't have to practice to make yourself miserable, so he tried to confine his thinking to the things that pleasured him. It was hard, and it took great effort at first, but he'd finally mastered it, so it was rarely that his remembrances disturbed him.

Spring pleasured him greatly for it was a time when the cowboy could cast off the idleness that winters produced, when he could do the things he knew best: working horses and cattle, free and unhampered by anything as foolish as four walls.

He'd been glad for those walls this winter, however, for he could feel every ache and each pain that accompanied moving in the morning. One finger, the fourth on the left hand, had been lost in a roping incident, and though it was two years past, he still missed the digit. When the cold penetrated to him, he thought the missing digit hurt like hell. His ribs were no longer as resilient as they had been, and his first deep breaths made the cartilage tear, or so it felt. Arms and legs were clusters of pain at the joints, and his muscles seemed to ache eternally. Ah well, he thought, if that's the price, so be it. You make one more day still on your feet, and it's one more day you got to your credit.

He looked up at the ceiling. He couldn't see it for the dark, but he knew every fiber of wood, every nail, and the scratches of all the cowboys who'd ever left their marks on the small shed. That ceiling had had to be repaired only once in all the years he'd lived there. Now that Tom Connors, he thought, was one helluva carpenter. Dodger had known many other dwellings in his life, but this one that Tom had repaired and loved was Dodger's favorite spot as well, and while he hated being indoors more than anything else, he was proud of the building and the man who had lavished such care on it because it had meant something to him.

It gave him a moment's pause to think that he used to be one of several cowboys that worked for Tom Connors. But those days were gone forever. Dodger was the only cowboy who would or could work the Connors Ranch, and so, when all had seemed hopeless and wiser men, or so they thought, moved on, Dodger stayed. He felt like a faithful old dog at times, and while he did not enjoy the feeling, he understood it, and knew that at his age he couldn't expect much more.

"Damn." He jolted himself off the bed, slipped into his levis, worn boots and old shirt. Than he lit his lamp, buckled on his spurs, which he removed nightly unlike other cowboys who were less particular about their gear, and grabbed his hat. As his body came to life, he left his home to shoulder out into the predawn wind that came out of the south for a change, shoving the clouds north to Canada. His long strides carried him to the small narrow barn that once housed a fine Sears buggy, but was now empty.

There was a qualification to "empty." The bitch, Patches, had chosen that barn to give birth to her fourth litter of homely pups, and it had fallen to Dodger to see that Patches' needs were met, simple as they were. Every morning he paid the bitch a visit with ground beef that was precious, but needed by the small brindled pups that were only days old and perhaps doomed by their appearance. Not that the pups would suffer on this place, for food would always be found for them, even if human mouths and stomachs did with less.

Dodger swung the door to the barn wide, and fumbled for the old icebox that held the ground beef, and found his treat for the bitch and pups. They knew the sounds, knew the scent of the cowboy at once, and began a hungry merking that continued until Patches had eaten and then, properly, allowed her children to take their turn at her exposed nipples.

The cowboy lit a candle for a moment, watched her gobble the meat down, then flop on her side and scoop the pups to her hairless belly. He smiled, blew out the candle, but before leaving, stuck his finger into the water dish, noted there was ample for the dog and stepped out into the dark morning.

He sniffed the soft wind that barely moved the grass, gazing off to the southwest where the faintest hint of light was showing through the narrow pass that marked the entrance into the Bear Paw Basin. His steps carried him to the larger barn opposite the two-story house that was dark, though it should have been lit up awhile ago, then beyond the barn to the horse corral, where he checked the animals in the gloom that comes before morning and found that they were fine.

A noise prompted Dodger to shift his gaze back to the house and he saw a light at the window, its warm and cheerful glow adding to Dodger's morning.

" 'Bout time," he said aloud and started his walk around the house to make sure that in the night the old windmill hadn't ceased its function, thereby causing alarm if the water in the house were turned on. When he could see and hear the windmill, he snorted and turned aside, mentally cursing the machinery that plagued him in all kinds of weather, driving him to great lengths, daring him to repair it. He could never find the parts he needed and rather than order them, resorted to jury rig, so that anyone familiar with conventional mills attempting to repair the hodgepodge of wires, shoelaces and leather from worn pieces of harnessing (he'd once used his belt to replace a fabric belt that had broken and it was still in service though he'd sworn to replace it many times and hadn't) would dissolve in a case of nerves.

Everything about the mill was wrong. The platform was too small and too far from the ground. The tower had been larger than standard because the blades of the mill at its normal height couldn't catch the high currents that came from the northwest. The thing leaned as though it would crash into the circular metal trough that caught the overflow and no one but Dodger had the nerve to repair the damned thing.

Well, he wouldn't today. Or so he hoped. He was damned if he knew anymore what each day would bring, so irregular had things been. There had been a time when he could plan out his days and he tried to remember just when it was. Then he recalled it was when he was only six, and thought, "Only a seventy-six-year-old man would be so damned foolish." He did not cherish thinking that he may have been better off seventy years before. A man likes to think he's grown.

There was no way for her to be sure if she had been awake the entire night, but she assumed she had for when she decided to rise, she was still exhausted, still unrecovered from the previous day's work. Her temper was already short, laced with impatience, and by God, she wasn't out of bed yet.

It had been getting lighter steadily. The night birds had given way to the thrushes and larks of dawn, accompanied by the sounds of the old man, Dodger, as he rose, left his shed and saw to the horses and dogs with routine authority. It was as if the old man's dignity were needed for the transformation. When she'd been a small child, she had thought there was some connection, and since nothing much had changed over the years, she somehow still felt it was true even though she was thirty years past the age of such beliefs.

It had been sixteen years since her father had died, and every morning of every day of those years she had awakened to the sounds of Dodger rising, listening to him age little by little, knowing the same thing was attacking her own body and mind. But she was damned if there was anything she could do about it, so she plodded ahead, ignoring time, and in her own eyes not changing a single bit. Oh, she grew harder, better at her work, but she felt that in her heart she was still a girl, still capable of dreaming.

She just never found the time to dream anymore.

The small clock on the dresser was barely visible, but 3:33 could be read clearly, and Dodger's sounds as he made his way to the barn were a sure sign the day had begun, so she swung from the bed and walked to the nearest lamp and lit it.

It was still early enough in the spring for her to see breath form on the glass of the chimney, but the quick heat dissipated it and Ella Connors held her hands around the glass as she always did, partly for reassurance, partly because it had become a habit of rising. All of her moves until she reached the shower were ritual, but this morning she paused before the commode mirror as she dropped the nightgown and examined herself, summing it up quickly with one phrase.

"Not bad."

A thin band of gold showed to the south and west singing out the promise of a fine day as Ella stepped from the kitchen onto the back porch only to find Dodger heading for the house wiping his hands on his chaps.

At seventy-six he was in better shape than men half his age, could ride better than most, still rope, though he was slow on the drop down and sometimes the cows or calves got up and away before he could get to them, but he had his humor and his hair and he was the best damned cowman she knew, not to mention her best friend in the world and a constant reminder that this life was about something after all.

When the old man spoke, he was pure Montana, probably from up near the Blackfoot Country originally, but he never spoke much about the time before he came to work for Ella's father, Tom Connors, fifty years before. Ella had been raised in a time when it was still considered rude to inquire if you were under twelve, and a damned sight dangerous if you were over that tender age and asking about a man's past. In either case, she never asked and he never said and that was all there was to it. Once—she was ten at the time—she heard her father and Dodger talking about a war someplace south in Wyoming, but it didn't mean anything to her at the time, and when she wondered about it now, which was seldom, she assumed they'd been talking about the Johnson County War. If she'd asked, he would probably have told her, but it was no business of hers and she liked the way things were between them just fine.

"You want me to fix us somethin' to eat, or you fixin' to starve us up to plantin' time?" he quipped.

"You eat like a damned horse, Dodger. Costin' me a fortune."

"Guess you make it up in what you don't pay me."

He hadn't drawn more than a small percentage off the few pitiful head they'd sold in the last few years, but the line wasn't delivered to make her guilty, nor did it. They both knew he was free to leave whenever he wanted. She owed him much, but they didn't place much value on that when thinking of their friendship. She was damned if she could figure out any reasons for him to stay with her as he did.

"That's 'cause we live the free and easy life, old man." As she said it, she noticed he was staring down basin toward the mouth where the mountains funneled down to let the river out, and now, as she could see, strangers in.

"Maybe free," he said slowly, "but workin' with you, Babysister, ain't never been easy." His eyes remained fixed on the rising cloud of dust that rose on the dawn wind and cut the rising sun, giving a rosy glow to the morning. Dodger looked at Ella, and saw a youngish woman still. And though toughened by years of impossible work, she could still confound him by dropping from her horse to worry over some sick wild thing. Most people took death for granted when they saw much of it, and working the range you saw plenty. But Ella cherished living so much, she wouldn't let a thing die unless absolutely positive there was nothing she could do. And that was only one thing that amazed the old man, who'd known quite a few women in his day and still had the desire and ability to love them well when he wasn't totally exhausted. She never missed a trick, seemed never to sleep, and was better with a horse, rope or just about anything else than most men he'd known. He knew he didn't have to discuss the dust cloud that could only be horses or cattle moving into the basin.

She hadn't been sleeping well recently. He'd heard her late at night, seen the lights on till dawn often enough, and furthermore, it was showing on her face. She was tanned from trying desperately to keep snow-bound cattle alive all winter, but it was like a patina to gloss the wear and tear and worry. It certainly didn't sit well with Dodger.

He wondered how much the worry dealt with the funeral today and the old passions and hatreds that would be shared once again. A swift glance at the concern on her face, and her next words told him it was more than it should have been.

"You suspect that Ewing's started his drive already, Dodger?" She said it flatly, as if already sure of an answer that would confirm her fears.

"Not unless he's buyin' new stock, and he's rich enough he ain't gonna make 'em walk none. You know J.W. well enough by now, Babysister."

When she made no response to him, he tried to put her mind to other things.

"Thought about makin' a run up to the meadows after the funeral to bring down the brood mares. Ought to be foaling any day now. You want to come along?"

She shook her head, swinging her gaze back to Dodger, watching him for a moment, then asking, "You think it was tough for Mark Ewing?"

Dodger thought, shrugged, and for a moment she thought he had no more to say on the matter, but he squinted off at the approaching dust cloud, spit once and nodded.

"More'n likely less he bought it quick. More's to the point in how tough it must be goin' for J.W." He noted a slight tenseness that sort of eased across her at the mere mention of the name. God knew what she'd be like at the funeral. In one way the old man was glad he was going along, but he knew how unpredictable she could be, and that gave him cause to question accompanying her.

"He still exists, Babysister, and not speakin' on him from time to time ain't gonna make him go away."

She almost smiled, but she just went through the motions and turned back toward the kitchen door.

"I'll see what I can scrape together for grub. You want to wash up, you can use the kitchen sink." She spoke the words quickly and with some embarrassment as she entered the kitchen, leaving Dodger to shed his chaps and drape them over the porch rail. He stared absently at the dust cloud, then turned and followed Ella into the kitchen.

Perhaps it was because they'd reached their goal in the middle of the night and camped near the main road into the basin that made them approach their start that morning with a great deal of leisure, but it seemed by the movements and obvious high spirits of the two young cowboys to be much more. They were making a ritual out of rising, eating and starting the cattle, as if no one had ever done a day's work before.

Frank Athearn, the older of the two by eight years, making him thirty-four, had been planning for this day for ten years. The inclusion of his younger partner, Billy Joe Meynert, was recent and brought about by the fact that a man can't ranch totally alone, and Billy was better than most even though a touch too young, a touch too eager.

But it was the eagerness that gave Billy his partic-

ular charm, and certainly his devotion was a great
asset as well. Devotion bothered Frank, always had,
and probably always would. He felt it placed burdens on both parties and it wasn't his nature to share
burdens that could be avoided. In Billy's case, however, it had brought them close together, had been
responsible for Frank's good health and well-being to
this very day. Billy was the first awake, the last to
sleep, never tired or if he was, he never let on. He
would find some inner reserve that drove him on
long after Frank's good sense told him it was time.

"Bill Meynert sorta grows on you," Frank would
say when questioned about the seeming mismatch. He
never admitted to liking Billy. He didn't have to.
Both knew the other one well, knew that what passed
between them was good, and never bothered to question the matter, nor did they really defend it. Billy
was a boy who by one unthinking act had thrown
himself into manhood and he was in over his head
now, with only Frank as a visible rock in a terrifying
ocean.

They'd met at Fort Dix, New Jersey, early in 1942,
and upon discovering they shared the skies, saddles
and animals of the western plains and mountains, became allies. Both were liked by the other trainees, but
because of the peculiarity of their speech, the basic
difference of their ways, were seldom included in pass
activity or anything else for that matter.

When Frank decided on Airborne training, Billy
cast his lot with his newfound friend, only to find that
Airborne included jumping from moving airplanes.
But while it didn't suit him to be higher than ten
hands from the ground, he went along without a word
of complaint, smiling and joking as usual, finding the
right words for the right occasion.

Even unusually tall horses bothered Billy, and while
it might seem strange to the outsider hearing of a
cowboy not liking horses, perhaps even fearing them
a bit, there was nothing unusual about it. Many cow-

ys hated horses and were only too happy to give
 animals when pickups and trucks would do the
. But Billy was a cowboy and knew the best way
 do his job was on horseback, so he kept his loath-
 for the biting, kicking beasts to himself, refrained
m showing it and rode, quiet and ever vigilant.
e horses sensed it, and did their best to build on
lly's fears. But Billy ignored his fears, or at least
pt them on a low burner, in jumping as in the case
th horses, and accompanied his newfound friend to
 jump towers and waiting airplanes.

North Africa followed training, then Sicily and the
inland of Italy, but it was the final step, the end
 the war for them, when they dropped into Holland
th the unit for the fatal invasion known as Arnhem.

In general, the war was something Frank Athearn
pt far in the back of his mind. He'd never be one
 those who would think of the war as the high
int of their lives. Instead, he'd been left a little
kened, a little disgusted and ashamed at what he'd
covered about his fellow man. He'd learned that
t all atrocities could be claimed by the other side,
d that his fellow man, when pushed and degraded
 enough, could revert far below any known form
animal life.

But Billy was a light in the gloom, which was why
 was here now, a partner and a friend.

Every waking moment spent with Bill Meynert was
 eminder of a time at Arnhem. Frank had been sep-
ted from the platoon, wounded and downed, un-
le to move in a totally exposed position as his unit
reated and the German counterattack moved to-
rd him quicker than he thought it was possible for
nbined men and armor to move. He considered
wling, saw it was hopeless, and saw that it was just
in foolish to fight it out. He was about resigned
 surrender when he caught a glimpse of khaki and
ve drab over his shoulder, and looked to see Billy

at the edge of a copse of trees, shedding his gea
sizing up the distance to Frank, the distance to tl
Germans beyond.

There was no hesitation when Billy started ru
ning, heading straight for Frank, breaking his stri
only to zigzag like the most beautiful broken-field ru
ner in the world, finally diving under the bullets th
by now were tearing up the field all around him. Tl
dive was poor, and he struggled for his breath whi
had been forced out in the fall, but he smiled
Frank, and grabbed his webbed belt with one hand
he struggled to his knees, quickly sizing up the Ge
mans who were pouring fire beyond them.

Some men from the platoon had followed Billy
the edge of the woods, and now were giving a cove
ing fire to Frank and Billy.

"About time," Billy muttered, and with one effo
stood, lifting Frank across his shoulder in a loo
version of the fireman's carry.

"You ready, pard?"

"Depends," Frank winced, "on what you got i
mind."

Billy laughed, started walking, testing his balan
with the new load, as bullets knicked up the groun
Frank, wounded in his right arm, lower left ank
and foot, was uselessly facing backward, toward tl
Germans, hoping for the best out loud, praying feve
ishly that they'd make it. Billy's steps increased i
distance and tempo and they began to cover mol
ground and quickly. There was no time for broke
field running now, but only the urgent need to reac
their own lines as soon as possible.

"One heavy sonofabitch, Frank."

"Montanans is solid, Bill."

"Shit you say." Then a bullet took Billy in the rigl
thigh, and they toppled to the ground nearly twen
yards from their own men, who were firing over the
heads at the Germans, but themselves being ove
whelmed by the heavier fire. The khaki and oli

shapes grew fewer and less distinct as they retreated.

As if the wound had only the effect of keeping him low, and slowing him down, Billy's hand clenched Frank's field jacket and he began dragging the older soldier behind him, cursing at their own men who were wisely dropping further and further away. Frank did his best to assist and they were two legs, three arms dragging themselves to cover.

Fifteen, thirteen, then ten yards to go when they had to stop. The Germans had veered off slightly, but one squad was still moving toward Frank and Billy when Billy dragged Frank's carbine from his shoulder and opened fire on the soldiers advancing toward them. Two dropped quickly, one dead instantly, the other yelling for help. The others scattered, flattening among the furrows in the field, giving Frank and Billy a chance to make the last few yards to cover without steady fire. The prey had teeth and the predators respected the fact.

The last thing Frank remembered as he started losing consciousness from loss of blood was Billy pausing as he gathered his gear to raise up on one knee and fire three long bursts at the Germans who suddenly refused to move.

There was no trace of that very calm young man who under pressure, under fire, had the grace not to break and run. Not now, for there was no reason, Frank supposed. He watched Billy begin his morning ritual with their prize bull, Buster, with more cheer than usual (the animal had taken a personal dislike to Billy, and the men decided Bill should be the one who should be his keeper) and as he watched this boy-man who'd become his partner and closest friend, wondered how it all happened. They were so different. Billy was possessed of many traits that Frank found to be less than desirable. He loved to spend money when Frank was frugal, he tended to drink more than was healthy and when he drank a quick temper would surface. It was said of Frank Athearn on the other hand that he could wait out a rock and that was about as close to the truth as you could get. Billy tended to talk too much while Frank was a listener. Billy loved roots that he could no longer handle and talked of those roots incessantly while Frank seldom spoke of his family, never saw them anymore, but loved the survivors, revered the ones gone and believed in a heaven and hell, if only the one that was his, personally.

Buster had broken from the herd, and was being pursued by Billy out of sight, back the way they came, so Frank slowed their small herd, bringing them to a walk, reflecting on how far they'd come. Out there in the basin, snuggled up against the mountains, was the land Frank had coveted, worked so hard to buy, and now they were within hours of home. He was impatient and then suddenly amused with himself for being so. He'd waited ten years for this day and now he was cursing poor old Buster and Good Ol' Billy and if he kept up that way he'd sour a perfectly good day.

He glanced at the sky. Almost day, he corrected himself silently. In time his mind drifted from the impatience, touching briefly on the trip from New York to Omaha on the bus. It was a shock after three years in the army. The country had changed greatly. You could read the signs everywhere. People had changed too. Frank could feel it, and Billy had commented on it, and they finally decided that it must be on account of the war. It seemed to them that every family had been touched somehow, that the emotion going in had been worn down by loss and word of loss. We were winning, but then we all knew we'd win, but not at the cost. The terrible cost. And it still wasn't over.

From Omaha, they bused to Chadron, Nebraska, still in the shocked state of returning vets. When they hit the ground in Chadron for longer than a pee break and a cup of coffee before changing buses, it

as like seamen ashore for the first time in three
years. They wobbled at sights and sounds that brought
back feelings that neither man would admit to, lest
they be thought overly sentimental, but both knew
what they felt, knew they didn't have to talk about
. The smell of the plains—cut grass, wildflowers that
follow the last of the snows. The sounds—a Great
Northern locomotive in the distance; you could tell
. by the whistle and it seemed to be bound northwest.
And in that instant both men thought of home, Billy
of the sweet highlands of the Bighorns in Wyoming,
and Frank of the high meadows of Montana. And
were they were in damned Nebraska, cowboys afoot
and rarin' to go, but as ill-equipped to follow their
instincts as a cat is to give birth to pups.

They were still in uniform when they made their
decision to purchase their herd, and that *was* a decision for they certainly felt disadvantaged bargaining
like cowmen when they still looked like soldiers. But
the deal went well, perhaps better than they expected
thanks to those very uniforms, and before dawn the
next morning, newly dressed in cheap but durable
clothing, they were on their way northwest, bound for
Montana, driving this cantankerous new bull, Buster,
and his harem of fifteen cows. They considered shipping the animals by rail, but the horses were prime,
the cattle fat from winter hand feeding, and their
spirits were so high they felt they could almost fly the
twenty-day trip on horseback in hours.

It took them twenty-three days due to the late snow
in the Bighorns, but by mid-April they were at the
base of the Bear Paw Mountains, beginning the last
day's climb to what would be their home. That was
yesterday.

Now it was just moments after sunrise and the low
morning clouds had begun their eastward sweep on
the light winds that came with birdsong to the basin.
More of the basin was visible than Frank remembered
on his last visit, but that had been a short one, solely

for the purpose of paying the price asked for the land he was now about to occupy for the first time.

Like every Montana cowboy, he'd heard of the Bear Paw, and longed to see the place. He'd been through the mountains called Bear Paw several times, once stopping at the spot where Chief Joseph of the Nez Percé surrendered to the United States Army, and the high peaks and upper meadows were lush, but not enough to cover the sadness of the place.

When he was out of work up near Fort Peck in the summer of '35, he took to the local circuit, hoping to raise some funds, hoping to make it big perhaps, in the rodeo. And while he was good, he knew the rodeo life with its show and falseness would never suit him. There was something wrong in using skill for entertainment to his way of thinking, but right in using that same skill to better yourself.

A show in Lewistown provided him with the winnings he desired, and the additional points accumulation gave him the all-around prize money as a bonus. Without a moment's hesitation, mounted on his solitary horse, Frank Athearn took himself off, up into the Bear Paws to see the fabled richest grazing land in the whole damned state.

So he'd come to the Bear Paw Basin, had fallen in love with the spot and in less than three days had made his choice, paid his price and bought the finest piece of land he'd ever seen in his life from the woman known as Ella Connors. For a moment, he reflected back on their one and only moment; he remembered that she hadn't said much and yet seemed so relieved to take his money that it made him wonder. It couldn't have been that the land was useless and it must be that she was in terrible need.

Had he bothered to find out, he could have confirmed his feelings and he'd always regretted he didn't know more about the woman and her business, but then it was not his way to push and insert himself if there were even the slightest hint that he might be rejected or scorned. He kept to himself, minded his own business and wished that other people would have as much courtesy.

Nothing mattered to him now except that he was there, sitting his bay stud, watching the navies of cumuli that swept north and east out of the Rockies of which the Bear Paws are a part, carried by strong winds, clashing with the calmer air of the great Judith Basin, then swirling off into the flatter, harsher regions of the land. Neither the fair weather, the clouds nor the vista moved him, but rather a sensation of need for this place. The beauty was secondary, the land was everything. His eyes took in the fact that there were no fences, nor any hint of them and the basin appeared as primeval as when great mammoths and dire wolves had roamed there. He liked the fact that he could see no fences, a fact that made him realize that if he were to survive this harsh, beautiful and rugged place, he would, against his own wishes and better judgment, have to fence, to put them where none had ever stood before. He'd long since made up his mind to keep that work to a minimum.

The heat was building already, the insects coming awake and alive as the sun dried, then split, the dew-soaked earth.

He could hear Billy cursing and Buster snorting angrily long before they caught up with the slow moving herd and he smiled to himself, glancing down the basin where the first rays of the morning sun reflected off the corrugated roofs of some of the buildings in the small town of Bear Paw. He pointed and Billy nodded as he drew alongside.

"Bear Paw."

"Bear Paw Mountains, Bear Paw Basin, Bear Paw City. Damn but don't you Montanans know but one name, Frank?"

Frank studied his partner for a moment, thought about the other Montana names, the marked affinity for sticking with a name that worked, such as the numerous places named over and over for Lewis and Clark and so forth. There was no answer, so he shrugged off Billy's question, and just sat there studying the great basin.

"Whyn't you sniff the wind whilst yer at it, Frank?"

Athearn was a name you didn't hear too often, Frank thought.

"Love this place, Bill," he muttered.

"We could be lovin' it more if we git goin'."

Frank nodded, swung his quirt at the cattle, forcing them back in line, and they headed for the last row of hills that lay between them and the basin proper.

"Trouble is, Bill, you younger breed of cowmen ain't got no real soul at all. You don't know how to savor nothin'."

If Billy had an answer, he didn't voice it, nor did he give any sign to his partner that he even heard. He had, of course, but he was damned if he'd let Frank know he was right all the time. After all, it could only go so far with a fella.

Frank Athearn and Bill Meynert reacted differently to the explosions which suddenly erupted around them, and not at all like experienced cattlemen. Billy froze at the first explosion, but quickly grabbed for his saddle gun, noting Frank had done the same. Soldiers first, cowboys second—at least this time.

The second explosion, seconds after the first, then a third and a fourth, all moving away from them, triggered a shift in their actions as they turned their attention to the cattle moving about five hundred yards away, when the fourth and last explosion died off.

A dust cloud lay across the narrow depression between the hills, and out of the dust came a sound, followed by a dusty red Jeep bearing the markings ATKO OIL. It roared toward them, the man beside the driver standing on the seat, gripping the windshield and yelling at the two cowboys, who stopped their work and watched him swing toward them.

"Get the hell out!" His high voice rang out, the air still now, very quiet as the Jeep came to a halt a few yards from Frank.

"Get out of here. Can't you see we're blasting down this valley?" He asked the question a shade lower but there was still the edge of panic in his voice and the two cowboys were almost amused at his alarmed state. No damage had been done except a little scare.

"I can see that," replied Frank, "but I didn't see no signs back the way we came sayin' you was blastin'."

"Well, they're there, all along the road." The man had taken on the defensive attitude with some petulance. He was embarrassed and annoyed, trying to hold his own. He studied the cattle as the older cowboy spoke.

"Mister, we ain't seen a road in over ten days. Come over the mountains." He paused a moment, glanced at his cattle then smiled at the Easterner, trying to put him at ease. "Ain't no harm done, Mister. Last time I was through this was government land and open to pass."

"It's still government land. It's just we're not used to seeing cattle on the move these days. Not in this country." He glanced down the valley, gesturing at it, then motioning to a rise just north of the valley. "We're wired all through that low ground, but the ridge is free. You won't have to go around."

"Obliged." Frank's eyes lingered on the oil company logo, then he studied the man. "Didn't know there was oil up here."

"It's here. Just took the war to make us get off our butts and go for it. A little help from technology." He smiled and extended his hand up to Frank. "George Bascomb."

"And I guess yer a geologist."

"Good guess. You know something about oil?"

"Some," smiled Frank. "Not enough to be rich."

The geologist swung his gaze to Billy, then he swept it over the cattle, lingering on Buster for a moment.

"He's mostly Longhorn, with Highland, Hereford thrown in for the bulk. Name's Buster."

"Yours or his?" quipped the geologist. Frank smiled in return, chuckled.

"No, mine's Athearn, and that's my partner Bill Meynert. Sorry, Mr. Bascomb, but my manners aren't all they should be these days. I been out of practice."

Bascomb considered pressing for more information, for he'd never laid eyes on the men and he'd spent three years in these parts, meeting with cowboys and landowners or else sitting in restaurants listening for something that might indicate the sure presence of oil. No, he didn't know these men, but from their equipment, and the cattle, he assumed they were settling in, or delivering the cattle.

He stored the information and the assumptions away, knowing he might be required to remember the men sometime in the future, but made no decisions about them other than they seemed decent enough, good humored, and bore him no ill will for an incident that might have had tragic results. He classified men as he did rocks and landforms, making no judgments until sure, and even then allowing for doubt.

"You were right, Mr. Athearn. There should have been signs down the valley. I don't make mistakes like that. Sorry."

"Ain't nobody perfect." They shook hands again, then Frank swung his horse off, moving wide around the cattle, bunching his group, joining them up with Billy's bunch and herding the lot toward the ridge.

Bascomb watched them edge slowly off, their own dust enveloping them, then he signaled his driver to take them back to the two red trucks already moving off toward the site of the next blast, satisfied by the parting of the cowboys that there was no harm done, no ill will.

For his part, under the calm, almost jovial exterior, Frank Athearn was troubled by the thought of oil in the basin. The world he sought to stay so far away from was creeping in here. Even here. And while he had few facts, and tended to worry only when he had all the facts, the possibilities annoyed and confused him. One glance at Billy told him the younger man was deeply troubled, most likely by the same damned thing. The men knew each other that well.

The cattle could be seen from the air as the small plane made its sweep over the eastern rim of the mountains and dropped from the turbulent air over the peaks to the calmer layers that hung in the basin proper. It had made this approach before, the pilot experienced in this mountainous terrain, knowing the sudden temper of the wind, and how treacherous that temper could be. To this pilot, his cargo was one solitary passenger in whose hands rested the pilot's future. But then, the airman grimly amused himself by thinking, I sort of hold his future in mine during these minutes and hours. And the pay was good. The young airman had been kept out of the war by this job, and he had a bright future, so what matter if he had to bite it every once in a while. He noticed the cattle as he swung low before making his final turn for a landing and considered that his lot must be better than those damned cowboys who had to work all the time, no matter what.

The youngish man who was his passenger had only glimpsed the cattle when he glanced up from papers as they were about to land. He gave the cattle no thought other than a dull mental note that they were there, moving into the outskirts of that miserable little town. He loved the West, but hated Bear Paw

City with a passion of Medici proportions. It was a
blight, a stink, an insult to the beauty that surrounded
it. He wasn't, however, thinking of the town this
morning; he was intent on how to play out this difficult day which he had originally planned so differently.

Neal Atkinson considered himself the most orga-
nized man he knew, and most who knew his ways
would have agreed. It was not a passion with him,
but part of the way in which he had been raised, first
by a nanny who alternately loved and tortured him
by forcing order upon a child whose nature was free.
His earliest inclination was to use his left hand for
everything, for it felt correct to him, but Nanny would
use every trick and bogeyman known to the human
mind to shame him into painfully using his right
hand. An appeal to his parents, who should have
known better, was dismissed perfunctorily. He gave
in, trying harder than ever to conform with Nanny's
wishes for cleanliness and organization, and for writing, eating, throwing and, in the long run, masturbat-
ing with his right hand. Nanny never lasted long
enough to discover this last mentioned, and certainly
most rewarding, discovery of his right hand, but had
she lived she most certainly would have. Her vigilance made Neal Atkinson a very neat, very organ-
ized young gentleman. His mouth and father turned
him into a very neat, very considerate shark.

The Atkinsons had been old money made public
by Jay Gould. They found their connections with
him, made public by the press during those years of
financial panic and railroad corruption, more than
annoyances. Before all this scandal they had been content to play with money gained before Lewis and
Clark ranged westward to the land known as Louisi-
ana, to dabble in ventures of every sort from Astorian
Support to piratical and smuggling operations all
along the Atlantic seaboard. A grandsire years before
had made the transition from darkness to respecta-

bility by choosing the right side during the contro-
versy concerning Aaron Burr. From that point until
the Union Pacific scandals in which they were involved, if only on the fringe, the Atkinsons lived in
quiet and plush isolation, associating only with those
who moved in that same protected world. Somehow
they'd managed to hand down from generation to generation of male heirs a sense of the rules by which
they'd played when they were not gentlemen, for it
was remembered that it had gotten them where they
were, and they shouldn't forget. You just never knew.

Neal Atkinson was schooled in the tactics of prob-
ing for weakness and dominating by indebtedness,
and schooled well, but by his generation another instinct had been self-groomed and came constantly into
conflict with the pragmatic side. He had somehow become a humanitarian and a libertarian or at least he
thought of himself that way. He weighed everything
twice, sometimes three times, each time dealing with
conscience. His grandfather harbored no conscience
when he emerged from the Union Pacific cat fight
with a fistful of land deeds and full title to one Montana railroad, and interest in three more including
the Great Northern. But Neal, who'd turned into a
fine businessman in his own right, was trying to apply
everything he had ever learned to organize what
should be a simple sequence of events. There was no
doubt that this business of Jack Ewing's boy getting
killed made it difficult.

Eighteen hours had dragged by since he'd gotten
the word in Omaha that what was to have been a
business weekend was to be turned into a self-effacing
memorial to the Ewings.

"Damn!" He nurtured the word aloud, and smiled
when the pilot didn't look over at him, for the man
must have heard. Atkinson's eyes ranged down to the
Atko Oil Company report that he now knew by heart.
George Bascomb was their best field geologist, no
doubt, but he was wordy and his reports rambled.

Nevertheless, Neal Atkinson absorbed every word, reading nuances in the report the more casual observer might miss. He was meticulous, and he chose meticulous men to communicate with him, to work with him. He'd stress over and over that information was essential to making proper decisions. He was like a young, fierce general in running the small oil company that he'd bought on speculation, become caught up in and was now dedicating nearly every waking moment to.

"Seat belt, sir." The pilot gestured to his own for emphasis. Atkinson nodded, slipped the papers in his briefcase and buckled his belt as the motors cut slightly and the plane with the ATKO OIL markings dropped to the dirt road that served as Bear Paw City's landing strip.

This whole day was turning into a disaster, slowly building to one great crisis for Virgil Hoverton as he checked his watch and thought, "We're never going to make it. Never. What the hell is he doing?" He shaded his eyes trying to find the small plane that had made one pass, then turned toward the western mountains and disappeared. He could still hear it, but he couldn't locate it. The sound of cattle and men and dogs made him glance down K Street to see two young cowboys moving a small herd of stocky mountain cattle toward the dirt road that was the landing field. He moved from his brown Buick coupe, waving at them, motioning that they should stop, turn, and that an airplane was approaching, until he realized he looked foolish and walked back to his car with a shrug, hoping for the best, checking his watch again and muttering to himself.

He'd never flown, never really been out of Montana, and therefore had no knowledge of how airplanes flew or maneuvered, but seemed relieved when the small craft hove into sight once more, swooping down toward him, touching the ground as the motors cut back and feathered and the plane gathered to a neat halt just yards away. Dust filled the air, mingling with the dust of the small cattle herd that had swung around the airplane under control of the two cowboys. Hoverton held his hat clamped on his head to guard against prop wash and half-turned as the cattle moved edgily by, frightened by the noise of the aircraft.

His anger and annoyance dissipated when he saw the older of the two cowboys and clawed at his memory for the name and events that went with the face. He was so intent on the cowboy at that moment, he only caught the last few steps of Atkinson's approach, and when he saw him, moved swiftly to take the overnight case from the oil man and heir to railroads.

"Hello," he ventured. "Was it rough?"

Atkinson smiled. He always felt benevolent around Hoverton, and tolerated the effort of small talk for which he normally had no use. He understood the limitations of these people, every one of them, with very few exceptions.

"There's always turbulence in the mountains. How's the family, Virgil?"

"Just fine," lied the banker. Perhaps things would change before he'd have to admit that Betty had left him, and if they didn't, he'd have time enough to manufacture a better reason than the fact that he was dull, which he was still convinced he wasn't. He tried to think of something wonderful that would rivet Atkinson's attention on him as they walked to the car, but could only point at the cattle and mutter about them.

Atkinson stopped near the car, appraised the cattle, then crossed the space between himself and the older of the two cowboys and stopped a few yards away, admiring their gear, their horses and the cattle, looking out of place, disappearing and reappearing in the dust that continued to eddy around the cattle and horses. Flies were fully awake now, stirred by the promise of a feast, and the sound crazily hummed in his ears. The sight of working cowboys and cattle still moved him, as it had when he was a boy of six coming out to grandfather's ranch, which was in reality a huge lodge, fashioned along the lines of some petty German king's hunting lodge. There were days of riding with cowboys, of hunting grizzly, or watching men on neighboring ranches work the cattle that were so much larger than the delicate boy. He loved the smells and the sights and the sounds, and these summers of youth were still among his fondest memories. Envy of their freedom made him constantly seek out cowboys even as a man, to pass some time with them, as if seeking answers to why these simple men were free, while he, so wealthy and powerful, was more confined than a prisoner in solitary. He tried to say that it was because they assumed few responsibilities, but in time he knew that was just not the case, and more likely, never had been. One old man told him once that it was just that working with cattle made nothing else seem like work at all, and after all, this was the life and the only way to follow it. He'd waited for more, but the old cowboy had said all he was about to on the matter and there was no further pursuit of philosophy. Could work be the reason for their inner peace? It wasn't for him, but then the stakes were different. But as he thought it, he knew that was untrue as well, for these were men who risked death or crippling each and every day of their lives, and accepted that as inevitable, so for them the stakes were the highest. He only found himself going through these self-searching periods when he was out here, among them. But he was drawn here, fascinated, and he found himself closer to Frank and Billy and the herd than perhaps he should have been.

Frank Athearn reined in his horse, signaled for Billy to keep the cattle under control, then turned his attention to Atkinson, appraising the expensive suit and shoes, the silk tie and perfect handkerchief. Hell, even the wind didn't muss his hair when the man removed his hat and smiled up at Frank.

"You must like dust, Mister."

"It goes with the country, doesn't it?" Atkinson motioned at the cattle. "Good stock. Early for market though."

Frank studied the man, not too surprised. He nodded thoughtfully, musing how a man's clothing could fool you these days. "Ain't bound for market yet. Jest settlin' in."

He studied Atkinson for a reaction but there was only that friendly smile that didn't quite fill the man's eyes. The man turned and looked over to the second man, and while Hoverton could not place Frank immediately, the cowboy knew him, remembered him in a second, going back years to the day when he signed his papers, collected his deed. Hoverton had done everything to block the selling of the land, had stalled for time, but failed in his attempts to stop the sale. But he wouldn't be forgotten. He moved now to the summons on Atkinson's face and walked to where the oil man stood beside the cowboy.

"Seen that name all over the place today." Frank motioned to the ATKO OIL logo on the side of the three-year-old plane that should have been pressed for military service and wasn't.

"That goes with the country, too." He smiled, then turned his attention to Virgil Hoverton who'd moved to his side. "You didn't tell me there was land for sale in these parts, Virgil."

"No sir, I didn't." Hoverton had made all the correct connections, and looked up at Frank, smiling, extending his hand. "You're Frank Athearn. I remember."

"Yeah. I remember too." There was no kinship, no humor in Frank's voice, no move on his part to shake hands with the banker, but then he quickly grasped the banker's hand almost as an afterthought, pumped it once and drew his own hand away. "But that was a long time ago, banker."

"I wrote you." Frank said nothing in reply and when he didn't, Hoverton tried again. "You could have amassed a fortune on that land. You should have answered my letters."

"Ain't no regular runs to a foxhole. Answer would've been no anyhow."

Hoverton checked his watch, annoyed at the inconvenience of everything, aware of Atkinson, listening to everything with interest. "You ought to rethink that decision. Price of land is going up. More now than ever. You can still make a fine profit if you sell now. You could get twice the land and stock someplace else."

"I ain't no speculator." Frank never took his eyes off the two men, but he knew Billy had maneuvered close enough to hear and that sooner or later there would probably be questions. He hoped his partner would wait until later. When they were alone.

"I don't blame you." Atkinson motioned at the mountains and basin with a sweep of his hand. "It's a magic place. I've been coming here for years."

Frank was beginning to make judgments on his first impressions of this pleasant oil man, and he hated that, so he watched his words. "For a man who sees the magic in this place," he said slowly after some thought, "yer in a terrible hurry to punch the land all full of holes."

Atkinson chuckled, nodded and thrust his hands into his pockets, a bit caught, enjoying this cowboy. "I have a romantic streak, but my business is oil. What else can I say?" He noticed Hoverton repeatedly glancing at his watch, fretting over their potential lateness to the funeral, the possible price he might have to pay in his relationship with J.W. Ewing. Atkinson took pity on the banker, quickly extended his hand, shaking hands with Frank and wishing him well, then turning on his heel walked to the Buick coupe. He slid into the passenger seat as Hoverton tossed his bag behind the seat and took his place behind the wheel, whisking them quickly off, away from town, leaving Frank and Billy to continue their push on to the new ranch.

II
DEATHSONG

The distance from the Connors Ranch to the old Ewing Cemetery was less than two miles on horseback across country, but Ella chose instead to drive, which meant taking the road. But for a reason she chose not to explore, pride made her choose the old black Model A she'd whimsically called Roncinante, and like Quixote's faithful steed, the old Ford seldom let her down and gave her good service in return for good care.

Dodger had anticipated her wishes, understanding the why of things with this woman who was his boss. Cleaning the black truck with disdainful attention, he muttered at the machine, talking to it, telling it that it wasn't half so good as the worst horse and while it had her fooled, it didn't fool him one damned bit.

At ten to noon that day, after Dodger had done his best to make some semblance of respectability out of his old clothing, slicked down his hair, trimmed the scraggly hairs of his moustache, he stood beside the Model A, waiting for Ella. Hell, let her take her time. He could stand there all day without moving, just savoring the breeze and the smell of early spring grass.

At eight to twelve, however, Ella emerged from the kitchen door and strode purposefully to the Model A, not really seeing Dodger, her mind drowning in anxiety over the next few hours. She headed for the driver's door, ignoring Dodger who obediently moved to the other side of the truck, and slid in beside her where he sat looking straight ahead until she fired the truck to life.

"Dungarees is all I got that I can look half-sober in, Dodger." It was said quietly.

"Ain't no business of mine."

She studied the old man, shifted through first into second as they rolled beyond the gates and down the road.

"You gave me one of them looks. I saw it."

Dodger shifted uncomfortably on the seat and said nothing. Of course the choice of clothing bothered Dodger. He didn't approve of women in pants, not even working, and most certainly not going to a funeral, no matter what you think of the people to whom you're supposed to be paying your respects. But he knew better than to voice his concerns on such matters. If Ella cared about clothing or how she looked, she never let on to him, but she was pretty to a point. Any man would fancy her on almost any terms, although, and he went over it again in his mind, she was looking more tired every day. He'd seen beautiful women remain that way in these parts, and then one day all the hardship would catch up with them and they would suddenly age. He glanced over at Ella, noted the set of her profile and decided that it probably wouldn't be so with her, but just the same he wished she'd made a little effort to show herself off, even if it was a Ewing funeral. Hell, he didn't know what he thought at times like this. He wasn't sure what he liked or didn't like.

The bulk of the Connors Ranch was mountainous, but the ranch grounds proper were on the flats of a high valley, and when you were on those flats, you could not see the entire scope of the seventy-mile-long basin of the Bear Paws. There was a spot, however, that existed on the road to the Connors Ranch that afforded a view, a sense of the enormous mountains and the incredible height and depth of the sky. When-

ever a stranger found himself at that spot, he would
have to stop and invest moments of his life in the
spectacle that stretched out to the horizon. Except for
the hottest months, there was snow on the peaks, and
in many years the snow stayed the year round. It was
a Bierstadt landscape, Neal Atkinson once said, but
there was more to it than that.

Now the Model A reached that spot, and would
normally have slowed only a fraction, for this view
impressed even Ella and she'd seen it all her life, but
this time she stopped, left the motor in idle and
pointed to the thin trail of dust that was perhaps a
mile away or so.

"Same ones we saw this mornin'." The old man
nodded. "Cattle. Movin' too close together, too slow
for horses. If it's Ewing, then he's headin' for our
land."

The old man swung around, looked harshly at her,
a bit angry, and trying not to show it. "Why'd Ewing
be moving cattle from the mouth of the basin to yer
place? And on the day of his son's funeral? Shit, Babysister, I taught you to think better'n that."

"Well then, who the hell is it?"

He remained calm, recognizing the tone of her
voice, knowing she was pressured. If he gave in at
this point she'd blow for sure, and that'd be a waste
of time. "We could forget the funeral, go check 'em
out, or we could go to the funeral and check 'em out
later. Movin' slow enough they won't make that second hill by three."

She looked at him, knowing he was right, knowing
exactly what he was doing to her. He knew her too
well and she wasn't sure she liked it at all, but there
wasn't much she could do about it anymore. They
were a little too tight for that. She expelled her
breath, thumped the wheel with the heels of her hands
and shifted into gear, forcing herself to move toward
the Ewing Cemetery.

The country was wide open before the two cowboys, just hills and shallow depressions that passed for small valleys. But the inaccurate map that Frank was following was not close enough. They'd run into high spots that weren't marked on the map, and streams in full flood, and so instead of being almost home, Frank was beginning to believe they'd be lucky to be there by sunset. They were, at this moment, on what he hoped was their last detour, heading for the pass he remembered marked the spot where his land lay.

Billy had grown quiet, murmuring about a second lieutenant in the army with a map. "Remember one, couldn't find his ass with both hands, Frank?"

"Map is ten years old, Bill."

And so it went through three tries, only to find the way blocked by signs marking the perimeters of the Ewing Ranch. Frank had heard of it. One of the great families in the state. Owned most of the land in the basin, though it had been different once. But this was over a hundred thousand acres by his reckoning, if the lines ran true and those great stretches of level grassland were indeed all Ewing land. It was impressive. Little by little their spirits fell, and by noon, Frank had decided to try to turn it around.

The cattle were moving well, though there'd been few stops due to their anxiety about "getting there" and Buster grumbled over interrupted love-making. Frank unslung and removed the oilskin wrappings from the old guitar that had been his father's and strummed and hummed until the instrument was in tune.

"Singin' ain't gonna git us there no faster, pard." Billy was just plain pissed. He was like a child in that his hopes were easily scattered, but Frank understood and smiled as he tried to remember the words he was searching for, already moving his hands to the tune.

"I ride an ol' paint, lead an ol' dan,
Gonna head for Montana to throw the Hoolihan. . ."

He sang, and then he seemed to forget the words, for he da-da-da-da-dad a few times while his hands strummed the melody.

Billy just shook his head and began to fish in his saddlebags for something.

"There's water in the coolies," he said to Frank.

"That ain't way it goes."

Billy looked at him deeply affronted. "Waaalll, I just guess it is."

Frank shook his head and strummed on while Billy fished in his bag and produced a harmonica and took a few tune-searching blows, then grinned at Frank.

"One . . . Two . . . Three." He blew the tune as Frank strummed, and when he stopped, they sang together.

"I ride an ol' paint, I lead an ol' dan,
Gonna go to Montana to throw the Hoolihan. . ."

Once again they were interrupted, this time by gunfire that came in three distinct volleys, broken by faint commands of load . . . fire . . . and they searched until they realized they were carrying on under the very hill where a military funeral was being conducted. Their own arguing and boisterousness made them ashamed, and their shame made each of them angry in his own way. In silence, they remained motionless for a moment, aware that there were eyes on them from the hill. It was impossible for them not to have been heard.

Frank quietly leaned to Billy, motioning for them to move on. "Seen too much of that, I guess."

"We was the lucky ones, Frank."

The first broken strains of a bugle blowing taps filtered down to them, and Frank looked up at the crest of the hill, noted the tall man in black standing apart from all the rest, assumed it was the father or close relative and felt sympathy for the man. He felt thankful it wasn't he, and aware that it could well have been, he urged his horse on behind the cattle, slowly wrapping up the guitar once again.

Except for the intrusion of the two cowboys, the funeral had gone well enough. Julie Blocker had looked across the grave at John Ewing who had not moved throughout the windy sermon by the Methodist minister. The minister had said little about the boy other than that he'd served his country well, as did all the Ewings, and Ewing's loss would be their loss in the long run, if not now. Blocker was a fine foreman but had difficulty with ambiguities, and he wondered if there could be another meaning to the words "in the long run." Could this mean that if the old man died, the ranch, the town and the entire basin would be lost to those who made their home there? Probably so, for without an heir, what would J.W. do? Then he looked down the line of cowboys beside him, stopping when he came to Emil Kroegh. For one so young, he had risen quickly to Blocker's side. Blocker had assumed all the attention lavished on Emil by Ewing had been because he'd been selected to replace Blocker someday, and this bothered Blocker, because he knew he was more than capable of running the ranch for at least another dozen years. It made him uncomfortable to have his own replacement at his side, especially since he and Ralph Cole, the Ewing top hand, had worked so hard to help the boy whose family had suffered so much. Everybody liked Emil, though all of them felt there was something wrong with him when he was sent home from the army. In fact, Emil had fallen arches and it wasn't discovered until basic training, and when it was he was sent home. But he was ashamed of this deficiency and said nothing about the reason for not going off to war, and was totally unaware that to this day people thought he was a bit off, and as a result treated him so, until he had actually lived up to their expectations. It was an unconscious choice made by Emil, and he would never have understood the reasons, even if they had been explained.

Blocker, although not brilliant, had insight into people. He had spoken to Ewing about Emil and thereby assured the boy of a place in the Ewing hierarchy. But for the past year he had not been comfortable with Emil. There was nothing wrong with the boy other than a misplaced sense of honor, and a temper that tended to carry him quickly to the heights of passion. Once started, he was not easily stopped.

Blocker noticed Ralph Cole behind Kroegh in the lineup of Ewing cowboys, and mused on how those two had always been close, that when one was in trouble, the other would be at hand. The hardened foreman smiled, for as long as he'd known Cole, and that was a sizable piece of time, he'd never known that cowboy to take to another living person. But Emil Kroegh had a strange effect on people and it was impossible not to like him, in spite of his shortcomings.

He pondered the other faces around the graveyard, remembering the ones long gone and looking at their relatives, near and distant, who remained behind. Some good men had died and far before their time, but this was a place that aged you quick and killed you quicker if you weren't vigilant. There had been no newcomers to the basin in years, so there was not a face that bothered Julie Blocker, not one unfamiliar face. Ella Connors's presence surprised him as did that of Dodger, but he was glad to see them honoring the old man. Perhaps it would take a bit of the edge off life, which for days past had been made dreadful by

Ewing's presence, his manner which was distant and at times terrifying. Blocker sighed inwardly, acknowledging to himself that he hadn't lost a son in the war, and would never know the feeling, but it must have been comparable to losing his second daughter, Anne, three years back. She was the light behind his eyes, and he loved her more than his own life, but it had been fated that she go and death had claimed her at the age of eight.

He assumed that losing a son, an heir, could be worse, possibly, but he was a simple man and didn't understand how that could be so. He'd seen so many young men go off to war and not come back, or come back maimed. Or come back disturbed, if they did not have some physical injury. So that now he even questioned his own patriotism that had been so high a few years back. He shared loss with Ewing, and protected the man, and at the same time, strangely, looked to J.W. Ewing for his own strength.

He wondered if the old man knew his son was useless as tits on a boar-hog, and that perhaps this shock was necessary to get the ranch back in shape. Perhaps Emil Kroegh could be groomed for the old man and it might do. It might.

The guitar sounds reached him before the duo voices of the two cowboys, just seconds before they were drowned out by the military salute afforded by a six-man military honor squad, made up of boys in cadet uniforms. The young bugler was Danny Lapp' and he couldn't have been more than fourteen. Blocker wondered what effect the singing had on Ewing, and glanced at the bearded man in the dark suit who barely turned to look down at the cattle and two cowboys. His eyes held on them a moment, then swung back to the grave. Blocker noticed that he looked up only once again and that was to study Ella Connors.

Ewing had seen nothing else since she'd driven up to the graveyard in that truck of hers, for like Blocker, he'd been taken off guard by her arrival, never expecting her to come to him on any terms. Not that she'd really come to him, but he regarded her presence as a form of make-peace, and overlooked that this could have been nothing more than common range courtesy.

When Tom Connors died, Ewing had gone to his simple funeral and burial, had even swung by the house to offer his condolences to Ella, only to be turned away, rebuffed coldly. And while Ella might be an enemy and rival, she was pure Montana, and had all the instincts of the best of cattlemen. He never thought of her as a cattlewoman, but always ranked her with the men he'd known in his life, at least when it came to cattle and ranching. But on every other level she was a woman, and because he hadn't seen her in months, although their ranches lay side by side, he was moved by her dignity, her beauty, or what he called her beauty. He regretted only that she didn't understand what had to be between them, perhaps would never understand. It occurred to him that he should remember that she was, in part, a Ewing, and Ewings were sometimes shortsighted. "Not me," he thought, "but I got enough vision for the whole damned world."

He glanced impatiently at the minister, wished the man would end the interminable eulogy, and that this whole thing would be over. He knew what he'd do, knew he'd have to make the first steps if this gesture on Ella's part was to be made fruitful.

He kept his eyes fixed on the grave throughout the service, only stealing a second here and there to fix Ella with his eyes, to make sure she hadn't slipped away. He hadn't thought much about the loss of his son since word had come two weeks earlier that Matt had died someplace in the Pacific. In fact, there'd been little sorrow, though he knew his men and friends would be thinking he was torn with grief. Let them.

If he suffered, it was under the weight of the question that ranged through his foreman's mind. What would happen to the ranch now? What if J.W. Ewing were to fall dead tomorrow? What happened then?

He went over those thoughts for two nights after word of Matt's death reached him, then shoved such thoughts away, lest they deter him from other plans. So much to do now. So much. But when he saw Neal Atkinson come up the hill where the Ewing family kept watch over their beloved land forever, it caused him to think of it again.

Ewing exercised total control when he shook Atkinson's hand, when he looked the other man in the eyes, smiled and murmured his thanks. They'd never been friends, but Neal was the son of a great friend, so he must be tolerated. But when Ewing looked at Neal, he could see only threat and domination on the face of the pleasant young man. The rancher wondered if he was getting old, getting senile and paranoid.

John Welsh Ewing believed in a powerful and vengeful God, a strong country, cowboy life and little else. He had no faith in any man but the ones he made and they were few. Enough for him, but few still, so Ewing was in the position of being a man alone in his own eyes, with a handful of supporters that he could probably trust under any circumstances, but possibly not.

Atkinson and the banker. Well, that fits, thought J.W. Ewing. That fits. Then he looked at Ella and beyond her, finally returning his thoughts to the ranch, masking his feelings by staring at the pine box that held the body of his only son, that worthless piece of buffalo dung.

The coffin was simple on the exterior, not much better on the inside, for the old man felt that anything else was rather stupid. If you're in the ground, you might as well be useful. All that copper lining crap was just that, so much crap. Sooner the worms get you, the better. The flag was a nice touch, he reflected, although Matt certainly didn't deserve all this honor. He hadn't been killed in action, but in an accident, a stupid car accident. Well, nobody need know, and since they won't give much of a shit for me when I die, we'll just let all this foofaraw do for me now, and I'll be honored. He wondered if he looked right, if he appeared to all these people, all his people, as the stricken father mourning his son. He was so good at pretending, he knew that he was as near to perfect as he could be.

He was only vaguely aware of the singing, startled by the instant volley of rifle shots, so deeply was he absorbed in his own thoughts. He was aware only of sounds, and he turned his head on instinct, saw the cattle and two cowboys below him, and at first dully registered the sight as nothing unusual since there'd hardly been a day in his life when he hadn't seen men working cattle. But in that same second, he knew all his men were here, with him now. And those weren't his cattle. They were handsome, but bred differently than his, built for a new herd, a durable rather than a large stagnant herd like the Ewings'. And he didn't think he knew the men, but couldn't be sure at this distance. But he knew horses well and he'd never seen either of those animals in his life before. They had to be strangers. And they were not just passing through, for in the years past when there were problems with horse and cattle thieves, every path for movement through this basin lay north to south and these men were moving west, crossing his land. He knew all of this in seconds, knew also that Blocker would check it out, that he wouldn't have to deal with the matter, so he looked back to the grave, jolted by the volley, and only looked up from the grave to watch two of the officer-cadets remove the flag from

the coffin and begin to fold it. Behind them, Ella
Connors stood, backed by Dodger, their eyes fixed on
the small herd moving away from the burial hill,
heading for Connors land.

Ewing accepted the folded flag from the officer-
cadet, nodded and spoke to the young man as the
coffin was lowered into the open grave. The cadet
stepped away smartly and softly ordered his men to
attention from parade rest, and while all other eyes
were watching the coffin disappear, Ella Connors
watched the small herd of range cattle and the two
cowboys and their dog head for the mountains, and
she realized where they were heading. It could only
be the high meadows through which ran the creek
named Wolf by Dodger when she was a small girl.
When they veered left and picked up their pace, she
was positive. There was no road out of there, no pass
through the mountains. It had to be the Wolf Creek
meadows.

From the grumblings behind her, she knew Dodger
had seen them, and had reached the same conclusion,
and didn't like the thought of trespassers in his favorite thinking spot. Deeds of yesterday were to be remembered there with particular fondness. She realized
she hadn't been up there in nearly eighteen months,
for the action of running the ranch had shifted to an
area easier to maintain even if the yield was low. She
had to force her thoughts about the ranch yield and
profits and loss and all such things away from her, for
when she reminded herself of the loss she was heading
for, it plunged her mind into panic and things became
cluttered.

Dodger's hand on her shoulder jostled her into line
behind other mourners and they headed to the spot
where J.W. Ewing stood and received their condolences, one by one. She hadn't planned on this, and if
she'd been fully alert, would have discreetly turned
away. She didn't want to face him, this time or any
other, and damn Dodger, he should have realized that,

but she knew he was a simple man with a dignity that would never allow him to affront courtesy.

Step by step they drew closer to Ewing, but only once did he glance down the line to see if she were there, and then, while she was thinking that she'd have to have a word for him and couldn't find one, the line moved away from her and she stood with yards between her and Ewing, unable to walk to him.

The rancher made the first move, and took one of her hands in his, saying, "I never thought to see you come . . . glad you did."

She wanted to say, I didn't come for you, J.W., but for your boy, but the words wouldn't come at all. She could only withdraw her hand, turn and walk quickly away without a word, leaving Dodger facing Ewing.

"Nice of you to come, Dodger."

"Sorry fer the loss, J.W." He clamped his hat firmly on his head, nodded curtly to Ewing and strode off after Ella, walking down the hill to the Model A truck.

Ella waited for him at the truck, scanning the horizon for some sight of the herd, but they'd dropped behind a rise and she assumed they must be watering since no dust rose in the air, and the year was promising to be a dry one even this early. If they were still moving, they'd raise dust no matter what. Dodger drew up to her.

"You think you can get a ride back alone?"

The old cowboy thought for a moment, looked at the faces filing down the hill to their cars, buggies and horses, then nodded. "Yer goin' up to the meadows."

"That's right."

He squinted at her as he fished for and produced his tobacco pouch, began filling an old pipe. He nodded once again, and concentrated on the pipe. "You sure you can handle it all right?"

"Don't worry about me. I just want to know what's goin' on."

"Yeah," he said and tamped down the tobacco

with the edge of his finger, carefully cleaning under his nail when finished. His silence always annoyed her. It was his way of laughing.

"You sure you can get a ride back?"

He nodded and held the door as she slid behind the wheel. "Ain't goin' back. Thought I'd try to bring in a few horses I saw down riverside this mornin'. Ought to be in about seven in the mornin' . . . I tol' you that."

She pointed at his clothes, "You goin' horse catchin' dressed to the nines like you are?"

"I got clothes at the line shack."

"Dodger, it's a long way to the line shack."

He nodded, then shut the door, checking the handle. "I got me a way. Besides, I figure you need time to think on what yer gonna do."

She assumed at first he was guessing about the roundup, but then she realized he could read her like he read signs. He'd been her playmate as a baby, her teacher as a young girl and adolescent, though she'd completed high school, and done very well with things other than cattle and ranch work. At one time in her life she considered going off to college, but that was long before she'd begun her junior year in high school. "And *what am* I going to do?"

He smiled. "It don't matter. You'll think of something."

She nodded, smiled and watched him take two steps back, then wave slightly from the hip as she backed the Model A away. She shifted, then aimed the truck down hill toward the road that led to her ranch and the Wolf Creek meadows beyond in one direction, to town and the headquarters of the Ewing Ranch in the opposite. The old truck protested second gear, and first as well, hinting at a possible problem with the clutch, but once on the road and heading for the meadows, she noticed that it ran just fine although the clutch was soft. She made a mental note she'd have to strip it down soon and take a look.

It was nearly three when they entered the thick stand of aspens that flanked the narrow road leading to their destination. At least Billy assumed they were almost there, if he could tell anything about it from Frank's behavior. People always hated to play cards with Frank Athearn for he could look at you and betray absolutely nothing, and when he moved, he exerted so little effort, or so it seemed, that his total state of apparent relaxation annoyed most.

But Billy noted that for the last hour or so Frank had grown increasingly impatient with the dallying of the cattle, and kept telling them that they were almost there . . . almost there. He was tense, and taking everything in, obviously enjoying the torment of the slowness. The younger cowboy recalled when he'd once seen a strip tease and it was so agonizingly slow that he'd reached several peaks of discomfort before it was revealed that there was nothing much to be excited about. That's how it must be for Frank, he assumed.

He liked what he saw about him, but that hadn't been the case an hour earlier and he'd voiced his concerns. They'd begun to climb, and the overgrown, once-graded road edged around a rock shelf from where they could see the basin floor. A few miles apart, but easily in view, were the remains of three other ranches that had once flourished, but were now aging quickly as heavy snow and fierce heat tore and twisted the old wood. There were other abandoned or burned out places, but they looked long given up. He knew from even his short experience that that could be an illusion, for nature took over quickly sometimes, and sometimes avoided man-made things, so one could seldom tell about a ruin. He saw the ridges, a few inches high, that marked where fences had been. Above the fence line, before the trees, he noted, the grass was a deeper shade of green, almost blue, and he knew it was the gramma he'd heard about, never seen. The buffalo grass that the great herds that crossed the plains harvested in their graze, planting seed by grinding it with their hooves, providing the fertilizer that nurtured the grass that grew by them and for them, and now that they were gone, stood no chance whatever. But the grass still flourished up here, perhaps because there had been no fences, but that couldn't be the whole reason. Billy's brain reeled with tiredness and he crabbed out suddenly, "You sure this place is worth the climb?"

"You'll see," came the patient reply.

"I heard what that bank fella said back there in town. We . . . you, could be rich. Why I heard of fellas turnin' a quick profit time an' again. We could have it easier than we thought, Frank." His head bobbed with enthusiasm.

Frank said nothing. He assumed it was the abandoned ranches that whipped up this flurry of road fever, knew that Billy's family had been involved in the range wars of the late nineties and early part of this century. Even though Billy was never a victim because of age, he had heard stories that must have left a lasting impression on a young boy.

Now Billy continued, "I know, I know. . . . Yer gonna tell me about the dream. You always go to doin' that. But Frank, I been in the saddle more'n I'm used to after three years afoot, and I get more pleasure thinkin' about bein' rich instead. . . . You understand?"

"I understand," Frank lazed, "that if bullshit was goosedown, Bill, you'd be a mattress."

After that, Billy remained silent, watching the excitement build in Frank, wondering if after he got some true rest, he'd share that feeling a bit. He pondered the question until Frank brought them to a stop and pointed to two old rotting gateposts that someone had used for target practice. A "No Trespass" sign with the faded name "Connors" hung loosely from one post, its end dragging in the dirt. "Needs a fence in some spots, but I don't want to cut this grass line, so we'll work outside the trees and tangles, only fence the open spaces, and we'll just have to see how it all goes." Billy nodded as Frank added, "Gonna put a guard and gate in here, I guess."

"You mean this is it?" The strain was showing.

"Almost there."

"I ain't no cow, Frank." But Frank Athearn just laughed and rode ahead, taking point on the small herd, urging them on and loudly. There was something in Frank's movements that infected the cattle, horses and to some extent Billy, though he hadn't thought he had the energy left, and they moved through the trees and along the path that opened out suddenly into a lush mountain meadow, a sight so impressive that Billy reined in and took a quick breath at the edge as if his presence might spoil the vista. It was not one meadow, but two, reaching back for perhaps two miles through the mountains. The slope was easy and the streams that were fed all year long from a north-facing glacier were slowed by the numerous beaver dams and lodges. That beaver in this region had survived the fur trade was a miracle, but they were there, and there would seem to be no reason for that to change. Elk droppings near the stream and the flash of German brown trout were signs of fertility, and the meadows were protected from the winds and snow by the mountains.

Aspen and lodgepole pine formed cliques, and while the beaver had made inroads, it would take thousands of years for them to damage it beyond repair. Thousands of seedlings were everywhere, and yearling trees and upward to maturity flourished in species unfamiliar to Billy. He did recognize the single most important thing of all.

"You never tol' me it was virgin land," he whispered, and clawed desperately for better words, and gave up. "Damn."

"It ain't virgin, but about as close as you can come. Didn't I tell you so?"

"Said it was pretty, but not like this." His voice dropped a notch; his hand swept across the meadow. "You was right. I never seen such a beautiful spot in my whole life."

Neither man said a word or moved for a full ten minutes, but stayed their horses, let the animals graze and watched the cattle spread out across the meadow in earnest investigation.

The remains of a cabin built over eighty years before was just visible under a tangle of undergrowth and trees. The work of beaver had exposed a portion of the rotten walls.

"Cabin ain't much, y'know." Billy had quite an eye.

"Didn't even know there was a cabin. Couldn't or didn't see it the last time I was here." Not that the old structure would be much good, Frank thought.

Billy stretched, then dropped to the ground and began pulling down the saddle and tack, carefully placing them on the ground beside the trail-weary roan. He murmured to her, then left her to graze with hobbles and wandered toward the cabin, climbing through some brush to see the words carved into what remained of one wall.

"Near to froze," he read, "ate mule this mornin' and to them who reads this remember that this is the devil's own land. December 1876." And then, a bit further down, his eyes discovered another carved line. "Blackfeet around the ranch. Holed here with Jake Mooney. Jacob Ewing, June 11, 1875." He turned to see if Frank had heard, and watched as his partner pulled their coveted bottle of Scotch they'd smuggled back from Europe and carried to the highlands of Montana. "Words like that don't lift my spirits, Frank."

Frank Athearn had heard stories like that all his life and worse, but he understood the concern of Billy and listened sympathetically as he uncorked the bottle. He gestured to the surrounding mountains, speaking softly. "Never said we'd have it easy, Bill. To listen to you, a soul'd think they had no winter in Wyoming." He got only a sour look from Billy, but he knew that the younger man was in actuality happy when he grumbled the loudest. He smiled. "Well pard, think on the bright side of things. The Blackfeet have settled down."

"That something you can tell me for sure?"

Frank thought about it a moment, then shook his head and murmured, "Ain't too much I can tell you for sure, 'ceptin' we got us one fine place here and I am grateful."

Moments passed without any words as they passed the bottle between them, taking small swigs, celebrating quietly.

"I'm grateful too, Frank. Thanks for including me in on this. We'll make it proud."

"Mean you don't want to sell off and git rich quick no more?" He knew he could needle Billy with comfort. The younger man showed his embarrassment through a grin as he shook his head. Another short space of silence fell over them, broken only by the sounds of the cattle lowing contentedly. "My Pap and Grandpap worked their whole lives as cowmen for the big ranches and never even owned hardly their own spurs." There was determination in Frank's voice. "We got one helluva chance, Bill."

Billy took a loud swig from the bottle, fought the burn of the liquor and watched as Frank stripped away the saddle, blanket and gear from his horse. "Soon as I can I got to write to my uncle and aunt. They always been dirt poor and this'd make 'em proud." Frank nodded, said nothing as Billy continued. "Why I knowed men, Frank, who'd been livin' the country so long, they knowed all the lizards by their first names, and ain't one saved hisself a shit penny nor done something like this." He belched.

"Jesus," Frank said, "that was a nice speech till you done that. Swear, Bill, you could fuck up a wet dream." And that started them laughing and remembering some light moments that had been not as funny in the past, but now, bolstered by good spirits and smuggled Scotch, brought them to the point of near hysteria. They had to set the bottle on the ground or lose it, and they were weak from laughter and gasping for breath when the Model A truck grumbled and lurched through the aspens and rolled to a halt a few yards from the cowboys, whose eyes were wet with tears.

Frank Athearn remembered Ella Connors the moment she stepped angrily out of the Model A and walked up to them, her face crisscrossed with doubt and suspicion. He knew she didn't remember him, or assumed she didn't, but after all, it'd been at least nine years since they'd seen each other. "Howdy," he said.

"Don't howdy me, you trespassing sonofabitch. Give you five minutes to git back on yer horses and underway with them mangy, damned sick-eye cattle."

She hated being so abrupt with them, for up close she saw they could only be common cowboys, though the older one looked somehow familiar. The younger one was a bit on the cute side, but she didn't linger on the thought. She couldn't go soft on them for she knew laxness when moving people off your land could be fatal. She still thought of this land as hers. "This ain't the basin for grazin' no strange cows. I mean what I say."

The older cowboy smiled easily, though it was plain he was not the smiler his sidekick was. "I'm sure you mean what you say, ma'am." When she didn't react, he continued, "Well, I guess you don't remember me. I'm Frank Athearn."

Absolutely nothing passed over her face, but when he spoke his name, her stomach tightened, soured and threatened to embarrass her on the spot. She fought for control and uttered calmly, "Thought maybe the war'd got you for sure."

"Sounds like you was countin' on it."

He was smiling, but she had no quip for his statement. Her eyes fixed on the younger, cuter cowboy and her voice was cold. "Who's this?"

"My partner and friend, Bill Meynert. Bill, Miz Connors."

"Howdy," said Billy, but she turned, ignoring him and confronted Frank. "I been usin' this land."

"Don't look like you been hurtin' it none."

She shook her brown hair, annoyed with this light attitude on his part. "I mean it was a mistake for me to sell it, and I want to keep right on usin' it." There was no plea.

Frank pondered the statement before answering, and his deliberate slowness infuriated her, but outwardly she seemed calm enough.

"Don't see how that'll quite work out." He knew what she wanted, and decided he'd have to be firm in a moment, but this was a handsome woman and it wouldn't hurt to stand here a bit and talk with her. It made him feel perfectly human just when he was beginning to wonder. He wondered how old she was, noting the lines around the corners of her eyes that had been permanently set by wind and sun. She'd changed little in nine years.

"I'll buy it back." She hesitated a moment, "I can't pay right now, but . . ."

"Ma'am, you sold me this land and you didn't seem to mind much then."

"It was near ten years ago." She said flatly, "I've changed my mind!"

He smiled and cocked his head to one side. "I ain't."

Ella hadn't expected him to agree, but then she would never have been so abrupt if she'd realized who he was at first. She thought through every word now. "You can go someplace else."

"Been goin' someplace else all my life."

There seemed no way of breaking his stupid resistance. She knew then she should back off and walk away, come later and do it right. It would take some time. "I don't bear you ill will, Athearn," she pronounced his name incorrectly, "but the land's been in the family a long time and there's been much blood shed over it. It means a great deal to me. I guess you ought to think about it." He just nodded slowly. She looked at the younger cowboy, whatever his name was—she had forgotten—and the boy nodded as well. "You'll go under and sell for taxes." She wished she hadn't said it.

"You hope," grinned Athearn, the damned smiling sonofabitch.

"Damned right," she said and meant it. There was nothing more to be said, and convinced she had played the fool for the moment, walked back to the truck and drove off leaving the two young cowboys amused and confused.

"Hell of a start." Billy watched her go, then whacked his hands together and hooted, "You sure can pick the neighbors, Frank."

For all of her determination Ella knew she'd never get the land back. She'd never admit it to herself, but when she passed the old gateposts, she stopped and removed the old, faded "No Trespass" sign and threw it in the bed of the truck. Her father had made and painted that sign along with all the rest in a blizzard in January of 1922 and all but one survived to this very day. In her own way, Ella Connors thought unconsciously that she'd closed the door on Wolf Creek meadows forever.

Upon leaving, Ella detoured through Bear Paw City, aware that there were things she needed desperately if she and Dodger were to start working cattle, if they were to be up in the hills for long periods of time. She'd also have to fill the tank on the truck, and began mentally to note where she had pennies and nickels stashed for emergencies. There might be nearly fifty dollars in the kitty, but she'd have to count it. She was sure she had enough now to top off the Model A and perhaps buy two cans of oil. Her ration tickets were in fine shape, for she only used the Model A when necessary, conserving the coupons and money wisely. Ella Connors had skillfully shoved her desires for things to a back burner whose flame had gone out. In fact, she needed little, thought she needed even less, but every once in a while longed for a dress or new shirt that might lift her spirits when they flagged. It would have to come later, she granted, as she swung the small dark truck into Bear Paw City.

Bear Paw City was a place where time had come to an abrupt halt someplace between the dawn of the industrial revolution and the age of electricity. It had a paved main street with telephone, telegraph and power poles and lines, but few homes or ranches that were distant from the town had such frivolities, even in 1945. One semaphore signal stood at the junction of Main and Kilgore Streets, the pride and joy of the community that felt big time with the addition of the contraption. The semaphore never worked properly and jarred heavily with the equestrian travel that still dominated the town, but everyone was proud of it nonetheless, for it marked them as progressive. The other addition to the two-horse town was a movie theater that always ran films over a year old, but was packed to the rafters at every performance. The bill this week was "My Darling Clementine" and "The

Prisoner of Zenda" and as she passed the theater, heading for Stadtlehoffer's store, considered seeing them, for she loved shit-kickers and had loved the Zenda book when she was a girl. Dodger or her father would read to her when she couldn't, and when she could, she devoured everything she could get her hands on. The only things she valued more than the land and the ranch and the cattle were her books, each one carefully selected for its own reason by either her father or herself. Her decision came quickly; the money could be better spent and she had books. Therefore, the hell with it. The Model A ground to a halt.

Stadtlehoffer's was the only store for sixty miles in any direction and did a brisk trade, making Johann Stadtlehoffer an independent man, or so he thought. He was not dependent on the Ewings alone as most of the businessmen were. As far as dry goods, groceries, auto parts and hardware were concerned, he had the trade all locked up and had since 1911. When it came to his feed and grain business, he had stiff competition in the body of Oss Loring whose newer feed and grain store stood one block away, at the edge of town.

For a moment Ella thought about stretching the day, of walking down to Loring's big red building and giving a pitch for a payment deal on feed that might be needed if they had snow flurries that might trap bunched animals. She was not so convinced that spring was there, but hoped it was, and that the snows would stop coming and killing her beef. It was probably after four, if the sky was to be believed. She could hear the thunder up in the mountains and knew that the light could stay awhile if the clouds broke, but then she decided it would take too long today to deal with Loring, and turned and walked into Stadtlehoffer's. She got the part she needed, increasing her debt to the German, and left, prepared to head straight home.

It wasn't hard to strike a deal with Stadtlehoffer, for he was partial to Ella for her own sake, and because he

secretly rooted for her, admired her courage to keep
going when so many others had given up. And he
owed the Connors a debt, for in the awful days of
World War One, Stadtlehoffer had been conspicuously
German and when young men would die in war, people would look to Stadtlehoffer for satisfaction as if
there were anything he could do. The German was, of
course, deeply offended at being blamed for the war
and the death, and could never understand the simplicity of the people who lived in this basin and blamed
him. Even old Jacob Ewing, with his own son fighting
in no-man's-land, or above it, for John Ewing had
joined a flying unit, led a senile, half-witted campaign
against the German, trying feverishly to drive the alien
out. But Tom Connors had sided with Stadtlehoffer
and talked patiently and quietly with the small ranchers and businessmen, one by one, showing them how
foolish they were. In fact, he did it partly for humanitarian reasons, for Tom Connors was that, but he did
it also because he could be defiant to the Ewings. So,
as a result, Ella Connors had an ally. She'd never
starve, but on the other hand she would never ask for
a thing, a shred of help, nor would Stadtlehoffer ever
help unless asked by her, for he understood her pride,
and revered it as well.

Ella dropped the small package on the seat of the
truck, but didn't open the door. Instead, she turned
and walked back down the street, not going anywhere
in particular, but walking and looking, because she
was somehow stalling for time, delaying the time when
she'd have to go back to the ranch.

The two-horse town had nearly twenty horses before the Lime House Bar and Grill, an indication the
Ewing cowboys had been given the remainder of the
day off. She knew Ralph Cole's bay, Jack Longworth's
sorrel, and thought how she'd never been in the Lime
House, how that particular place had been Ewing's
ground forever. She thought she'd like to walk in just
once, go up to the bar, have a drink and walk out,

but she drank seldom, hating the taste and wasn't that curious after all. But just once it would be nice. It made her feel strange to think that in the place where she'd been born there was a spot she'd never seen, and had no idea of its character.

Considering the length of the Connors-Ewing war it was astonishing that not everyone had either died off or moved away, for there was such great bitterness it seemed there was not enough kindness in the world to quench it. The irony was that it was the small ranchers that had suffered the most while the Ewings and the Connors waged the war. It had seemed that way to everyone, but only the ones who knew could have said how much suffering there was in the Connors household.

And during the long, bitter range war that divided them, the Ewings grew powerful and prosperous, while the Connors lost men, animals and equipment to the elements and the Ewing men. Court cases were ultimately settled on a more personal level, and the simple people who were friends and allies of the Connors were burned out, killed off and run off of land they'd put their lives into. The tougher ones stayed until it was too late, the wiser ones left with their lives and some property. The town of Bear Paw was touched as well.

Because of the violent nature of the war, the railroad had stopped running to the town, and in 1929 it was decided the line was too costly to maintain. In 1939, when there was rumor of war, men came and took up the tracks, leaving only the ties, which were soon used for firewood. It was said the steel rails would be needed soon, and so the hopes of Bear Paw City died, but long before this, the town had divided along Connors-Ewing lines.

The feuding forced five consecutive lawmen to leave

town, and the businessmen resented the violence. They didn't resent John Ewing, who was responsible, but cast the blame on Tom Connors, saying that he ought to quit, to sell out to the Ewings and move on. It didn't take them long to find having a pariah around sort of took the edge off things. When something went wrong, you could blame Tom Connors, for he was crazy more than likely. As often as not, they felt better when they said it.

To this day when she walked the streets of Bear Paw or even passed within view of it, Ella was reminded of those days, which hadn't changed all that much.

A dress in the window of a local shop caught her eye before she crossed the street and walked back toward her truck. But then dresses did catch her eye, and from time to time she would wish for one, then dismiss it with the thought that fashion was foolish out here anyhow. To the women of Montana, the highpoint of fashion was looking at pages of the Sears & Roebuck catalogue at a church social. She sighed wistfully, however, and then, annoyed with her own double-mindedness, walked back to the truck, climbed in and drove off, more troubled than when she'd come, but satisfied she'd killed enough time and that Ewing had come and gone. If that were the case, then she could relax; if not, then she'd have to be more vigilant than she liked.

Sunlight was only barely reflected among the clouds that had moved north over the mountains and clung to the light. Her father had called it an Indian sky and she'd always thought of it that way. The winter, thank God, hadn't been so bad this year. But the fact that the snow was light, that there'd been a thin pack at best, meant that in early July they could have the beginnings of drought. The summer storms would

count for nothing other than a refreshing cool that
would linger for a moment before leaving the basin
to its heat. She'd worry about that when the time
came, for there was no predicting the weather in these
mountains and they could have snow up until late
June, and it could start snowing again in early August. It had happened only two years before.

As the Model A truck rounded the last corner of
the road approaching the ranch, it moved in near-
darkness. Ella could see the outlines of the house and
barn roof as the light faded to blue-black. It faded
quickly, and the sundown winds made the descent of
night more chilling.

There were no lights in the house, for she was not
the kind to waste the precious oil needed to run the
lamps. Nor would she, for she loved the old house
and feared one thing more than anything else imag-
inable. Fire had destroyed her mother, had trapped
the woman and killed her when their old truck had
turned over. Ella was eight at the time and never forgot the sound of her mother screaming, the sight of
her clawing helplessly at the windows until the long-
bed Model T exploded, leaving Ella helpless and terrified, her father injured and just gaining consciousness on the ground beside her. She hoped that one
day electricity would be feasible, and that would, to
some degree, allay her fears. But until then, no wel-
coming lights would burn untended in the Connors
house.

John Ewing stood in the darkened living room and
watched the Model A laze down the road with the
headlights out, though on that road, for safety's sake,
they should have been on before dusk.

"That's just like her," he said aloud, although there
was no one to hear him. He needed no light to show
him the effects of time and age on the two-story,

wooden frame house that he'd once helped build and willingly. It was a damned shame to see that she'd let the house go like everything else, but he felt no pity for her. It was rather a cold appraisal, the only thing moving him being a photograph he could hardly make out, but knew well, of Tom Connors, John Ewing and their wives, with Tom holding an infant Ella. The photo had been only a snapshot from a brownie box camera, but J.W. had it enlarged because in those days the Ewings and the Connors were kin-folk and friends, and it still moved John W. Ewing to think about those days when there was little bit-terness.

He knew she hadn't seen his Packard for he'd stopped in back after swinging wide around the house looking for Ella. She hadn't returned after the fu-neral, but then neither had he. He knew his house was crowded with well-wishers that he didn't wish to see. Not this night. He'd done all that he chose to at the funeral and while his guests would be fed well, and given plenty to drink, he felt certain that Blocker and his assistant, young Emil Kroegh, would see that everyone was cleared out before the old man came home. He knew they called him the old man, and didn't care, in fact rather liked the appellation. It made him feel fatherly and patriarchal, which were two emotions the man thrived on. He watched as Ella swung the car to a halt before the house, still un-aware of his presence, watched her get out. Then John W. Ewing shoved the screen door open and stepped out onto the wide front porch, his appearance stopping Ella, rooting her to the ground.

"Door was open. Helped myself to a glass of water." His voice was so soft that only certain words reached her, for he stopped on the porch with a glass of wa-ter in his hand, and there was a distance of fifteen yards between them. "You always did have the best water around." He came down the three steps and closed the distance between them until he stood less than a yard away, looking down at her, but Ella wouldn't let herself move back or avoid this contact, wouldn't give in to the apprehension and fear that ate at her.

"I seen the old clock was missing. . . . Been in the family a long time." He referred to a clock given by Jacob Ewing, his grandfather, to Tom Connors and his wife on the occasion of their marriage. It had been carefully brought all the way from Germany before the turn of the century and was a beautiful piece of workmanship, standing over seven feet and with chimes that held Bavarian air still. It had run with perfection and no care whatsoever but when there had been interest due on the note on her ranch last quarter, she'd sold it, and Ewing knew it within hours. She didn't have to say that it lived in a pawnshop in Great Falls and had brought ten dollars more than the note interest due, and she didn't have to say that it was none of his business, for he knew this about her as he did most things. And for her part, while she was tempted to pepper him with words, she chose instead to remain silent and say nothing as Ewing drained the last of the contents of the glass and set it on the hood of the Model A, giving Ella and the Model A a consideration that spoke nothing in their behalf.

"You got to sell off everything that matters, don't you?" He showed his annoyance, but it was controlled. "You think I don't know you sold Wolf Creek to them two soldier boys?" She felt a bit lost, but still remained silent.

"Ain't you done enough to spite me?" he queried when he'd waited about long enough for a proper answer, and still she said nothing. It frustrated him, annoyed him and pushed him to a point where he thought he'd explode. He felt heat in the back of his neck, at his temples and behind his ears, but he appeared calm as he studied her from head to toe and back again, then he looked about him at the darkening ranch grounds.

"Used to be quite a place, Ella. . . . And look at you." His eyes covered her face in detail. "You got a line for every bad year and a crease for the ones you broke even."

She still would not respond, and his voice grew quieter, forcing her to strain to listen. No matter how much she hated him, something drew her to his words. She knew the quiet was the calm before his rage boiled out, but she would not and could not say a thing.

Ewing looked down at her, a concern she'd never seen before flashing into his eyes, then out. "I never wanted it like this." He gestured to where the hills hid the respective family cemeteries from each other and from public view. "It's down to just the two of us now."

He hoped she'd say something, for the silence was impossible to read and he needed to know she was hearing him. He needed for her to understand him now, as never before, but he felt that as usual he was failing with her. He always had the urge to shake her, and had fallen prey to the urge more than a few times, and he understood that she feared him for that reason. He deliberately took a step backward to allay her fears, but she still didn't move or make a sound.

"You don't even know why we're fighting all the time," he said. "You jest get yer back up when you see me or hear of me and you don't know why anymore!" And regretted having said it, for it sounded to him as if he were whining.

His manner changed and it became difficult for him to speak. He scanned the ranch as he fought for the words. "I ain't never done anything to be ashamed of."

She wanted to stop him, cut him off, for she'd heard this before, and it wasn't possible to hold back her anger at his lies. Of course he'd done things that any human would be ashamed of, and to her, but he never

seemed totally aware of others when his emotions and
drives were in high gear. And she took that for a dangerous trait, one to be wary of. Although his voice was
calm, his manner quiet and reasonable, she knew she
had more than one reason to fear him at that moment.
He could turn like a grizzly bear, without warning,
and kill with one blow, for he'd done it and felt little
regret, even after time had passed and a man with
normal conscience would have shown some contrition.
J.W. Ewing had no idea what contrition was, for no
one had ever taught him the meaning of the word.
And knowing that, Ella still did not move, did not
speak, did not tell him to get off her land as she
would at almost any other time, knowing that every
moment he was here, alone with her, increased her
own peril.

Ewing looked at her now, the lie done with, and
wished he'd either act or move on and leave her alone.
But he found himself continuing to talk, hating it,
but unable to stop himself. "You should've married
me. We'd have had a child by now." He looked for,
but received no reaction from her other than a cold,
uncaring stare, but still he continued. "He'd be heir
to everything then. Everything."

"My God." The words slipped past her lips, but
were said so softly that they went unheard. Ewing
stared off into the night. It had been a year and a
half since they'd last met. She had carefully avoided
any contact, for she knew that the sight of her would
draw him to her at once. But it had been so long,
that she had surmised he'd decided to abandon the
passion he had for dominating her, decided to wait
for her to fold all on her own. He'd always expected
it, always figured she'd have to come to him in time,
but years had passed and she remained, a blight on
his basin, an obstacle to making the entire region his.
She wondered how long he'd known about her selling
the land, and why he hadn't said anything about it
before now. Wolf Creek was as precious to J.W. Ewing

as it was to her, but now it was beyond the reach of either of them. The thought of it gave her a small amount of consolation, but not much and not enough to dispel the fear that this meeting between them was not going in her favor in spite of her silence. He was carrying on madly about marriage and children, not recognizing her hatred, or ignoring it, which was even more infuriating, as if hating him didn't matter.

"I said, it ain't too late." His words made her blink for she hadn't been listening. She'd heard him talking about Matt and his loss, but there was no sorrow and she felt no pity at all. "Got only each other now. A child between us would make this basin one, forever."

The coldness of him made her wonder if he'd already bought out Athearn. He'd certainly had time, but then she thought about Athearn's attitude when she'd pressed him, knew it well, for it was shared by her, and decided that it hadn't been the case. There was no doubt in her mind that he meant what he said, insane though it sounded, for she'd heard it before and it was beginning to sound familiar, almost comfortable, but frightening. He seemed to know exactly what he wanted, as he always had. Her hands were very cold, the palms moist inside her gloves, and her throat was thick when she spoke. "There ain't nothin' inside my fences with the Ewing brand and there never will be."

He smiled, shrugged off her answer as he shook his head, "Got to give you credit. You hung on longer than anyone else and you put up one hell of a fight, but it don't take no genius to see it's yer last year." They both knew her financial status, but then Ewing always had, even when her father had been alive. He had owned the bank at one time, and even now had great influence and could have her note called at any time, but chose not to, wanting her to find out on her own how much she needed him. "I don't want to have to ruin you, Ella."

That's nice, she mused, wondering what the next

move would be. There was no place to go from here, but he'd said it all and she knew he'd say no more. The next move would be his, and it could be lethal. She knew that and it drew something out of her, for there was a certain strength and courage she got from the adrenaline surging through her when she faced him, and it pushed her further at times than was prudent. Only strict control prevented her from speaking and now the edge slipped from her control.

"I ain't goin' under no matter what you think, J.W. You want to talk ruin, go croon it to yer bull calves when you turn them into steers."

Ewing studied her eyes, unable to see the light reflected in them any longer, and suddenly, he couldn't remember if her eyes were blue. It was impossible, he really couldn't remember. He could remember the scent of her, how there was always the essence of the mountains you can never pin to one plant, but is all the smells of all the flowers and grasses that hover in the mountain air, the fragrance of pine and spruce, and he recalled suddenly that when she was a young girl, her hair had been the color of aspen leaves after a frost, had darkened through the years and was still fetching.

She was very much like Tom, he thought, too much for her own good. Better she'd been like her poor mother. Better for her in the long run, certainly better for J.W. Ewing. There was an absence of anger suddenly, and when he realized he'd lost that edge, and couldn't get it back, he pivoted away from Ella and walked around the house, heading for his Packard.

It couldn't be over that easily, Ella thought, but then she understood that it was, that he'd turned away with a marked absence of malice. If she could read him right, there was sadness in his first steps, but they strengthened and toughened as the darkness swallowed him up.

Ella took several steps toward the front porch when

his car started and eased around the corner of the house, its headlights hitting the edge of her barn, the corral, then flashing out over the sloping plain that rolled away from the house, scattering quail into the sagebrush. He looked at her as he passed, but turned his attention to the wheel and the road as the Packard carried him away from her ranch, off of her land, and hopefully he wouldn't return. She held few hopes on that, but then her life ran on slim hopes that sometimes paid off. She could hear his car even when he'd dipped out of sight and something in the sound of the motor as the wind caused it to die and rise in volume made her wish that Dodger hadn't chosen tonight to go for the horses. She dropped her small parcel on the porch, then picked it up and walked around to the back door and set the auto part inside the kitchen door, and after such an elaborate move, wondered why. She was lax about security, in that she seldom locked doors, thinking there was nothing much to steal. But she feared for her personal safety sometimes, for the West had changed and strangers passing through had done irreparable harm to range hospitality.

When she moved to the corral, the bitch, Patches, scooted out of the buggy shed and trotted beside Ella as they went about feeding and watering the two horses. The bitch loved her woman. She knew the old man fed her, but loved the woman and had sat vigilant at the crack in the buggy wall, watching her woman and the man who spoke to her. Although she understood nothing, she could detect a mood that disturbed her. Now Patches stayed close to Ella, partly for comfort, partly for the reason that she was tired from the attention her pups needed constantly.

When everything but the feeding of Patches was done, Ella walked slowly toward the shed, and only then did Patches move away, heading instead for the back porch and taking a spot she'd all but worn down with her body.

"Don't you want yer food, Patch?"

The dog wagged her tail, but eating meant the pups would be on her, and they were like their father in that they were rough, and while she loved the roughness in spurts, over a prolonged period it became tedious. Patches had little inclination to move and could only demonstrate her feelings passively, which is what she did, and the message was soon understood. Ella entered the shed, mixed the food and set it out, but did not command the bitch to feed even though the pups whined in confusion.

For all its cracks and fractures the buggy shed was remarkably warm. The hay was accumulated there and it was still used for the winter feeding of the horses. It had a wonderful, rich aroma, and Ella lingered there for a bit before stepping out into the night chill.

She offered the dog admittance to the house, but the bitch's tail wagged happily as a sense of duty told her the coyotes and foxes would be on the prowl now and her pups might need her. Ella smiled and closed the porch door and screen against the spring night air.

Ewing's car gathered speed as he swung off Ella's road and onto the star route that cut across the Wolf Creek parcel, angling to the northern perimeter of the Ewing Ranch, cutting it where a stream called Two Mile splits and divides a wide, flat meadow into three lush portions. He slammed the car into high gear as he knew the road well, knew its limits, and plummeted into the night with the thought that he might be able to outrun whatever it was that disturbed him. He still had sight of the Connors wire, and was tempted to drive the big coupe through it at fifty miles an hour. Let her try to fix that. But though he might feel pettiness, he would never express it in such a way, for that would demean him in his own eyes.

"I'm a fair man," he said aloud, fingers fumbling the dial of the radio but picking up only the static of distance and shifting winds. Still, he was content to let the sounds block his thoughts and he drove methodically, trying to control his confusion and building rage.

Before he crossed the lower end of the Wolf Creek range a light in the mountains caught his eye and he slowed the car. He wondered if this could be a blaze beginning, but he saw the light remained steady and he suddenly remembered the two young soldiers. What was the name Hoverton had said at the funeral? Athearn. He'd heard it before, and hadn't liked the sound of the name. There'd been troubles with some ranchers named Athearn over near the park about thirty years before. Hoverton hadn't said how old the cowboy had been, but he'd quickly decided there must be a number of Athearns in the state and these couldn't be the ones that had concerned the Stockgrowers Association. Anyway, he'd laughed; that had been a long time ago, and it didn't matter much anyhow, and all the men who stood around him near the graveyard nodded and agreed, knowing how difficult it was to survive in these parts, which was why they were all Ewing's men, if not in fact, in spirit.

Now the thought of the two young cowboys on that land bothered him and continued to do so as he started up the car, picked up his speed again and brought himself home. He was thoroughly angered, the anger compounded by the frustration and the sense of loss that he felt at his son's death, though he couldn't admit it even to himself. Matt was everything people assumed him to be, but he was blood seed, or had been, and now there was only J.W. Ewing to carry on and for what? He sat with the motor idling before the great log and stone house that stood on a rise surrounded by the outbuildings, bunkhouses and quarters for the married ranch hands. Instincts long honed without the interference of intelligence made

him control his rage and despair. He looked at his
ranch grounds noting only that it seemed a small city
out there for all the lights. The hands had no sense
of cost. Damn, but they'd let lights burn all night
long, and to hell with the fact that he had to foot the
bill. For his men, he granted, the electricity was a new
thing, a toy, and he fathered and frequently spoiled
his men, so there'd be no words to Julie Blocker this
night. His fingers moved from the wheel, flicking off
the ignition as he shoved open the door and walked
up the stone stairs to the great house his grandfather
had built so many years before.

It was taken for granted that the Ewing house would
always be open to Neal Atkinson, and the same would
be true if and when the old man ever visited the
Omaha house or the New York apartment, which he
never had, and in all probability never would. One
room with two large beds was always kept for the
Atkinsons and it had been so since the families were
linked nearly a hundred years before; the Ewings with
land and cattle, the Atkinsons with the railroad, both
keys to their survival in a hostile world. Indians, rus-
tlers, horse thieves, and just plain troublemakers were
fought as much by the Atkinson money as they were
by the blood, and anger and dedication of the Ewing
men. It was a mutually satisfactory arrangement that
secured, in time, much of the basin for the Ewings,
giving the Atkinsons a refuge for the early years, an
investment to satisfy the lean years, and a future for
eternity if they didn't make a mistake, which they
didn't.

It was business in the beginning, but as things go,
the relationship between Jacob Ewing and Neal Atkinson's father grew because they both loved the same
things. They fished and hunted together, accompanied

each other on trips, threw lavish parties in each other's honor, and had a keen sense of history and destiny, which was, perhaps, the single thing that made the two men friends.

Those were the things they loved, the things they had in common. Because of those things, there was always a room for the Atkinsons in the great log and stone house that seemed out of place and time even in the West.

Atkinson had remained downstairs with the guests who had come to pay homage to J.W. Not finding him, they relaxed and enjoyed the party for what it was, regardless of the fact that Emil Kroegh and Julie Blocker stood around with long faces and silently damned them for not being down in the dumps at the death of that worthless boy of J.W.'s. Atkinson had listened to them skillfully avoid any mention of Matt Ewing until each and every one had the one drink too many to stay discreet. Then they talked too much, became a little rude for the tastes of Neal Atkinson, and he excused himself to go up to his room and write a few letters.

Three hours had passed and he'd heard the door open and close downstairs, motors fire clumsily to life, and then, for about forty minutes there was no sound at all other than the faint clatter of trays and the clinking of glass, telling him the party was over, the cleanup in progress. He listened as he wrote his letters, and when he heard the Packard drive up, he put away his leather writing pad, closed his fountain pen, and straightened his bathrobe before the mirror as the front door slammed. He lingered in his room for a moment, studying the local paper that came to the ranch once a week. There was nothing that could interest him in the three-page sheet, making the glance a time-wasting look, but he felt comfortable indulging himself with waste every now and then. It was never a habit, merely an occasional treat.

He was waiting, allowing Ewing to settle in, to relax, and after a few moments, when he heard voices, walked to the door and quietly slipped it ajar.

The great house had simple beginnings. When Jacob Ewing first came with his tiny herd of cattle and his teenage wife, infant daughter and three mestizo servants who had grown tired of life in Texas, he built only a single room, a large one-story cabin. But it was built on a stone foundation, and was the beginning. Blackfoot, Crow and Flathead Indians came to him in the hard times to trade for food, and because in those early days Jacob Ewing and his family depended on the good will of the Indians to survive, he gave to them freely, sometimes forcing his own family to suffer some. Not much by certain standards, but there would be a meal missed, and sometimes two. But the family survived in this wilderness and in time prospered, so the house grew, slowly but solidly.

A second story was added, then a wide porch, but still there was not enough room for the image of Ewing. So Jacob removed the ceiling of the original room, opening it up to a two-story affair. He built a new fireplace and chimney out of granite boulders that washed down the moraines from the high peaks. A balcony ran completely around the great living room at the second-story level and off of that, over the wide porch that surrounded the house, additional rooms were built, so that each door opened out over the living room, and one had to walk to a six-foot-wide staircase, built in St. Louis, brought to the Bear Paw piece by piece and assembled at one end of the living room facing the fireplace. The next addition was a new porch added outside the existing one, giving the house, large by any standards, massive proportions, so that by the turn of the century, when it was reaching its present state, the locals who didn't belong to the Ewing system referred to the place as Ewing's Castle. From a distance it seemed that way still, only the outbuildings contradicting the illusion.

Atkinson could see the back of Ewing's head as the man stood before the fireplace warming himself, could hear Julie Blocker talking quietly. "You been countin' on the by-God time, and it ain't done much good as I can see." Ewing's shoulders hunched slightly at the inference, but he didn't turn from the fire.

"She had no right sellin' them that land, Julie. No right at all." He turned to face Blocker who was out of the line of Atkinson's sight, and the oil man could see that Ewing's face reflected anger, while his voice was quiet but distant. "The land was given that family and you don't sell off a gift. By God," his voice rose, "I worked too hard to put this place back together, bit by damned bit, and I'll cut her down before I see it go back the way it was, family or no." He took a long breath and said something that Atkinson couldn't hear, then the old man's voice rose again as he moved to a chair, out of sight. "Want it done tonight. Soldiers or not, I don't need no fixtures in this basin not of my makin'."

Another door in the room downstairs opened and closed, there was a mumbled greeting; Blocker's voice, Ewing's voice and one Atkinson did not recognize at all. He remained by the door, standing far enough back to avoid discovery, but maintaining his partial view of the living room. Ewing spoke again, some of the tension leaving his voice as he made plans. "Pay them what it takes, whatever, but I want them out tonight. I won't be spit on by that woman."

A young blond man Atkinson recalled as Emil Kroegh moved to the bar and poured himself a drink, then stood there listening attentively as Ewing spoke.

"You don't remember how it used to be, Emil, but it was things like this almost killed the basin. Loners would come in, good intentions or not, and in time they'd put up fences, ruin the land for years to come by overgrazing or just plain stupid management. Then when it was all played out for them, they'd be down on us with a fury. We wouldn't have no protection from the law, 'cause they wasn't hard-type criminals, but *poor folks,* they said, down on their luck, but *not* too proud to steal from folks who worked hard and had respect for the land." He spit out the words. "My family and yer families built this basin, almost lost it, and now we near got it all back again, but it ain't been easy." Ewing came into sight, on his feet, and moved to a yard from Kroegh, facing him. Blocker moved into view, pouring himself a drink behind Kroegh, listening to Ewing.

The powerful rancher's voice had changed, his range accent gaining control, for Ewing could be polished when he wished. "When my grandfather first come out here, everything was like this basin. Rich in game, rich in grass. It wasn't the cowboys and cattle that spoiled this land, but the pitiful ones who couldn't stand the stink they'd made of the cities, and the farms they'd killed off." He stepped closer to the young man, emphasizing his points with radical gestures. "Was greed killed off the East, same thing's near to wiped out the West. Soon the whole damned country ain't gonna be fit to drive or ride through, but there'll be oil wells and refineries and sloughs where there were streams, great ugly holes in the ground where they mine for coal. . . . You seen the rest of this state. Hell, since you was a boy, you seen all these things happen here."

"Yessir, I have." Emil Kroegh's enthusiasm itched in his throat. "Thank God it ain't happened here."

"It could, boy. It don't take much to set it in action. All it takes is one person to start it all in motion."

Kroegh nodded his understanding, though the drink had passed through the warming stage to the ego level and all he could really hear was that he was being confided in, given the responsibility of understanding. It made him proud to have another man give him his fears and loves laid out like a dressed steer. "I ain't never let nothin' happen to this basin, nor you either, Mr. Ewing."

Atkinson grew uncomfortable listening, but remained where he was and made no move to shove the door closed. The words he heard bored him and alarmed him at the same time. He knew a half-time shuffle when he heard it, and wrote it off mentally as propaganda, but knew there was something in Ewing's speech that indicated he possibly believed the crap he was spouting. It wasn't likely, but with J.W. you couldn't be too sure, mused Atkinson. He was dangerous to blind-side and many had suffered that realization too late. Atkinson had seen it happen over and over, this uncontrollable rage of righteousness that indicated to the oil man the rancher was in need of help.

Neal Atkinson, who made his judgments from what he read, which concerned business and the arts, an interest in politics, and years of experience with numerous psychiatrists and analysts, seldom let his emotions cloud a decision. He felt he had his remaining life under control no matter how foolish his youth. He had always regarded Ewing as a quaint, old-fashioned conservative who was rooted to the free life, but bound to the land. Now he was beginning to question the state of Ewing's mind, to question his involvement with a man who'd been under business and personal pressure to the point that a lesser man would crack. He'd have to downplay all his decisions regarding Ewing and the ranch, and for that matter, all discussions of oil and the basin. It would be a time of putting the rancher at ease, while trying to find out the condition of his mind. Atkinson's earlier impatience gave way to caution.

"I ain't sayin' other folks ain't got a right to land." Ewing's words shifted Atkinson's thoughts. "But I won't have anybody comin' and tryin' to take over my land or this basin unless they can prove to me they got a right and they ain't made a mess out of where they left."

Blocker watched as Kroegh nodded earnestly, and

thought of things in years past, the things that annexed his life forever with Jacob Ewing and his grandson, John Ewing. He wondered if this boy who was second generation Bear Paw had any concept of what the old man was talking about, and figured that he didn't, for that knowledge comes with years, not the written or spoken word.

"How's yer family, Emil?" Ewing's tone shifted, and there was concern.

"We had Pa to Great Falls last month. The boys took him down, and there was feeling in the legs, the doctor said, so things are lookin' up. Rest of them are fine. Ma's doin' well and sends you her best."

"Yer mother's a sow grizzly, Emil. I guess you know that."

"Yessir."

"Always had a fondness for you, even when you were a pup. I remember you an' Matt once got me up in the middle of the night to bail you out of the Lewistown Jail. Twelve?"

"Thirteen, sir," Kroegh corrected.

Ewing nodded, sizing the boy up and down. "You an' Matt always had a streak of wild in you. I hear from Blocker and the shopkeeps in town you still got yers."

Kroegh hung his head, sheepish to the point of embarrassment.

"Hell," Ewing teased, "I'm jest glad you don't tear up my house like you do them bars in town when a touch of the old firepiss gets to you."

"Yessir."

"Don't git me wrong, boy. I like that fire you got." He clapped the boy on the shoulder, then moved away, back to a spot under the balcony where Atkinson could no longer see him, nor were his words as distinct. "I know you boys won't let me down."

Atkinson saw the enthusiasm and pride all over Emil Kroegh, saw that Blocker seemed more than aloof, more than unconcerned as he kept his eyes on the youth. Then Blocker moved, downing the last of his drink, quietly moving off to where Atkinson knew the door was that led to outdoors. Kroegh stammered a goodbye to Ewing, turned and quickly followed Blocker from the room. Neal Atkinson moved away from where he stood, checked his appearance in the mirror, then headed out along the balcony and started down the magnificent staircase.

John Ewing sat in a high-backed chair, just under the balcony, staring at the fire, a limp drink dangling in his hands. He was aware of Atkinson's descent, but paid no attention until the son of his late friend crossed the room and stopped a few feet away.

"Looks like that drink could stand some life."

Ewing glanced at the drink, nodded agreement and held out the glass for Atkinson to take to the bar and renew. When Atkinson's back turned, Ewing's eyes followed him, then went back to the fire. The fire was certainly more comforting.

"Scotch, or maybe a little brandy?" asked Atkinson.

"Don't matter." The replies came flatly and singly, in short bursts. "Jest make it red. And straight. Brandy's locked in the small cabinet. Key's under the bucket."

Atkinson followed the directions, sniffed the remnants of Scotch in the glass and played safe by repouring Scotch for Ewing. He took brandy for himself, then came to sit in a chair facing Ewing, setting the old rancher's drink on the table beside him. Neither man spoke for a full three minutes.

"I wish there were something I could say to ease your burden, J.W. I suppose you've had more than enough sympathy."

"I suppose." There was no encouragement in his voice.

"He was a good boy, Jack. It's a loss."

"For you or me?"

Atkinson was cool. It wasn't uncommon for Ewing to take the initiative. "All right then. Let's say it's a loss for the ranch. I know you have the good of the ranch always in mind."

Ewing silently regarded this young man and wondered if he despised him for his manners, his coldness or for the hold each knew one had on the other. He couldn't remember when the pleasant young boy had turned into the coyote-like man. There was almost no resemblance to old Jim Atkinson, who was a pirate in stock and a man of great warmth. He was one of the boys and a good old one. But his kid was different. Atkinson reminded him that everything he knew and loved was changing, not necessarily for the better. Something in Atkinson's manners, his way of speech, his way of dressing reminded him of that change, and under most circumstances would treat the man with civility, even with good humor, but not today. He remained silent, speaking only when forced.

"In many ways I was closer to Matt than you were. You always suspected that. The only problem Matt had was in how he could please you." Ewing sat impassively looking at the oil man as he spoke, the steady silence unsettling Atkinson, making him wary. "He loved you, maybe more than was healthy for him. But he never knew you didn't like him."

"You don't know a damned thing about it."

"I know that just because he looked like your father you treated him as if your dad was in that very body."

Ewing never realized that Matt had confided anything personal to Atkinson, but had suspected some underhanded business dealings, for Matt was always in need of money. He had flashes of another Neal Atkinson, but they were jealously herded away by stronger passions, and he drained the glass of Scotch, expecting it to be brandy. Anticipating one thing, sensing another, he made a sour face. He hated all surprises.

"Why'd you give me Scotch?"

"You were drinking Scotch."

"Yer scared to death of me, Neal boy."

Atkinson weighed the statement, sipped his drink and then smiled. "That's right. I feel like a coal black Negro in the midst of the Ku Klux Klan with a white girl on my arm when I'm around you."

Ewing laughed, stood up and moved to the bar. He started to pour Scotch, then set the glass down, reached for the brandy and poured two snifters, making his a touch smaller than Atkinson's. "I ain't that bad."

Now it was Atkinson's turn to watch Ewing, who had changed quickly, radically, to a man with energy, fire and determination.

"I don't hate you," Ewing lied, "but I sure git some ugly thoughts about you every once in a while. I guess what I come up with most is you jest ain't yer daddy, but then as you pointed out, neither am I. That's why I'm as successful as I am. I guess I shouldn't judge you by my prejudices, but Neal, I just ain't got none other." He came back to his chair, handing Atkinson a snifter, then taking his chair. Each man lifted his glass to the other, but neither said a word.

"Yer daddy was a fighter. In every way." Ewing sipped between the phrases, shutting his eyes and savoring the burning taste, the aroma. "If he saw something he wanted, he'd come right out, go for it. And when he lost, which was seldom, he showed great grace. He was a wonderful man, an' I was always proud to call him friend." Ewing grew thoughtful, thinking back on how, when he'd been in trouble beyond his control, there'd always been help from the Atkinson family. Neal was like Matt in that neither was like his father, but to his own son there was no debt. To Jim Atkinson there'd always be a debt to repay, but damn, it was so difficult with this little snot. He forced himself to smile. "I'd like to call you a friend, Neal."

"You've always been like a member of my family, Jack." He warmed considerably. "When I was very small, I thought you were Uncle Jack."

"You 'member the time we went huntin' griz?"

Atkinson recalled that day with horror, but showed his teeth in a grimace that could never pass for a smile. Ewing remembered the boy had panicked when the grizzly charged them, terrifying the horses, downing two men, and when Blocker and one other cowboy, whose name eluded Ewing at the moment, roped the nine-foot, thousand-pound piece of rage and death, the boy, Neal, had screamed and jumped from his horse. (He'd seen the bears, watched them from a distance and loved their power and strength, horrified from the beginning that he'd see an animal killed and hating the prospect.) As horses screamed and thrashed for freedom, men cursed and one, a cowboy caught when the ropes were drawn tight, fell before the wounded, defiant bear as it slashed at the ropes. Then it turned its attention to the man on the ground, and mauling him with seven-inch claws, bit off his scalp in one swift move. Spraying blood filled the air as Ewing, Tom Atkinson and a few cowboys poured rifle and shotgun fire into the silver back of the bear, who was now defensive and fighting the pain that would soon stop. The boy had no place to run, could only stand on the ground screaming at the sights and sounds, stricken by all his worst nightmares come true.

Nineteen shots hit their mark before the grizzly, with the last strength it could muster, charged the hysterical boy at twenty miles an hour, covering the distance in less than a full second, attacking with bleeding, massive jaws. Its moves were so quick, the cowboys had no time to react, but watched the bear knock him senseless. But while it began mauling the small, limp body, it'd lost so much blood that there was only the gesture of violence left to the beast. Compound lacerations and a few broken bones kept the boy hospitalized for over a month, then bedridden for another, and sessions with plastic surgeons when he was well enough supposedly made Neal Atkinson all well. Ewing remembered it as a stupid and foolish act, and that maybe it taught young Atkinson a good lesson. God knows he needed it. But then he thought that perhaps it was only a vague memory to Neal.

As if Neal could ever forget the accident or the fact that he'd been scarred facially at a vulnerable time in his life, and still felt scarred, even if the visible signs were gone. As if he could ever forget that the damned bear was stuffed, and standing to its full height beside the fireplace to remind him. He tried to tell himself he didn't hate the West, that he truly loved it. And there were things he loved, but that hunt had damaged his feelings about Bear Paw, the Rockies, Montana, and the West. He felt a paternal, sophisticated affection for the West, but would not be unhappy with the changes that surely would come.

"Y'know, Neal," Ewing said, "I been watchin' you move yer interests closer to my basin."

"Yes."

"It bothers me, son. Bothers me a lot."

They were both avoiding a confrontation. Ewing was testing, feeling, but had no intention of dealing with their problem.

Atkinson spoke slowly and softly, "It's my business, Jack. I can't ignore oil when it's right under my nose."

"What about when it's under my land, Neal?"

"Please . . ."

"Please what? Damn, don't you think I know you got that damned Bascomb man sweeping through the mouth of the basin about once a month, actin' like he's at Anzio and the basin folk are Germans or Japs!" Ewing snapped out the last words, unable to believe he was doing this now, when seconds before he'd sworn to cut this off. "I know you got to do what you chose to do. I don't want it done around me. We git that understood between us, and we'll get along."

Atkinson considered any answer to the indictment an admission of guilt. "I'm not here to discuss this. I came hoping to be of help at a bad time."

"You are so full of shit, they was to cut you open,

they could fertilize the whole damned state." Ewing poured another drink, moving quickly from his chair, and took a few sips before coming to stand near the fireplace and watch Atkinson. "But I don't know a man who isn't. All right, son. We'll accept it at that, and I'll thank you for the consideration. I won't be your fool, that's all." He finished the drink and stayed by the fire, not moving, and he looked at and through Neal Atkinson until the younger man broke off the stare, smiled and stood up, thrusting his hands into his bathrobe.

"I'll be flying out in the morning. I'm sorry we have this misunderstanding, but this is a bad time to work it out."

"There ain't nothin' to work out, son. I think you know where I stand. Can't think you'd be as unwise as to try to shake me from that spot."

Atkinson rolled the threat around, shrugged slightly and turned to go back to his room. He stopped at the bottom of the stairs, turned and saw that Ewing hadn't moved. "Do you love this basin and this ranch enough to keep it from dying?" He flicked an edge in his voice back where it belonged, continuing before Ewing could answer. "You say you do, but you can't, or you wouldn't be letting it happen."

Ewing said nothing, did not even blink, for he felt what Atkinson said was so utterly false that to acknowledge it would give life to the lie. Atkinson, content with having made his point, or at least a portion of it, continued up the stairs, seeing Ewing still watching him as he headed back to his room. The old man's eyes never left him until the door closed quietly behind the houseguest.

The wind that came after sundown lingered for three hours instead of flowing away, but it only caused

Blocker and Kroegh to stop their horses and don their heavier jackets. Blocker was trying to work the buttons with his gloves on, not succeeding at all, when he heard the distinct sounds of a shotgun broken open and two shells set side by side in twin chambers. The moon was up, but behind clouds and low still, so he couldn't see, but the sound was unmistakable and it angered Blocker somewhat. "No need for that."

"There may be. You heard what he said."

"Emil . . ." Then Blocker decided a long answer was useless and beyond the boy, so he shook his head, ripped off the gloves and buttoned up. They traveled the last hour to Wolf Creek meadows in total silence.

Night had engulfed the meadows, and the two young cowboys had made a final check of the stock, and finding the cattle grazing contentedly, returned to their camp and picked up with singing, and the talk that would break the music when one or the other told a story or tall tale. Like most cowboys, they'd been reared on tall tales, and as each region had its own particular lore, neither had heard the stories of the other, so each time they talked it was a new and happy experience. It was perhaps the thing that bound them most, for while they knew each other well, each had a deep cellar of secrets and ideas, which they shared freely.

They'd given "I Ride an Old Paint" another stab and created their own set of ribald lyrics, then they fell into one of the long silences. After he'd thought of everything that had happened that day, and was beginning to speculate, Billy played a few notes on his harmonica, then stopped and looked at where they'd been clearing brush from the remnants of the cabin. "It don't matter the cabin's fallin' down."

"It don't," said Frank, less proud by only a cloud

of weariness that swept over him. He counted quickly and realized they'd been hard at it nearly sixteen hours.

"And it don't matter you could drive the Fifth Armored Division through the holes in the fences."

"No. It don't matter."

"It don't matter it's gonna cost us near a thousand dollars to fix it up . . ." It was said with humor and taken with none.

"Billy, it don't matter cause it's all our'n."

The younger man looked at his partner, agreeing, but still needling. "But it could be less a toilet, right?"

"Whyn't you stick that harmonica up yer ass and blow us a real tune, Bill?"

"I guess it's cause yer so touchy you ain't never had yerself a woman. Far as I can see yer gonna be lovin' old lady five for a long time, you go sportin' that disposition."

Frank Athearn sat up, held his partner in a fixed gaze and thought. He spoke when he finished thinking, and not before. "Matter of fact, young Meynert, I had a few in my day, which is why I'm so cautious now. Ones I knew spelled nothin' but trouble for me, and they warn't too faithful, and in the long run I figured it jest warn't worth it and raised my standards, and found fewer and fewer women that could fit my standards."

"They musta been tough."

Frank nodded, "Tough as tits on a tank." He settled into his blankets, propped against his saddle and holding his guitar like a baby on his lap. "But it's the tough ones make the greatest impression. I remember once . . ."

"Yeah?"

"It ain't necessarily the ladies. Could be cars that makes them wild and wicked."

"Cars?!!"

Frank thought about it and gave a bob of his head to mark that indeed it was probably cars. "I was

workin' for my pa and I remember he got this brand
new '32 Chrysler. It was a Cabriolet with side mounts
and he'd won it from some dude over in Billings.
Three Kings did it fer the dude, and three Aces fer
Dad gave us the Chrysler. That was in '33 so you can
imagine how proud we was. But soon Dad got embarrassed at drivin' it, and stuck to an ole "T" and
gave me the Chrysler. Damn if I wasn't king shit with
the girls then. On my way home from Great Falls one
night with a touch too much of red whiskey in my
belly, I ran head on into an old Chevy truck loaded
with Blackfoots. Nobody got hurt and fat lotta chance
that truck of their'n would show any damage, for it
was already held together with stolen barbed wire and
wooden crates. It had no doors on the cab, nor windows neither. And more damned packing boxes and
fruit boxes for seats. It was a Blackfoot Bus. And there
were about fifty of them and jabberin' away and all of
them hoppin' mad. The gal with me was from Chicago
and I was squirin' her around all gallant-like and
fixin' that very night to get her down for the first
time. Oh, we'd done all the ritual things and she had
let me know right off that this was indeed the night.
I knew, because she was playin' shiftin' gears with me
when we hit them Injuns. Near to tore my pecker off
at the impact.

"Now there ain't nothin' that looks as mad as an
Injun when he's on his way home from town on a
Saturday night with about one gallon of anything
he can find tucked somewhere between his hat and
moccasins. Unless it's an Injun who's on his way *to*
town on a Saturday night. As I said, the Chevy's body
could stand the damage, but when we hit, the motor
tore loose from its mounts and was beneath the truck,
the little fan still spinning stupidly. I guess you might
say I was detaining them Blackfoot.

"Beverly, for that was the Chicago gal's name,
muttered something about rape, and then I guess
started lookin' around fer the most suitable one. He

was there in an instant. About my age, shy like they always are, damn them. Mad and shy at the same time. How good an act can you get? She made him a few eyes while I was over dickerin' with the man who owned the truck, and the man they had quickly designated the leader. Now, this was in the days before I learnt my trade as a bargainer. And besides, they was holding all the cards. I stole a glance at Beverly and didn't exactly feel like a man bargaining for a woman's virtue. She was making some good time with that Blackfoot. But deep down inside, the real reason was that they were fixin' to lay into me, right then and there and there were just too many of 'em. I handed over the keys to the Chrysler and they thanked me profusely, told me they'd take good care of it. They all loaded in, but I don't know how, for there were Injuns hangin' all over it when it pulled away. But the bastards could've left me with Beverly. Hell. Don't suppose it would have done any good anyhow. For all I know, she married that buck for I never saw her again.

"Several days later they found the Chrysler up in Browning and when we towed it home it was fit only fer the junkyard."

While he was spinning the story, he'd picked up the sound of horses moving through the woods, but it was hard to assess the distance in the mountains for sound carried and echoed, sometimes throwing a whispered conversation in a narrow canyon over a mile, even if distorted.

Billy's attention was on the story, not the surroundings, and he heard nothing at all. "Ain't a single woman can make a hinny out of a good man, Frank. They's got to be more."

Frank half-smiled, still able to hear the horses, and knowing they were heading in their direction. "Hell, there was a lot more than her, but she was sort of typical and the one I remember the most 'cause I set my cap for her and was sort of bound and determined.".

The sound of horses was clear now, and Billy heard it as well for he cocked his head, his eyes searching Frank's face. Frank nodded a confirmation, then strummed a note on the guitar.

"I guess it all adds up and you find yerself a bit gal-shy after a while, but I really ain't had no luck."

"Not with women you ain't."

The horses had stopped in the woods and there was nothing but the sound of the wind, and occasionally the sounds of cattle lowing happily in the meadow.

"I will, someday, Bill. Matter of finding the right one."

"Frank . . . they's some horse folk out there in the trees watching us." Billy spoke just above a whisper.

To say it made them uncomfortable to be watched from the darkness is an understatement. The rule in this country was that you never rode up on a night camp without identifying yourself unless you were bound for trouble, in which case stealth was the only solution. The two young cowboys sat by their fire apparently relaxed but both were waiting, tense, and trying not to show it. Billy warmed his harmonica, Frank the guitar, and played the music to "I Ride an Old Paint."

Blocker and Kroegh sat their horses and watched the night camp for a full ten minutes before a word was exchanged. To Blocker's way of thinking, caution was always best and while the two young men seemed innocent enough, he knew what he was doing violated every rule of range etiquette and therefore put them in the right and him in the wrong right off the bat. There was no saying how they'd react, though he noted that there'd been no change in their attitudes except they stopped talking and began making music. Neither was bad with an instrument, but neither of them was great either. Still, it was good to hear and took Blocker back two dozen years when he'd sat around a fire like that. They were happy days.

"They ain't goin' away, we jest sit here watchin' 'em, Julie," Kroegh spoke quietly.

"You gonna tell me how to do my job, Emil?"

The young man was irritated by the rebuff, but shook his head and said no more.

"They know we're here. Ain't no way they could help but hear us, all the noise we made. I'm goin' in there alone to talk to them. You stay here and don't do nothin'. You understand, Emil, nothin'."

Kroegh ignored the older man, studying the stars as an act of defiance. Blocker only shook his head and started his horse out of the woods, calling out as he rode into the perimeter of the camp.

"Hello, the camp." He saw Frank motion him closer, and rode on in. "Howdy, boys. Safe to come in?"

Frank smiled lazily, motioning to the bottle, but never taking his eyes off Blocker's face, and Blocker's massive hands which held only the reins. The Ewing foreman did not dismount, but sat his horse before them, unmenacing, in fact open and friendly, which was never an act with Julie Blocker. It made Frank a bit more relaxed, but not completely. "Well, we ain't got more'n a thimble-full in the bottle, but you kin light and help yourself to coffee of which we got plenty."

"Thanks, boys, but I ain't in need."

"Took a helluva chance ridin' in like you did," chimed Billy.

"Sorry, son, but I wanted to git you boys whilst you was still up. Saw the fire." He waited, giving them a chance to question or even ask him to leave, but they were still, just watching and listening. He continued, "I hear you boys got a good strain of beef. Tell you,

you don't see young men startin' off on their own enough these days. Yer to be admired. Afore the war, boys yer age only wanted to go ride the damned rodeo. Nothin' else."

While Billy was charmed by the warmth of Blocker and as a result, totally relaxed now, Frank was not taken in completely for he was always strong on preserving a fragment of doubt. It kept you alive a bit longer he believed. In the case of Blocker, the ring of the man's voice was true, but the words sounded familiar to Frank, who'd heard all of his life of night riders, of the powerful men who wanted no competition. This big man could be one of those, he speculated, but showed a friendly smile.

"You got a name, Mister?"

"Jules Blocker. Folks call me Julie."

"Julie. I'm Frank . . ."

Blocker's smile waned a bit. "I know who you are."

Now all three were silent and Billy's vigilance returned at the sound of Blocker's voice.

"I hate to bring you boys bad news."

Here it comes, thought Frank.

"Don't see many young men these days. You boys in the war?" Blocker's tone was friendly again.

"You know who we are, you know we were in the war." Frank waited, but when Ewing's foreman didn't speak, he continued with a touch of agitation in his voice. "Go on. Say what you have to."

Blocker genuinely liked this young man, the older one named Athearn. Liked his relaxed way of dealing with things and the directness that seemed missing in young men now. He didn't enjoy having to do this, and never would, for he'd done it before and in all probability would do it until someone took offense and he would meet his end. He didn't think this would be the time. "Ella Connors sold you a piece of land some years back that's caused more problems than Tojo has teeth. It's gonna bring you nothin' but headaches and grief."

"We kin handle a little grief, and I don't get no headaches, Julie." He thought for a moment, glanced over at Billy, then back to Blocker. "Yer the second person today's said somethin' like you jest done. If yer the welcome wagon, you ain't funny."

"I ain't tryin' for humor. . . . I can make you a good offer, there's no problem with that. . . . If I had a son, I'd tell him the same exact thing. I'd do anything to convince him there ain't no land worth fightin' for."

"Then what the hell have we been doin' the last few years?" Billy came to his feet, moved closer to Blocker. "Ain't one person told me anything but we was fightin' for this land, and now you say it all ain't worth it? Don't like to be thought fools, Mister."

"Billy." Frank's voice calmed the younger man, and yet he wouldn't move, but remained by Blocker's horse, looking up at the foreman.

"You boys ain't fools, and I ain't talkin' about the war, but about this piece of land. It ain't worth it."

Frank strummed a few notes, studying the frets, and talking at the same time. "You must never've owned a square inch, Julie."

Blocker was growing edgy, wishing it was daylight and that Emil Kroegh was not within hearing distance in the woods. It was Blocker who was beginning to feel foolish. "I know how you feel. You done yer bit, you jest want to settle down. Well, fine I say, but I say do it someplace else."

Bud, the cowdog, had seen Blocker come up, and while he seemed harmless to the dog, another instinct told him to be wary, so he left the herd for a moment, drawn by a stronger sense of duty. He trotted around the herd, checking them out, making a wide approach on the camp unseen by the man on horse and then dropped to the ground a yard or so beyond where the fire gave an aura of warmth and light. From that spot, where he could be effective if needed, the black and white and brown cowdog watched and waited.

"I don't think so, Julie. We like it here fine."

"You won't."

"Well, we're gonna try."

"Then yer a fool, son." With those final words, Blocker turned his horse, and rode back into the trees, disappearing. The dog, however, stayed beyond the rim of the camp, just in case, for his senses were aroused and he could watch the cattle and his humans from right where he was.

John Ewing sat in darkness broken only by shafts of moonlight as they played across the wall of the small room, dancing in and out of the heavy clouds. His shirt was open at the neck and beads of cold perspiration clustered in the two small pits that marked the spot his collarbones joined. It was cool, and the breeze came through the cracked window, but he still sat with touches of sweat holding his shirt to him. He had seen everything in this room a thousand times and still could not get enough. Everything in this room was a delight and a torment, and it was impossible for him not to feel both passions tearing at him as he sat in the high-backed chair, waiting.

The flowered, delicately striped wallpaper, the family photographs, the clothing so carefully tended and folded. There was no hint that the woman in the bed, sleeping fitfully, could be anything but the most caring and meticulous of people. The rest of the house was decaying from neglect and lack of necessary funds, but not this room. Oh, he thought, it was old and faded, but carefully loved and tended by the woman he watched in the bed within an arm's reach. The photos on the wall were ghostly images of better days when the Connors and Ewings were family and friends and allies, and there were picnics and parties and hunting trips that they shared and loved. He had loved and still loved the people in the photos, living and dead, but as he loved them, he hated them, and wanted them back in his life to fill the bitter void he'd inherited.

He'd never understand this woman any more than he did his wife who'd died twenty-one years before, or the other women he'd met on a business or personal level. Men were something else to Ewing. He knew that, recognized his strengths and many of his weaknesses. He could bully men, could joke them into just about anything, could hold the power of life and death in the form of work over their heads, for his word carried far and the system of blackballing a cowboy until he moved so far away he died from the radical change of climate or he committed suicide in one form or another was still in effect. There were very few old cowboys; fewer still were the old cowboys who'd retired. So John Ewing had power over men, could command affection from them when he wished, could destroy them like they were ants by not ever knowing them again, and yet he had no idea of how to deal with women, for at heart he was a common cowboy overcome by the power he sought. He'd worked so hard, he'd never had the time or the desire to investigate the world of women. Childhood had been short and quick, for when his mother died young, John, age five, had only one friend, Tom Connors, and by seven years both were expected to be fully knowledgeable in the ways of men, for life was hard and you couldn't fend for yourself early enough. His life was that of a small adult from his eighth birthday forward, his world a world of men. It was a place and time where women were thought intrusive and not wanted. Period. "They ain't good for nothin' but you-know-what," his grandfather would say, "and poontang ain't never worth the curse, Johnny."

He hadn't understood at the time, and the first sexual arousings were on him at the time, so he went into fits of confusion wondering if that were the case of his own mother. He went through a time, about a month after she died, when he couldn't remember her dark skin and brown eyes, and the smell of sage she seemed to exude from her skin when she held him. His mother had lived apart from the rest of the family, for she was a quarter Cheyenne and thought to be less than the rest, though her son was treated like the crown prince by all who encountered the youngster. Jacob Ewing, cursed with a dolt in the form of his own son, John's father, loved the grandson and hated the father, hating him even more for making John less than a true Ewing.

Everything was done to erase the memory of his mother by the family. Her clothes were destroyed or sold or given away. He never knew. Her prized tortoiseshell mirror was the only thing he found, and was able to spirit away. There was a small, simple funeral, with John, Tom Connors, and a young man who was like an older brother to both boys. The young man took charge of John, favoring him, for he knew the boy needed the attention and affection. Besides Tom Connors, the young man named Don Garman was one of the few people who would listen to John and treat him like a equal, and Don was the only one who seemed to understand how he felt about his mother, the only one whom young John would dare show his tears to when he felt the loss. It was so long ago and had dimmed through the years, so he was stunned by the clarity with which he recalled the time, and what he felt was anger at losing the days of youth, and at being made to remember that he'd lost them. It was only because he was here, in this room, that he remembered. He studied Ella, sleeping in the bed, and wondered what it was that made her so fitful. He decided it wasn't due to any sense of conscience over the damage she'd done

him through the years and he reached out and shook
her once, but she only moved away from the touch,
made a small angry sound and slept on. His fingers
then touched her shoulder lightly, as a father might
with a child, to wake her.

That she was able to sleep at all was strange. Word
had come that there'd be no further extensions on the
note that hung over the Connors land like the plague.
No longer would the bank be satisfied with a payment of interest, postponing payment on the principal. The times were hard, for the war was almost
over and money was already tightening. While the
price of cattle was high, with the war coming to an
end, and the demand to feed a standing army de-
creasing, the prices would plummet. The Connors
land was too much in demand to allow it to go to
waste, and the bank could see only that they would
never get a return on their investment. September 1,
1945, was the impossible deadline.

For ten nights since Ella had learned all this, confirming what she already suspected, she slept fitfully,
unable to fall off completely, and when she did, she was
bothered by nightmares—visions of herself, wrapped
and dragged in wire, torn by the wire, visions of
everything going up in flames, an apocalytic view
with Ewing looming over her, unsmiling, but tri-
umphant. And when awake, she was unable to remember the dream, but was left with the terror.

Through all the years of fighting she felt herself
free of domination by Ewing, but when she was in
doubt of her own existence, her own future, he returned to her dreams to haunt her. And while she
fought sleep, forcing herself awake when the dreams
came, exhaustion and a touch of curiosity dominated
and she slept, poorly but with a sensation she hadn't
felt in some time. It was the old days returned, with

the excitement you feel only when fronting a fierce and powerful opponent. While she hated her dreams, she thrilled to the strength she got from them the next day. If she didn't understand why she made the decisions she did when awake, her mind received clear signals when sleeping, and the next morning she would be more determined to survive, more set in the decision that she'd win this battle.

Just surviving wasn't enough. Not any more. The years had crept by and the work became an effort to fulfill. Things had spiraled downward. There wasn't enough money to pay hands to go up in the mountains and bring out her cattle that were half-wild in some cases, totally in others, and because she had neither money nor hands, she was unable to have a real roundup. The cattle had bred and run free for six years, with Ella and Dodger working alone just to skim the few they could catch, take them to market and get only enough to pay the interest and fall behind a bit more each year. They were surviving, but barely, and while everyone felt that for her own good she should pull out and give up, for a woman running a ranch alone was bound to lose, they secretly admired her, for they had watched everyone they knew give up and give in. Ella became an unspoken-about hero to men and women alike. She knew it, of course, but it didn't help. She could take no help from any of them, and they wouldn't give it, for like Stadtlehoffer, the storekeeper, they knew her well. They could only stand back and watch the fall and hope it would never happen. People who loved this woman hoped for a miracle they knew would never come.

So Ella carried on, but for her own sake, not for the benefit of a bunch of well-meaning, but sadly soft people who had given up the thing that once made them strong.

She knew what she was, knew her strengths and knew her weaknesses even better. She also knew her enemy, John Ewing, and feared him. It had been a mystery to most why he never went for the Connors land as he had all the others that once filled the basin, but it was not a mystery to Ella. The basin folk assumed it was because they were family, but she knew it was for other reasons. This very day had confirmed it, and now as she slept the image of Ewing standing before her and asking to marry her, to have a child with her, then leaving as quietly as he did when she refused, disturbed her and gave her no satisfaction. Her dreams returned this night as they had on the other nine, and she saw herself a young girl on horseback, riding across a broad meadow going yellow as the days shortened toward fall. The weather was summer, but the light had changed. She rode the old gelding, Brownie, and wondered where she was bound, as curious in her dream as she had been when a girl of sixteen. Then there was a part she could never dream, and it would be voices and sounds, then the sensations of violence, and Ewing would be looming over her, a giant, feet planted on the peaks of the basin walls, stamping on everything that moved. Then there would be more sounds and voices she couldn't place, and her dream would dissolve in flames, with Ewing towering over her. It was the same every night now and it was because of the dream that she attended the funeral, hoping that seeing him after so long might revive the hatred and squelch the fear, but she dreamed the same dream, tossed fitfully the same as before, and wakened suddenly as she had before, to see him standing over her in her room. It was that way; the image of the man would linger after the dream, before waking fully, but would fade quickly.

Only this time he didn't fade, didn't disappear, but remained standing over her as she lay in the bed, not moving. Ella knew it was reality and not a dream, and could feel the fear tightening her back and arm muscles.

Her reactions were honed by years of working cattle,

her moves sharpened by the toughening that comes with the need for quickness under the worst of circumstances, and she was out of the bed, racing for the door before Ewing could stop her. But he followed quickly, caught her by the hair at the top of the stairs and forced her to her knees, twisting the hair tightly until it felt as if her scalp would tear loose. Her hands were striking wildly at first, but fists, then claws tore at Ewing's hands and face until the pain in her head was so great she had to stop. He let her slump to the floor a second, then jerked her hair once and dragged her up to her feet. He just held her, staring at her, then forced her back into the bedroom and threw her across the bed, and pinned her there with massive hands. His knees worked at her nightgown, forcing it up past her legs, bunching it around her waist. As she felt him work at his own clothing, she struck quickly with one leg, bringing it up between his, into his groin, but the injury was minimal to him, disastrous to her. He hit her and held his hands around her throat, forcing her to submit, telling her he'd kill her and almost doing it, choking off the life slowly until she stopped struggling and gave in to him.

At first, he took her against her will, and hurt her mentally and physically, but then something in him changed and as he raped her, something was aroused in him he had long thought dead, and something in her she wished was.

Hands that hit her now caressed her, held her and tenderly brushed a sensitivity to life she fought to control. But as he kissed her, whispering into her mouth and ears, his hands touching her, she hoped for rape again, and fought as before, trying to hate him.

Ewing ignored the blows, and brushed her hands aside, pinning her to the bed, making love to her slowly, arousing her gradually.

Toward dawn, when he left her, John Ewing said only one thing. He had dressed, and looked at her where she lay curled in a ball, deeply ashamed, and filled with revulsion for him and for herself. He was cold and distant, not at all proud or victorious, and he sat on the edge of the bed and turned her head with his hand, and looked at her.

"I own you and you know it. It's just a matter of time." She thought he was finished when he rose and yet he continued on, "I told you years ago it'd be like this."

And he was gone, leaving Ella with her doubts and fears.

When Julie Blocker rode off, he went past the stand of woods where Emil Kroegh sat his horse in devastated quiet. Blocker never even thought of the younger man until he heard the padding of horse hooves moving through the woods to his right. He marveled that Emil could be that quiet, but then the boy was a hunter and could track lizards on concrete or so they said. Blocker spoke to his horse, touched the reins and the animal slowed, then stopped, and the two of them waited quietly as the horse came closer but not out of the woods. A paint horse, so he was sure it was Emil. "Let's go, Emil."

"Man jest pissed in yer shoe, Julie." The words cut the still night air like a scythe. There was silence, and when Blocker said nothing, Kroegh rode his horse out of the woods and stopped. "Wouldn't believe it, I didn't hear it myself."

"Ye of little faith," Blocker replied, a wry comment he hoped would ease the discomfort he felt under the scrutiny of the younger man. Then he added, "It don't matter what he said. Now shut the fuck up and come along." He turned his horse and started back to the Ewing Ranch, knowing Kroegh would follow, which he did for about a mile, the two of them quiet for almost an hour.

"It *does* so matter, *Goddammit,* Julie!" Kroegh's voice echoed. They reined in their horses and sat there as Blocker calmly rolled a cigarette.

"Calm down, Emil." The foreman barely spoke over a whisper, but the authority was there. "Now be a good boy, Emil, and don't bad-mouth me no more, 'cause you might ride fence a few months this winter, favored boy or no."

"I guess I know what J.W. said. You truly disappoint me, Julie. I always heard you was stud bull hereabouts, but I sure as hell can see you gone to seed."

Blocker felt no need to answer this acorn calf posing as a man, but he'd set the boy straight when he cooled off. "You got the spirit of an aborigine soaked with rum, Emil. You put that with what I know is a good mind, you might have yerself something to be proud of. Know what I mean?" He left it at that, knowing Kroegh had no idea what he meant. "You ready, now?"

Kroegh sat subdued, reins held loosely in his hands, nodding in response to the first question, mulling it. Then as he thought about it, he snapped into a snarl. "I ain't ridin' with you. Not now. Never. You can't even move them along like you was told. You ain't fit to be a foreman and you certainly ain't fit to ride with me." He began to back the horse clear of Blocker, angry where before he'd been hurt and confused. He was, unfortunately, smarter than Blocker thought, and had a strange insight into a code that had blurred to conform with the times.

As the boy reined the horse away angrily, Blocker thought how much Kroegh was like a trained leopard, chained and happy when left to lie, but when aroused, a fury of fang and claw that would maim its owner. Yep. Emil was like that.

Blocker watched Kroegh disappear toward the ranch. Taking three drags on the cigarette, he snubbed it on his thumb and shoved the butt in his hat band.

The foreman felt a hard ride, while bad for the horse, would more than likely cool Kroegh down. And the horse was Kroegh's horse, not a Ewing mount, so whatever happened would be on the boy's head. Screw him, he thought, for he's a punk and deserves whatever happens to him. He spoke to his horse and the bay mare eased down the road, taking her time, enjoying the night, hoping this would be the pace all the way.

As the fire died, and the warmth it gave fell off, the two cowboys considered that it had been a long day, perhaps too long, too filled with clashes and temperaments, and they were exhausted. Several times they'd talked about turning in and that led to more words, more memories, and soon another hour had slipped by. Billy talked about the days when he'd worked in Texas just before the war, and the pros, but mostly cons about Texas cowboys were batted back and forth. It reminded Frank of John Clay Tubbs.

"Who?" queried Billy with booze and exhaustion slurring his words.

"Never tol' you about ol' John Clay?"

Billy shook his head, hiccoughed, and shook his head again. "No."

"Everybody has a John Clay Tubbs, Bill. Everybody. But I guess in cowboyin' the man that teaches you is just about the most important man in yer life. But he was more'n that. Taught me more'n cowboyin'." He thought for a bit, enjoying some distant thing that flashed through his mind, and then he was serious and quiet. Billy, tough under the weariness, fought to stay awake, fought to listen. "John Clay was a reader and gave the habit to me, though aside from the pleasure I get from books and magazines, ain't a bit of damned good ever come of it."

No sound came from across the fire, and Frank

looked over at Billy, noting that while the young man was sitting upright, his head was bowed to his chest and the harmonica had slipped from his hand and lay on the ground. Frank rose, grabbed a blanket from Billy's roll and draped it over his partner, then he settled back down and studied the fire, alone with himself and relieved by it.

Billy moved, opened his eyes, then closed them and slept a bit more. The other man watched him as he poked at the fire with a stick, willing more warmth, but refusing to add fuel so late at night. His face was void of expression, his senses taking over. He thought he might have heard another horse out in the woods, but was unsure, for he was tired. He rose and walked to where he could see their horses and cattle, dim shapes on a night sea of grass. Nothing was wrong, but he was uncomfortable as hell. He listened again and heard nothing, but still watched the sleeping cattle and horses. He thought: I hope we make it. God, I hope and pray that more than anything else.

He climbed into his blankets, feeling the numbness start in his lower back, spreading quickly over his body, flooding his mind. His eyes shut, and he was floating, hovering between sleep and not sleep, wondering why a loud chicken was cackling in the dream. A laughing, cackling chicken in the woods.

Emil Kroegh's left hand held his hat to avoid breaking branches, to avoid making noise. He had left his horse downstream by a torn piece of old barbed-wire fence, tying his gelding to the wire. He waited until the animal began to graze, then when he was sure it would not knicker for him, took a Remington he'd had since he was a small boy from a scabbard that was strapped to his saddle, and went into the woods. He took his time, just sauntering to watch and look things over for himself, he would have said.

He'd seen the fire before and thought he knew where it was, but considerable time had passed since he'd ridden off angrily, and he hadn't thought the fire might have been doused by now. And now was too late, for he was lost, stone blind in a forest of aspens on a night after the moon had gone down. All sense of direction was suddenly thrown off. He calmly stopped and tried to get his bearings. His words with Blocker had compounded his anger, while his decision to ride back and see if he might be able to roust these punk cow-kissers made him edgy, for it was a bold play, even for Emil Kroegh. Now, if all *that* weren't enough, he was lost. It had never happened to him, and he'd never have believed it possible, but once in the aspens, there was no north, south, east or west in the night. Just soft green leaves, white-barked trunks by the hundreds, close together. Just a few steps and he was lost. A fear he couldn't explain came over him slowly, and he walked until he felt cold and stopped again to gain another blind sighting.

He tried to remember if he'd made a circle. He didn't think he had, but he wasn't sure. He had heard stories of things like that happening. He began walking, and then remembered that a few years back a cowboy lost in the woods had wandered over an embankment, broke his back and died. Kroegh stopped walking again, changed course directly to the left, and in five yards came out of the aspens, onto a bluff lined with undergrowth, through which he could see the remains of Frank and Billy's fire. He could also see the faint outlines where Frank slept lying down and the younger cowboy, whom he remembered had been so mouthy and sass-filled before, slept sitting against his saddle and gear. He couldn't see the cattle or horses, but assumed they were out in one of the two big meadows. Kroegh checked where he'd come out of the woods, noting a probable return trail he'd missed before. He quickly calculated where his horse was tied, and began to edge along the bluff closer to the camp, stopping where he was concealed from view by brush, but clearly able to see the camp, fifteen feet below him and thirty yards from the base of the bluff on which he stood. He was clammy, but not sweating, could see his breath, but wasn't cold. He felt very good, but still under the influence of what Blocker had once called "his goddesses, rage and stupidity." He thought he was cool and collected, but a loud noise would have terrified him, if unsuspected.

He thought: Those chicken shits! Look at 'em. Think time in the damned service gives 'em special rights. Well, we done our part here and then some, feedin' chicken shits like these, and I'll be go to hell if I'll see the place I was born ruined by the likes of you. Chicken shits!

He didn't speak. He cackled, bowk-bowking softly, then laughing to himself, giggling as he bowk-bowked again, twice and louder. He laughed aloud. "Bowk." He drew air into his lungs and watched as Frank Athearn sat up from near sleep and listened. "Bowk, bowk, bowk. Chicken shits." The voice echoed against the far wall of the meadow and came back, confusing Athearn as he swiveled his head slowly, trying to fix the bizarre cackling, the yelling man he couldn't see. "Move it on, chicken shit GI."

Billy came awake, didn't move, but listened, then looked over to see Frank sitting up, listening, looking around slowly, so he whispered, "He's in the trees." Billy still hadn't moved and Frank's head nodded imperceptibly.

"Hey, chicken shits! Hey!" Crazy cacklings and crowings came out of the woods, went past Frank and Billy and bounced back again.

The dog, Bud, hadn't moved. He had lain for two or three hours in the same spot between the cattle and men, alert. He knew where the sound came from but it was unlike human sounds he'd heard before and he cocked his head to one side, then the other. He was tiring, but stayed vigilantly close to the camp. He saw the person named Billy begin to rise.

"It's a kid, dammit, it's a kid!" hissed Billy.

"That ain't no kid!"

Nothing came from the woods now. There was no sound in the meadows at all. No wind. No night birds. No thrush songs, and there had been some before. No songs, then Kroegh's voice cackled and crowed and laughed at the two cowboys from the darkness, almost a song. Chilling.

"Bastards," Billy muttered.

"Easy, pard."

Billy couldn't be stopped. "Easy on the way up, tough to pull down," was how his uncle Merle had described him to Frank. His fingers touched the rifle against his leg, but didn't take hold. He rose from a stiff kneel, leaving the gun against the saddle leather, and shouted across the clearing to the bluff that rose facing him, "I don't know a upright, well-meanin' man who'd call a man out from the holy goddamn shadows, less he's some kinda fool. Come on down here, motherfucker, and call us out!"

"Bowk, bowk, bowk, bowk! Ain't callin' you out, chicken shits! I'm sendin' you out!" shouted Kroegh.

"I'm tellin' you, Frank, that's a damned green kid! Ain't no grown man gonna act like this. Hell, it's damned nineteen and forty-five, y'know."

He was stopped by more crowing from Kroegh, but there was more anger to it now, less fun, and it would break to allow phrases so garbled as to be unintelligible. It *did* sound like a hysterical child, refusing to be calmed.

"You ain't seen that many grown men yet, pard," said Frank Athearn. Under the covers his hand closed over the handle of a knife but he made no move. He watched the woods, checked his partner and called out, "We ain't got no reason to fight with you, Mister. Whyn't you come round in the mornin'? We'll talk about it some over a cup of coffee."

A shot chunked up dirt near the fire, a second took the coffee pot and whirled it into the darkness of the meadow where it landed beside the dog who had risen and was moving slowly to the camp.

"Hold it!" Frank spoke, but saw it was already too late. Billy was moving for the old rifle that his uncle had given him. A third shot took him in the head, the fourth high in the throat, and he fell backward into the fire, not moving, not quite dead. Mercifully, he went before the pain penetrated the shattered brain tissue.

The fifth and sixth shots took Frank where he was and he fell back against his saddle, still holding the knife under the covers. The shooting was over in thirteen seconds, but it seemed like one second and one hour to Bud, who froze at the edge of the camp, knowing the smell of death all too well.

Emil Kroegh was not surprised he felt little remorse for his act. Rather, he was stunned by the feeling of elation he experienced with the first two shots, then the sudden surge as he saw the impact of his third and fourth shots on Billy's body. He took quick but deliberate aim on Frank, squeezing off the last two shots carefully, driving them into his target, the high chest. It had been so easy, he marveled he had never done it before when he considered the moods he had been in when armed in the past. He had a very good reason for his actions, and knew it, but hadn't expected this bone-shaking feeling of power that came over him, taking away the anger he'd felt before. He reloaded the Remington, then made his way down the embankment, already feeling better about Blocker.

When angry, he had been prepared to go straight to Ewing, to tell the old man how Blocker had shamed them all that night and not even tried to carry out his orders, and pal or not, it'd serve Julie right. He was getting old anyhow and Kroegh was convinced that he was next in line for Blocker's job, and lately had even begun to consider himself a possible replacement for Ewing's own son. Why not? he'd asked himself, but ignored any negative reason.

Now the anger was gone, and while at first he lied skillfully to himself, he began to be less convinced he was in the right. He was wondering what the next step would be. He could go to Blocker, tell him what happened and the foreman would become part of it, lest the old man think he was losing control, letting his cowboys shoot up the world any time they wanted. He was instantly less than convinced of that. Why *should* Blocker back him? Or the old man for that matter? He knew he'd have to get rid of the bodies and tell the old man he'd run them off, and take all the credit for himself. But it wouldn't much help the old man get the land, he suddenly recognized. No one was alive to sign over the land, and it would be five years or more until Ewing could get it for taxes. He tried to recall the orders, what Ewing had said to him, but he couldn't remember. He'd been off in shit city, or so he thought, now. He moved into the camp, crossing from the base of the bluff to the fire circle and the two sprawled shapes he knew were dead. There was no movement from the one against the saddle and the other one was smoldering as the fire smothered under the body. Still, he was unsure, and levered a shell into the chamber of the rifle and lifted it, firing one into Billy's head, the head and face taking a strange shape, distorted beyond recognition. He slowly levered a second shell, took a deep breath as the weight of what he was doing came down on him. He hesitated as the power fell off sharply and things swarmed into focus all too quickly.

The hesitation was all the dog needed, taking three short steps, a longer one, another and leaping as

Kroegh raised the rifle and took aim at Frank, know-ing now he'd gone too far, but forced by fear to go further and driven to be absolutely certain he wouldn't be discovered. Bud struck the cowboy near the right shoulder, and slipped free, but Kroegh, shocked by the attack, knocked off balance, quickly recovered as the dog turned, lunged at him, snarling and snapping, trying for the throat. Kroegh threw himself to one side and swung the rifle, cracking the dog on the spine, knocking him away.

At first, Bud could barely whimper. He had hit the ground, and spasmed wildly, shaking, feet rigid. The dog was stunned and unable to move as Kroegh rose to his feet, picked up the rifle, then cracked the cowdog's skull. He took a breath and stood over the dog, waiting, searching for a sign of life, and for one split second thought he heard a noise, but before he could turn Frank Athearn came up behind him, a strong left arm going around Kroegh's throat, pulling him back against Frank's weakening body as he drove the knife between Kroegh's ribs.

"Sweet Jesus!" Kroegh screamed, then cried and screamed to God to help him as the barlow knife flashed again, this time shallowly finding its target. Frank held it with all his remaining strength, pulling the taller and younger man against him, and he could feel Kroegh's strength as the larger man fought fu-tilely for freedom.

When his legs buckled under him, Frank shoved his knees against Kroegh then fell, dragging Kroegh over on his back. The impact drove the knife the last quarter inch to penetrate the heart. Kroegh kicked, his hands clawing for air and then the struggling stopped. There was no strength left in Frank, no de-sire to move, nothing that could help him slide away the heavy body that pinned him to the ground. He could feel everything going to black in his head, and knew he was dying. His last thoughts were damning

III
STARGAZER

Dodger crossed from the Connors land to the Wolf Creek meadows with some concern. He'd thought he heard shots just after two in the morning, but it might have been later. He hadn't thought about it, for it could have been someone after a coyote, or it could have been a distant car, though he'd thought it was unlikely. Now he came up into the meadows, aware of the buzzards circling lower and lower, aware of something dead or dying. His horse could sense it and shied. A horse he recognized as a Ewing mount grazed at the edge of the lower meadow, and the old cowboy could see the cattle and horses belonging to the young cowboys undisturbed in the upper meadow. Strange, he thought, but it seems quiet enough. He could see the camp, could see what at first he took for sleeping shapes, but as he got closer he could see the bizarre angles at which the bodies lay, and then saw Emil Kroegh, face contorted, a hand clutching the hand of Frank Athearn's that held the knife, and knew this was a place of death.

He studied everything from horseback, and no stranger to violence himself, soon read the signs and understood all that had happened. Too bad, he thought. Too damned-fuckin' bad. Something would have to be done with the bodies, but he supposed he'd better leave that for the sheriff. Fat lot of good that'd do. Might as well eat ants and hope to live as count on the sheriff to do anything about this. He started to turn his horse, to ride off, when the dog moved slightly and whimpered, and the hand of the cowboy left the knife in Kroegh's chest and flopped at the dog. Then the fingers moved, clawed the earth and Dodger knew that one of them was alive. He slid to the ground, ran to the two bodies and heaved Kroegh's lifeless form from the other cowboy, kneeling and holding the other man for a moment. "Hold on there, gonna git you some water." He laid the young man down carefully and moved back to his horse, taking his canteen from the pommel and bringing it back to Frank. He held it, poured some water into his hand and dribbled it onto Frank's lips. There was no longer any sign of life, so the old man dropped his head to the chest of the wounded cowboy, listened, then muttered "Yep" and scooped the younger man in his arms and lifted him as if he weighed no more than twenty pounds. Walking was more difficult, swinging the inert form across the saddle even more difficult. He knew he wasn't young anymore, but this was harder than he remembered. It had been a long time since he'd carried a wounded man in his arms. He forced the memory away as he breathed and gained the wind to mount and urge the horse off. He looked at the dog, would have shot it, poor beast, ending the pain, but hadn't the time. He swore he'd come back. He put spurs to his horse and they carried Frank carefully but swiftly to the ranch.

From above, the buzzards watched, driven skyward by Dodger's presence. Now they saw the old man leave, and satisfied they'd be left undisturbed, swooped in to feed on carrion. It was a bountiful meal, and soon there were dozens of the birds covering the camp, more on their way, but Dodger was already crossing the old fence line that split Wolf Creek from the Connors Ranch.

It wasn't the first time. Not by a long shot. You've been hurt by him before. You've got to keep on going, and standing there, feeling sorry for yourself isn't going to do a damn bit of good. You're acting like a woman, Ella thought as she washed and dressed before the mirror, and that's exactly what he wants you to feel.

She was happy the bruises on her face were slight, and was glad suddenly that she wouldn't have to face Dodger. He'd probably roll in after noon sometime and she hoped the swelling would be down by then. Makeup never crossed her mind, nor would it. Lies would have to suffice if ice packs wouldn't do the job, and the hell with what he thinks, she thought. She wondered what would have happened if Dodger had chanced back, seen Ewing's car or horse. Dodger's presence might have kept Ewing away, but she doubted it. She realized she hadn't heard him come or go, had no idea that he moved so silently and wondered if that was part of her dream. A bitter laugh escaped her throat as she quickly dressed and hurried downstairs, away from the bedroom. She had stripped the sheets and pillowcases, hanging the mattress and pillows out the bedroom window to air.

For a bit she thought of postponing washing the sheets, but changed her mind. She might need them when she was tired and knew how it felt to wash when you were exhausted. So she prepared to do a laundry, a thing more distasteful to her than housekeeping, though she dealt with both chores with resignation. She carried the sheets and other things that had accumulated inside the kitchen door to a large tub where she washed by hand, carefully working each piece on a washboard that had been used by her mother.

She was awkward at first, resisting the work, but as she worked, she developed a rhythm that made the chore disappear and enabled her to do it without thought or regret, but that freedom gave her mind a chance to wander over other thoughts, and she wondered after a time which was worse. It had been after seven when she began the laundry, and now, aware someone was riding hard for the ranch, was surprised to find it almost nine o'clock. She thought: I've rubbed these things a thousand times. Fool.

Her eyes followed the dust as the rider fell behind a hill, and after moments reappeared on the flats that marked the approach to the ranch. Her hand went to the bruises on her face as she realized it was Dodger, and she tensed, knowing now there'd have to be an explanation, or lies, or both.

It was strange for him to be in such a rush, and the thought of some possible problem made her forget herself as she started toward the gate that lay past the windmill.

Dodger's horse stumbled once and they almost went down, and she saw he was carrying something or, as she soon realized, someone in his arms. When they came through the gate, Ella ran beside the horse, reaching up to take Frank Athearn from Dodger's arms as he brought the horse to a stop. Dodger dropped to the ground and together they lowered Frank and knelt beside him as Ella checked the extent of his wounds, muttering "Sweet Jesus" over and over. She looked up at Dodger, wished she had a telephone, for she thought the cowboy who was her neighbor was dying. "Take the truck. Git the doctor and right away." Dodger nodded and motioned for her to help him carry Frank to the narrow buggy shed forty yards away. The load was heavy and they had to stop once to rest.

"Pardner's dead as a stone." Dodger saw the dark marks on her face, but averted his eyes, saying nothing. He nodded at Frank instead. "Don't think this one'll make it."

"Not if we stand here talkin', he won't." Ella wished she'd bitten the bitterness that came out, but understood without asking what had happened in the meadows, didn't doubt it for a second, and were it denied, she still would believe it. She knew this and what happened to her were to be laid at the feet of J.W. Ewing, and she knew that in both she shared a portion of the guilt. Whether it was just or not, she shared the guilt, and now prayed for the life of the young man whom she half-dragged, half-carried to her shed with Dodger's help. She wished she'd said something to them, warned them, but she hadn't and now could only hope he wouldn't die.

She remained with Frank, cleansing the wounds, working carefully, as Dodger left, driving off in the Model A. She remained until the doctor returned almost two hours later. The doctor spent a long time alone with Frank, while Ella and Dodger waited outside.

"What time you think it is?" Dodger queried.

"About 1:30. Maybe 1:45."

The old cowboy looked at her face and noted the bruises were all but gone. He pulled a bite from the chaw he held and wrapped the black stick, shoving it into his vest pocket. "Doctor could treat half the world in the time he's took."

Ella leaned against the '38 Dodge coupe and wondered why the doctor had painted his full name on the side of the car, when most docs, including vets, just put a red or white cross. Maybe they'd stick the letters M.D. on either side, but this one put all of it on, like he had something to be really proud about. ALEXANDER JOHN MCGOWAN, GENERAL PRACTITIONER, M.D. Just then McGowan appeared from her shed, as if her wondering this had brought him out. He was apparently finished.

A lanky man with great meaty hands, indicating he'd once had a more powerful profession, McGowan came up to where Dodger and Ella lounged against his car, set his bag down and drew his coat on. "Broken ribs. Bullet deflected down, and he had an exit wound near the hip." He pointed just above his kidney line. "He was lucky, lost a fair amount of blood and he'll be dizzy for a while, but he should live easily and mend to working shape with few problems if any." He fished in his pocket and drew a chain with two dog tags out and handed them to Ella. "He was in the service. These weren't his first wounds, nor his worst. Keep these for him until he's better, maybe a couple or three weeks. I'll be back in a day or so, but when he wakes, keep him quiet for Godsakes." He looked sternly at Ella, saw the irritation and doubt, knew he had stepped too far out and sought to withdraw some of the sting. "You don't mind, do you?"

"I do," she said quietly, glancing back to the shed.

"Ain't gonna hurt none," volunteered Dodger and got a harsh look for it from his employer. He shrugged, and spit once at a swift ribbon that wriggled through the grass, wondering if it were a king snake or garter.

"He really shouldn't be moved, Ella." The doctor wished he'd been more tactful before and now used his best and most effective manner on her. "I've never heard of you so much as refusing a wounded wolf cub. You gonna tell me you'd make a human being chance his life?"

"I might," she said flatly, still annoyed, but also bothered that Athearn's wounds were somehow related to her, "but I won't. He can stay for a while, but you better try to get him someplace else pretty soon. You hear?"

Doc McGowan patted her arm, gave it a squeeze and nodded his way into the car and away from the ranch before he went out on a limb and agreed to do as she asked. The cowboy wouldn't have money for a hospital room, and wouldn't take charity anyhow. He was sure of that, so Ella was the answer.

Dodger had started toward the shed as Ella watched the doctor drive off, but stopped to wait for her and heard her say, "Jesus Christ! Don't that beat it though." She shook her head, and as Dodger came back to her, looked up at him, saying, "Athearn's got my land and now I got Athearn."

The old cowboy looked levelly at her, not smiling.

"You better know," he said. His eyes flicked to the traces of the bruises and he hesitated.

"I better know what, Dodger?"

"Warn't jest Athearn an' his pardner up there in the meadows." He wondered if he should go on, but did, before he reached a decision. "Emil Kroegh was there with a six-inch barlow knife that Athearn there stuck in him."

"Emil Kroegh wouldn't've done it without Ewing sayin' to go ahead."

"You don't know that," Dodger commented.

"Don't I?"

Dodger hated the expression in her eyes, looked away and shrugged. If he didn't know what caused the bruises, it wouldn't be so hard. But he knew, and knew he couldn't do a thing about it. He had to remind himself that it was none of his business. "What I meant was that Kroegh was a nearsighted rattlesnake all by himself, regardless about J.W." He wanted to reach out and hold her as he'd done when she was small. "It ain't yer fault what happened there. Who'd've thought?"

Ella nodded, then when seconds fell away, muttered, "Yeah." She stood watching the wind play across the sagebrush, and thought about the events of the last twenty-four hours and wondered why things always came together, and how come there were no easy decisions? "Gonna begin roundup, old man."

"Figgered."

She looked at him, tempted to smile. The old man knew how things concerning the ranch were: the state of the market and the need to raise enough cattle and sell them to pay the loan. They wouldn't have to discuss it. Still, she felt obligated to explain. He asked the amount of the principal, for it had slipped his mind, was told and whistled through his teeth, then listened until she was through speaking.

"My, my, my!" he said quickly.

"Guess you know this'll be the worst season we ever have had. Gonna hold the worst kinda work." He nodded, but said nothing, nor did he look, but stared out at the horizon, then swept his gaze up into the mountains. He motioned for her to follow him, led her into the corral and motioned that she take one horse while he take the other, and he tossed her a rope that hung on the wall of the shed, taking one for himself. Ella slipped out a loop, swung it around her head several times and threw it over the head of one horse as she talked on to Dodger. "Worse'n last year even."

Dodger just looked, nodded and spit as he swung his loop and dropped it over the horse he'd chosen. They led the two animals to the rail fence, tied them, and began grooming them with brushes that Dodger brought from a watertight shed at the side of the barn.

"You ought to know you're free to pack it in right now if you want." She said it quickly and watched him straighten, look at her. She hated the look. Since she was a child she had hated it when he'd show he was hurt.

He dropped his brushes into the box and walked around the horse to stand facing her, thrusting his hands into his pockets, rocking back and forth on his heels as he spoke. "Babysister, each year I git a little less prime, but I can still do the job, and I guess you know that. Now you want to be upset about Athearn, then I guess that's between you and God, but don't take it out on me."

She started to protest, knew he had her and nodded, then fell silent for a long time before continuing. "They're sayin' it's my last year, Dodger. Sayin' I'll go under before fall."

"Said it before, I recollect right."

She hesitated, about to let it go, but she'd watched him move, knew he ought to be taking life easier and knew that he'd go on until he dropped dead. "It's different. This time, I believe it'll happen. There ain't no way just the two of us . . . Ewing's . . ." She stumbled over the words. "He's just waiting for it to happen, then come down and gobble it up. When that happens, won't be no place for you."

"You want me to go?" He was not hurt, but matter of fact, and she knew from his expression that she had but to nod and he'd pack and go. She shook her head.

"You think we got a chance, Dodger?" She looked at him with no expression.

Dodger knew she wanted to hear his opinion, knew that it did not matter at all. He could tell from the way she approached him she was already determined. He shrugged. "A chance. Maybe."

She reminded him as he thought over their situation, "You remember, we barely turned enough for note payment on the interest alone and we had weather breaks last year."

"I recollect we had a few bad breaks with regard to bones." He was recalling a fall she'd taken, and once when he'd broken his ankle toward the end.

"I guess you had your share," she said, smiling for a second, "and yer older and brittler this year, old man."

"Yeah, and yer cows are one year tougher, one year wilder. You got cattle ain't never heard of flat land." He spit, grinned and wiped his hands. "Shoot, might as well ranch mountain goats."

They gave up on the horses, turned the animals loose and walked from the corral. Dodger had his hands locked behind him, head bowed in thought, and for a while she thought he wouldn't speak, but when they reached the entrance to the buggy shed, he stopped and regarded her calmly. "The deep water don't hurt, y'know, it's the feelin' of being dragged off the cliff that kinda gits you." He winked.

"You can say no, Dodger."

He shook his head and stuck his thumbs in his belt. "Nope. Made m'choice." He thought and grinned. "We got us one old man, and one banshee woman boss." Still grinning, he shook his head, turned and walked off saying, "Like a fart in a windstorm."

She was tempted to agree, for it was just about as effective as the two of them even having a chance. But he'd agreed. They did have a chance. And he chose to stay.

In his shed, Dodger packed slowly, for he'd grown used to the four walls and while he longed for the out of doors, knew he'd miss this place. It would be a long time up in the mountains, and when he wasn't working nights, pulling double shifts as they both would, he'd be in the line shack and the thought didn't thrill him, for the old shack was filled with scars of unpleasant days. They'd sworn each year to build a new one, but had neither time nor money, so the square cabin stood a bitter reminder of times past.

He took only a few things now, but he carefully laid out and packed up everything that'd soon be thrown into the truck and hauled up to the camp at nine thousand feet. He was glad he'd used good sense and brought those horses down when he did. It would give them more time for cattle, and the horses seemed fat and healthy.

I ain't sure we can do it, he thought, but I sure enough guess Babysister ain't sure neither. Might be a way, we was to get enough to sell and hire hands. . . . He suddenly remembered that Frank was there, and wondered how the boy was doing, then assumed that Ella would tend to him, no matter how loud she protested. Still, he thought, it wouldn't hurt to look in on the boy later on. He sat for a bit on the wood-framed cot and thought about what must have occurred between Ella and Ewing the night previous and grew sullen, a mood uncommon to Dodger. He cursed his silence, his willingness to allow it to be her business, then fell silent, wondering what she would say if she knew he wanted to help, and what would he do if she said yes.

His limbs felt weighty and his head was stuffed with thoughts that collided with the exhaustion he'd felt since morning. He'd tried always to fight sleep in daylight, but now craved rest and put his head down for only a moment, vowing five minutes rest and no more, but he slept quickly and deeply, not waking until early morning.

Ella prepared a light supper for herself, to share with Dodger. Carrying a tray to his shed, and finding him asleep, she left silently, leaving the tray on a chair just inside the door. It was a rare act for her, but she was moved by the simplicity with which he'd answered, and by his loyalty, which was unfathomable.

She was tempted to pass the buggy shed without checking on Athearn, for she'd been there twice and he'd still been unconscious. But she remembered Patches and the pups were two hours past feed, so she walked to the shed, swinging the door wide. There was no light, but she could hear the pups and knew they were indeed far past feeding. So she lit a candle, and moved to the icebox, following Dodger's instructions, scribbled on a piece of cardboard, written to remind himself of the way he prepared the food. She went by the numbers, looking over once or twice where Frank lay sleeping, but otherwise ignoring him, as she was determined to do no matter what.

He made a noise in his sleep but she only glanced at him, lifting the candle in his direction, satisfying herself that he was fine. When she had Patches' food all mixed, the dog devoured it, and went through the nursing ritual with her pups.

As the pups squirmed in the candlelight Ella marveled that anything so ugly could be living in this day and age, and smiled as she imagined what a pervert the father must have been, with God-knows-what in his blood.

Instead of going out when she rose, she moved to the back of the shed and stood looking down at Frank Athearn, noting the doctor had done a professional job of bandaging. A blanket had fallen on the floor, and she bent to get it, then spread it across the young, sleeping cowboy. Then she thought that there was tackle she might get now when he was asleep, rather than later, when he would be awake and would want to talk. She stuck the candle so she could see, and began to lift the coils of rope and harness equipment from the pegs.

As she turned with arms laden with the first coil of gear, her eyes passed over Frank, hoping she hadn't disturbed him. She tossed the gear near the front door of the shed, then turned back to the wall, passing over him a second time. She did it three times, and as she turned for the fourth and last coil of gear, she was aware of something behind her. Then an arm circled her throat and pulled her to the floor and she twisted to see Frank at her ear, his arms braced to snap her neck. With a short, swift move, she jabbed her elbow to the spot on his chest where the bandage encircled him and he winced, doubling in pain, releasing her. Ella stood against the wall, rubbing her neck, watching him, ready to react with a kick for the head if he moved again. He looked at her and raised one hand; then as pain swept him, followed by nausea, he found he couldn't even drag himself back to bed, but collapsed beside it on the floor, unable to rise. Ella watched him, tempted at first to help, then afraid as she tried to breathe past a bruised throat which had been originally hurt the night before. All memories of that night came back suddenly as she watched Frank try to pull himself back on the bed.

His hands could grip, his legs could work, but there was not enough reserve for him to pull himself, and the more he knew it, the harder he tried and the more injury he did himself. When Ella saw dots of blood on his bandages, she quickly came to his side, trying to lift him, overriding her own fear and doubt, helping the cowboy. Frank shouldered free and slapped her to one side, not hurting her, but surprising her totally.

"What the hell is wrong with you?" she demanded loudly.

Frank turned, holding himself, and saw her, but had no strength to speak. His mouth moved and his eyes closed and for a moment she thought he'd passed out. She waited and he opened his eyes, then nodded and held out a hand, allowing her to assist him back to the bed. He was sweating heavily and she wondered what to do for him. She poured water she'd set aside earlier for the purpose of giving him, then held the cup to his lips and allowed him to drink. He nodded and closed his eyes, letting his head drop back on the coarse pillow.

Ella stood over him a moment, considering if there might be anything else, when his hand shot out quickly and held tightly to her wrist, surprising and startling her. She twisted and pulled free, springing back from him.

"Goddamn you! You ungrateful bastard!" Her voice carried anger and surprise. She stood out of reach watching him try to form words.

For Frank, since opening his eyes, all had been a blurry vision of past, present and future rolled into one. He'd spoken to her, had words with her over the land, had no idea who the man named Blocker

worked for, and knew only that he'd been shot, and
that he remembered Billy go down. In his confused
and painful state, with only a few memories and facts,
he assumed Ella was somehow connected with it all.
He tried to form full words, but only a painful, rasping collection of sounds came out at first. He tried
again and put one word before the next as if learning to walk. "You . . . do . . . this?" He tried to point
to himself.

At first she didn't understand his meaning and was
about to ask him to try again when it hit her. "Not
me, you stupid sonofabitch."

"Got . . . reason enough," he managed.

"If I didn't, I got reason now, you bastard." She
turned and headed for the door, but Frank stopped
her and she stopped to listen as he formed the words
asking about his partner. She was about to ignore him,
then knew that would do no good.

"He's dead." She said it quietly, but Frank heard
it and shut his eyes. She seemed bound to stay, but
wanted to run, to get out of here. She wanted to offer some words of comfort, but knew she had none
to give.

"Look, Athearn . . . I'm sorry this happened, but
you must know I didn't have a thing to do with it."
He looked at her, saying nothing. "You think I'd
have you here at my place if I had shot you all up?"

He looked at her, and nodded as if confused, shaking his head lightly. He saw and heard only particles
of light, slivers of sound now. The room was going
around him and he had no control. His eyes opened
one more time and he saw Ella Connors come closer,
a look of concern, as she spoke to him.

"You hear me, Athearn?"

And then everything was blackness for him.

What finally brought him around was the smell of cooked food, and once, after it was light, he opened his eyes fully, expecting to find himself a small boy of six at home with his mother cooking on the great black and white stove that was her pride, but he looked out on an unfamiliar world, one of rusted stirrups, broken leather and worn saddles. He was in some sort of barn or shed, unsure of which. At his head was a wall with cracks where he could see through into the large barn attached to the building he was in. The smell of hay made him comfortable, but he couldn't place where he was, or where the smell of food was coming from until the door bumped open and Ella entered carrying a tray, and the night and day before came back in a bitter avalanche. He tried to move and found himself in pain so great it hurt to keep his eyes open.

He saw her carry the tray to the bed, and eye him with caution, and he remembered vaguely that he'd gone after her or something like that and frightened her, and felt sorry, but wouldn't waste words on an apology at this time. He felt he might pass out again at any moment, and wanted to stay awake long enough to know what happened. She watched him, but stepped back, as if expecting foolishly for him to feed himself.

"You can go on an' eat."

He shook his head, trying to form words.

"What's wrong with it?" she asked, stepping closer.

"Nothing," he managed.

"Oh, I see. You expect me to feed you, is that it?"

Frank couldn't answer, he just looked at her, not liking this woman at all.

"Well, I ain't about to. We ain't got no nurses around here an' I ain't about to become one." She gestured at him, then the food, "You sit up and feed yerself." She waited, but he said nothing. "Jesus, Athearn. It's only broke ribs."

He saw she meant what she said, and held his
breath, hoping he wouldn't feel something tear as he
tried to shove himself up to a sitting position. The
pain was not located in any single place but went racing through his body, in and out of his brain, and he
gave up, grimacing, trying not to show what anguish
he felt. He looked at the woman and saw her watching him curiously, waiting.

"I ain't gonna help you none, if that's what yer
waitin' on, Athearn."

"Why're you doin' this?" he rasped.

"You was a horse I'd've shot you. Don't need no
cripples around here slowin' me down. More it hurts,
more miserable things is, faster you'll get well and be
on yer way." She sat on a stool against the wall and
watched as he tried again and finally made it to one
elbow, taxed beyond any ability to eat. "Trouble is,
Athearn, you come here at a bad time, and I just
ain't got the time. Sorry. You got the best I can offer."

He looked around, made no sounds, but the look
said it all. The shed was dilapidated, and showed
neglect, whether deliberate or not he couldn't tell.

Ella watched him study the shed, saw him sniff the
food disdainfully and remarked, "Got the feelin' yer
gonna be one pain in the ass."

He shook his head and took one bite. He was content with a taste, giving him the warmth of the first
bite. After a moment, when the porridge in the bowl
had cooled, he tried again as she watched him.

"If it makes you feel better, most of yer cattle are
fine, but my . . . foreman"—she said it with some
hesitation—"says they'll wander out unless watched,
so he's gonna see to them for you. All right?" Frank
nodded. "Yer bull already wandered over here and
got after my cows, they tell me. Only one day and
he's after my cows. You hear?" Frank nodded again,
took another bite. "I suppose it don't matter lest you
figure on claimin' the offspring. What my cows birth
is mine."

She watched him take two more bites, then aware he was being quiet because of her aggressive tone, she relented. She smiled and scooted the stool closer, but Frank only glanced up and shoveled another bite into his mouth. "He is one horny bastard, that bull of yours," she ventured nicely.

He studied her before answering and it made her very uncomfortable. "Guess you kin tell."

She maintained a cool facade, better than most at banter. "Knowed a few."

Frank said nothing, but half-smiled and lay back on the bed, staring at the ceiling. She watched him for some time before speaking, aware of what must be running through his mind.

Her tone was kinder, softer. "I reckon yer stayin' on in spite of this." He looked at her, then nodded slowly and she found herself silently cursing him for being unreadable. She hated unreadable people, but fancied herself that way often, and many times it was the case. "Ewing," she continued, "the man that did this to you . . . well, he ain't gonna allow you to start up." Frank said only that he understood, so she went on, "I know what I'm sayin' though you might not think so."

"I ain't arguin' that you don't know what yer sayin'," Frank offered. "You jest don't know me."

"Stupid," she muttered. But it was overheard.

Ella Connors rose quickly and took the tray, seeing he was through. Her manner had changed and she was abrupt and business-like as she gathered up the things.

"Look now, Athearn . . . you can't be moved until yer fit and I guess that means I'm stuck with you, but mind you now, I ain't cut out to be no hospital." She thought about leavin' it at that but decided she was too uncourteous, yet she really didn't feel she owed him an explanation. She sighed, biting her lip before continuing. "See, I got a roundup to start. I can't be too bothered with you. I'll see you got food

and water, and you kin tell me at night if there's anything you need that I can provide, but I ain't rich,
and times are hard, so keep that down. But one thing
you got to remember is that you are gettin' fit, then
on yer way, 'cause I don't need you around and that's
it, you understand?"

He could only nod for the flood of weariness and
the pain combined to drive him out and under once
again. He tried to nod, but slipped off to sleep before
she could leave the shed.

A full day passed and Frank spent it lost in dreams
of cattle and land and partnerships and friends. Then
when he wakened to find light pouring in through
cracks from the west, he realized he must have slept
the entire day away. He shouted once for Ella, calling
her Miz Connors and waiting, but there was no sound,
so he assumed she was out of hearing and sooner or
later would arrive. He heard the pups who wakened
at the sound of his voice, and yipped and whined. He
tried to see them, but couldn't and decided to calm
them by whistling softly, keeping a nonsense tune.
The pups quieted and he was rewarded further by
Patches who left the pups to investigate the whistle
and sat now looking up at him. He stopped whistling,
opened his eyes, saw the bitch and stuck out a hand
hoping she'd come to him, but she scurried back to
her pups, leaving Frank without company, without
friends. He stayed on the cot and tried to remember
how everything had happened but could only remember how it had been between Billy and him in
the war, and on the trail.

The sound of an automobile caused him to snap
from the reverie and he listened to the droning sound
as it came closer, and wheeled into the area just outside of the shed. He could see the black and white

outlines of the sedan, wondering what sort of car would be painted crazily like that. Movement flashed, and he saw the star move past a line of cracks and knew the law was just outside. he lifted up on an elbow and called out, softly at first then louder, hoping to be heard. It worked, for in moments he heard the sounds of footsteps and the door swung wide, allowing the setting sun to blind Frank.

Two men, nothing to him but dark shapes, with one wearing a star, moved into the shed. The man with the star, spoken to quietly by the larger man, remained by the door as the first and larger man came to stand over Frank.

"I hear a terrible thing happened to you," said the man. "It's a damned shame."

Frank nodded, was about to speak, but the man continued.

"It'd seem yer lucky to be alive. Very lucky, considerin'."

"My pardner's dead though. I think I got the one that did it."

"You did."

Frank nodded, looked up at the man and studied him. The face was kindly, and the hands were large, indicating the man was powerful, and had worked hard. The sun had creased his face into furrows that made his eyes and mouth appear eternally laughing or smiling. "Yer the law. The man that did this to my pardner an' me is named Ewing. You gonna get him?"

The man smiled thinly and shook his head. "I ain't the law." He pointed to the man by the door. "He's the law. The man you killed worked for me." He placed one foot on the stool and braced against his knee.

A terrible lost feeling began at the base of Frank's spine and spread over his back and arms as he fought saying any more. He knew he was on dangerous ground now. The man facing him was too friendly, too calm, and not at all concerned with Frank or his problem. The attitude was clear. The man spoke, confirming Frank's doubts and concern.

"I'm John Ewing." He waited, but there was no reply, and Frank showed no indication of anything but instant hatred, but kept it wisely under control. "If I had wanted you dead, we wouldn't be having this conversation, son." Ewing's voice was calm and unhurried. He studied Frank, noting that the young man looked like he'd spent a hard life at work, that he knew horses and cattle and under most situations would be regarded a good man, not an outsider and interloper. But not here. Not now. "I'm damn sorry about yer pard, sorry as hell that it all happened, but sometimes things go that way." He gestured toward the sheriff, then looked to Frank, his manner affable, but laced with warning. "Now we're disposed to give you the benefit of the doubt when it come to the charge of murder. In that way, you might say you're very lucky." He reached into his coat, produced a wallet and slipped a check out, handing it to Frank, who took it, examined it and turned it over in his hands as Ewing spoke. "You take that. It's more'n enough to give you a good fresh start somewhere else. Git someplace where you got a chance."

"Guess now I understand how all them other ranches we seen on the way in went bad." Frank never took his eyes off Ewing.

"You don't understand shit, son." His voice grew hollow and he stood erect, as if ready to pull Frank from the bed. "This ain't no git-rich-quick basin. Ain't never been a small ranch succeed up here."

Frank shrugged, turned the check over in his hands as he spoke. "You want me off the land, you better gun me right now, 'cause you won't get no better chance." He smiled, then moved the check to his lips, and gripping part of it with his teeth, tore the check in half with a swift jerk of his hand as Ewing looked on. He dropped the pieces on the floor and waited for the explosion he expected to follow.

It astonished Ewing that he should feel admiration for the cowboy in the bed, but he knew it took guts to rile him, and it took even more guts to turn down a check like the one he'd just handed over. But he was never one to let admiration interfere with his plans. "If I wanted to shoot you," Ewing smiled, "I don't guess I'd have much of a problem." He looked for and got a nod of confirmation from the sheriff, then turned back to Frank. "You can't like playing the fool. . . ."

Frank made no sound, made no move, but allowed his silence to say all he had to say.

Ewing turned and started off, then looked back to Frank, pausing long enough to speak a few short words, his voice barely audible. "Ella had no right to sell you that land. Won't bring you nothin' but grief in the long run. A man who serves his country deserves better." He studied Frank for a time before speaking again. "Seems I might be able to trust my back to you, Athearn."

"I was wonderin' exactly the same," said Frank quietly.

"Son," smiled Ewing, "you better know you can now."

He surveyed the shed, shook his head at the state of things and turned out through the door, the sheriff stepping aside for him, then following him out, closing the door behind them.

Frank was grateful for the interruption, thankful it had ended as it had, for he was in no condition to have had it any other way. Now he was grateful it was over and he had the comfort of darkness to compensate for the rage he felt at being as helpless as he'd been.

Billy, he thought, I'm sorry I did this for you. I hoped for better for us both, and look at what I brung you to. He closed his eyes and rested. One thing was certain, there was nothing he could do now, and worrying wasn't about to get it done. Everything bothered him, from the Connors woman to the man named Ewing. Nothing fit. There was no reason for what had happened to him, and he knew this was all a nightmare and then realized there was reason enough, that he had land that two families wanted, that his partner was dead and he was laid up, perhaps forever. The thought that he might not recover a whole and able man caused him to throw everything else out of his mind, and he began to formulate how he'd get on his feet, how he'd force away the weakness that held him fast.

In the days that followed, Frank saw Ella only once. She'd come back from working the horses when he would be asleep and be gone after leaving him some food, each time a bit further from his bed, with a note that would read to the effect of get-off-your-ass-and-walk-or-else-you-starve.

But one afternoon she'd come in with a truck, stopping outside, and just mumbling at him as she ran into the shed and then quickly out paying him no mind, getting the first aid kit that hung beside the door. He waited for her to come back, but she went instead into the barn where he could see her through the cracks in the wall. He slid closer to see what she was doing and watched as she prepared a bed of straw and blankets.

"What's wrong?" he asked.

"Sick colt," and then she went outside and reappeared a few moments later carrying an undernourished colt in her arms, bringing it to where she made the bed, making the young animal as comfortable as possible. She was aware that Frank watched her from beyond the fractured wall, and while it bothered her, she tried not to admit it to him.

"He ever walk?" he asked through the wall.

"It's a filly." She was annoyed and hurried as she spoke, hoping furiously they would be the last words. "Today's the first time I saw her. Bringin' in my horses and I saw the mama hide her out." She worked for some time without a word, but everything she did seemed not to help. The colt was already in the late stages of malnutrition, for the mother had tried to wean the filly too young, dried up and refused to allow the youngster to nurse. Now the animal was all but beyond help; still Ella worked to save its life.

Among other things, in the last few days Frank had thought about this woman who owned this ranch. He realized he knew nothing about her whatsoever, yet here he was living in her care, and while she put herself out little, she asked nothing in return. He watched her through the crack near his head, resting comfortably, wondering if he should show her that he'd been on his feet and taken his first steps in the last few days, but decided this would not be the time and remained still as she worked over the colt.

"Seen a few colts, and never saw one as far gone as that one," he ventured after a while. He saw her tense and knew she'd forgotten about him for a bit.

"Leave me alone and don't watch me," she said loud enough for him to hear, firm enough for him to believe.

But he persisted, "I'm sayin' that colt ain't gonna make it and I'd be glad to . . ."

"I can save her," she said unconvincingly.

"I don't think so," he ventured softly.

He knew the colt couldn't make it and wondered what drove this salty woman forward to a futile conclusion. Well, he thought, it's her business. He confirmed it in his mind, and took one more glance through the fractured wall and settled in to rest and keep the vigil with her, even if he was unwanted.

"Have it your way," he muttered as he closed his eyes and rested. There were several things the woman didn't know, among them, that he'd forced himself to move, to stand and walk a few steps, that while it was difficult it had rewarded him with the knowledge he could do it. He felt it would please her, and then didn't care if it did or not. He hadn't asked to come here, hadn't asked her to care for him, yet here he was and now he owed her and there seemed no way to pay her back.

Ella cooed to the colt, trying to feed it from a bottle she kept for such emergencies. While the colt would take a few drops it had no strength in reserve and the weakness made it difficult to hold its head up. She would hold the head in her lap, stroking it, holding the bottle to its lips. The colt shuddered in her arms and she tried to feed it again. And so it went past midnight and into the small hours of the morning. The colt hung on until just minutes before four o'clock when it died.

She could only sit holding the head, looking at the little animal that had given up no matter how hard she worked, wondering if this would be the way of this season—hard work, only to lose in the long run? She shook off the doubt and looked to where she knew Frank was huddled beyond the wall that separated them and called out softly, "Athearn?"

No answer came, for in spite of his good intentions to keep vigil with her, he'd fallen asleep before midnight and slept now like a baby.

She called again, but when no answer came she rose and moved to a shovel that hung in a rack by the barn door and moved out into the cloudy predawn light that came from the southeast. She walked to a spot where she'd dug before and broke the hard earth, beginning to dig, with steady strokes.

Frank stirred at ten to five in the morning, sat up, and when he remembered the night that had passed, looked through the crack. Seeing no sign of Ella, he wondered what had happened. He rose slightly, listened and could hear the sound of digging that came muffled through the door. He sat up on the edge of the bed and using a five-foot two by four he'd scrounged, lifted himself and hopped toward the door, each step a blow that racked him with pain. He reached the door to the shed and swung it wide on a new morning that was already lightening the sky. It promised to be a wickedly hot day. He followed the sound around the shed and stopped at the corner as the sound quit and he saw Ella standing over a shallow, open grave, in the process of lowering the body of the colt into the hole. She stood there a moment, head bowed, and Frank watched as she began to fill in the hole, going on with the rhythmic strokes as she threw dirt on the tarpaulin-wrapped body in the grave. Frank's curiosity about her built as he watched, fascinated by the way she worked, thinking, she's more like a man in the way she uses her body. Must've been at this all her life and is hardened to it. He'd never known a woman who could shovel and maintain the hours this one did and not even rest.

A quick glance around the ranch grounds, for this was his first time out of the shed after learning to walk, told him they were shorthanded. There were a number of things needing work, and he was sure from watching her that it had nothing to do with laziness. The place needed work, no doubt, and he felt that maybe, just maybe, when he was fit enough, which should be soon, he'd do a few of the things needed doing. That way he'd be a little on the road to paying her back for some of the trouble he'd caused her.

Ella's digging ended and she turned abruptly, and saw Frank watching her, supporting himself on the two by four. But she said nothing, merely shouldered her shovel and walked directly to him, stopping for a second, then going past him without a word, heading for the barn, and coming out without the shovel. She carried the first aid kit to the shed, left it, saw to the pups and Patches, then went directly into the house.

Frank pondered a moment, going back over the last few days and sorting out what he knew about this strange woman who seemed all alone. Few horses, a Model A that while dependable should have long since been replaced, no other animals but a few chickens and two geese he'd heard, but not seen. And now that he'd surveyed the rest of the ranch, no hands unless the two distant sheds held cowboys who might be up in the mountains. What was it she had said about starting her roundup? He looked at the mountains and while he felt disoriented, knew only a few days had passed, and mid-April was certainly early to start a roundup unless you were bone desperate for hands and had to do most of the work yourself. Still, he pondered, a woman couldn't run a ranch by herself.

Recalling when he'd last met her, almost ten years earlier, he tried to recall if she'd had hands then and could remember only the old man whom he'd thought to be her father, but learned was a hand. So he knew she had one hand then; but now?

He hobbled back toward the door of the shed as Ella came out of the house carrying a large chest by two brass handles. She set it down beside the door of the shed as he came up and opened the lid to a fine toolbox with a handy set of tools and knives for carving inside. Ella pointed to the two by four under his arm, "You want to use those, to work down that hunk of wood yer usin', then be my guest."

He nodded and squatted with difficulty to inspect the tools. "Yours?" he asked.

"Belonged to my pa," she replied tightly.

"Musta been one for workin' with his hands. These are fine tools." He rose and smiled at her. She was a nice-looking woman, he thought, though she could do with a little fixin' up. He noted her hands were sinewy and dark from the sun, but they were tapered and thin, not broken and twisted like many women who drudged over a ranch. He wondered how she kept them that way, and knew he'd never understand women. "I thank you for the use of them, and if there's anything I can do to help out and give you a hand, just let me know."

She looked him up and down, her expression saying she doubted if he could do anything but hobble, then she shook her head and made a sweeping gesture with her hand. "Just git yerself well and off my ranch, will you please?"

She turned, quickly walking back to the house. He dragged the toolbox closer to the door of the shed, removed a draw knife and sat on the toolbox, to begin working on the two by four. He slowly drew the knife along the grains, beginning to form a shape. He worked for two hours without stopping, forming the board into a rough crutch, moving only to select a new tool for the proper cut or slice. His mind went over and over what had happened to him, and he thought about Billy, though he'd tried not to speculate on that until now.

She had left him a note telling him that Billy had been buried, but he hadn't asked her where or how it was paid for and decided that, no matter what, the boy would need a gravemarker. And then there was the matter of writing to his aunt and uncle. He put aside the crutch and sat thinking for a bit, dealing with the remorse as it came to him, thinking about how it could have been for Billy and how it had turned out.

He took the rough and half-finished crutch and shoved himself to a standing position. He'd overdone that day and knew it, but decided giving in to fatigue was no answer now, and moved himself to where he'd seen some cedar planks earlier. He found the boards, selected a piece about four feet long and about fourteen inches wide, wondering who had milled it, and deciding the woman might have done it herself for all he knew. He chuckled as he imagined her eating trees and spitting out planks, for it fit with his philosophy that you need your sense of humor when your spirits are low enough. He wondered if he'd ever be able to make this ranch work, and as quickly decided he'd just have to and that was it. There was no other solution to his way of thinking and he knew it would not sit well with this Connors woman nor J.W. Ewing either. Still . . .

He dragged the plank back to where the tools sat in the sun that had now come around the corner of the shed and he tanked up on a drink of water and settled in to warm himself and whittle on the plank.

By arrangement, Ella and Dodger had chosen this day to bring in the horses that Dodger had located, to corral them and prepare the animals for the roundup they were about to begin, or as Ella would say, "Already begun, but ain't nobody gonna know yet." For that reason, there was no need to go out, and the night spent futilely laboring over the colt had left her spent. She ran water, took a shower and tried to sleep, but doing so in the middle of the day didn't suit her and soon she was up, tending to paper work she'd long neglected, carrying the books and records and receipts to the kitchen where she could watch a soup she'd begun about eight o'clock in the morning.

A glance out the window told her Frank was hard at work on his carving. She noted he'd switched to a piece of cedar and wondered what the hell he was doing with that. She also wondered what it could have been that brought him to his feet so quickly when the doctor had figured more time than this, and felt a bit guilty that her short temper and nagging might have forced him beyond his limits. It occurred to her, though, that he might be on his way earlier now, so the sympathy waned and she went back to her papers, ignoring him and not moving from the table until the sound of hooves could be felt in the frame house.

Dodger had worked the horses down the mountain slopes for almost two days. He'd not slept in twenty-three hours and was delighted to see the ranch appear as he topped the rise that was last on the trail before the long flat plain that rolled gently downhill to the ranch grounds. His spirits, while vigilant, had been low for the last two hours as he fluctuated between hunger and a passionate desire for sleep. Now, with the horses under control, and moving easily, his spirits soared at the thought that he was minutes from his destination.

He gave a high-pitched yell, waved his rope and started the horses racing for the ranch, feeling they'd run off some steam and be easier to handle. If they didn't know he was coming, they'd know now and damn, but Ella'd better be quick about swinging the corral gate wide. He thought he saw her, then noticed the figure he was watching moved awkwardly, with halting movements and what appeared a bum leg or a third. leg, and he realized it was the cowboy, Athearn, not Ella, moving to the corral gate. He also saw the cowboy wouldn't make it before the horses.

Ella appeared on the porch and ran, passing Frank Athearn, swinging the gate wide for Dodger and the horses as the old cowboy brought in the twenty-six head like threading the eye of a needle. While the horses were excited, they seemed happy indeed to find food and water waiting for them and accepted confinement readily even though they'd been running wild for a month.

Frank came up to the corral and studied the horses as Dodger came out, dismounted and stood watching

Ella make a check of the horses as she tied the gate shut.

"Howdy, Buck," said the older cowboy. "See yer up afore they said you'd be."

Frank returned the greeting as he moved to the corral fence and watched the horses inside. He remembered Dodger as the old cowboy who'd been with Ella when he had purchased the land so many years before. He supported himself on one leg and his makeshift crutch and shook Dodger's hand.

"I understand yer the one who brought me in." The younger man still held the older man's hand as Dodger nodded his answer. "Then I owe you my life," said Frank, simply.

"Call it square. You got a chaw of something? Left m'stuff up the damned mountains." He patted his old, worn clothes for emphasis as Frank reached for the tobacco he kept in his shirt pocket and passed it to the old man who broke off a chunk and popped it into his mouth, eyeing Frank Athearn up and down, then handing the package back to Frank. "Don't look half so bad you did the other day, young Buck." He smiled but then sobered and thrust his hands into his belt. "Sorry about yer partner, and I guess you know the dog bought it as well."

Frank shook his head, indicating he had no idea. He was saddened as he thought about what a good dog Bud had been. He'd come with the cattle, a virtually priceless gift who'd become a good friend in a short time. "Who the hell'd kill a dog?" he murmured.

"Didn't look like it could be helped. Emil Kroegh, the man that shot you, was torn down from the shoulder. More'n likely he killed the poor thing when it went after him."

Ella stood listening to the two of them, wondering what it was that kept Athearn on his feet. She thought he looked a little pukey but was damned if she'd try to tell him.

"Buried yer pard on yer land, though there was some stink to have him planted in the cemetery." Dodger worked the chaw in his mouth, shifting sides for comfort, then going on. "Thought you'd ruther have him near where yer gonna live. That is if yer gonna stick it out."

"I'm gonna stick." Frank studied Dodger for a moment. "I owe you a lot . . ." He didn't know the old man's name.

"Dodger," chimed in Ella, wanting this greeting quickly over.

"I owe you, Dodger." Frank looked at her, then back to the old man. "You mark the spot so I can find it?"

Dodger nodded, spit and demonstrated with his hands. "When yer ready, I'll take you and show it myself, but I put him in the best spot I could find and marked it with a cairn of stones."

Frank observed he used the word cairn, indicating some Scottish lineage. He knew there were Scots working cattle up north near the Canadian border, and assumed Dodger may have hailed from those parts originally. He nodded his agreement with the idea, and then watched as Ella and Dodger walked off, leaving him by himself, allowing him to make his way back to the shed. He lingered by the horses for a bit, then went back to sit on the toolbox and work with a knife on the cedar plank.

Two meadowlarks played around the eaves of the house, swooping out occasionally, diving at Frank as the light fell off to the southwest. He'd forgotten how the sun traveled in the arc it did at this time of the year. He remembered Italy when it seemed the sun was always overhead, and it took time for him to re-adjust to things that had always been natural to him. His hands still worked at the wood, fingers forcing the knives and chisels to fashion the words on the small plank. He stopped only once in the afternoon and that was to drink water, and he noticed then that he hadn't seen Ella or the old man since they'd walked away from him in the morning, each going his own way, Dodger to his shed and Ella into the house. He presumed they were bound for bed, for each seemed walking and talking in a dream state, and now, as the sun fell, he wondered if they still slept.

He noticed that the door of Dodger's cabin showed signs of life as light flitted from the cracks, indicating that someone was walking between the light and the door. Well, the old man is up, he thought.

His ears picked up the sounds of what he took for glass or metal being rattled in the house and assumed Ella was moving around as well, and he thought that just maybe the reason he hadn't seen or heard them might have been because he was lost in thinking of how it might have been, could have been, and such. He seldom looked back, seldom lived in regret, yet here he was doing it for a day and just when he thought he'd gone over it as many times as he could. It did him no good at all and he forced himself to think of other things. His eyes flicked to Dodger's shed and he watched as the old man dragged a chair outside and then went back inside for a guitar that he brought out and began to strum. He nodded at Frank once, acknowledging he'd seen him. Dodger strummed chords and notes, then stopped and tuned, and while he tuned Ella came out of the kitchen carrying a tray, walking straight for Frank. He tried to rise.

"Sit down, damnit." She was curt and set the tray before him, saying, "Nice enough out here for you to enjoy an outdoors meal unless you don't care for that."

He took the tray, laying the board and tools to one side, and set the food on his lap, tucking the napkin

in his shirt to save it. When Ella remained, he moved
over on the toolbox and indicated there was room for
her to sit. "Yer welcome to join me if you want."

She looked at the box, then shook her head, not
once looking at him.

"All right then. Do what you want. Just thought
you might like to keep me company." He was annoyed
and it showed.

"Why?"

"What?" he asked, the confusion showing.

"Why would you want me to keep you company?"

"Never mind," he muttered and took a bite of the
food, which was fair and nothing more. He tried to
ignore the fact that she hadn't moved but was standing there, and he knew she was watching him. He
glanced over at Dodger tuning his guitar and wondered if the old man had such a time with her, and
if so, how come he was still around. It went on and
on, and still she stood over him, finally saying,
"Well?"

Frank looked up, puzzled, his mouth full at the
moment, making him unable to answer.

"Well what, Ma'am?" he spoke nicely, though he
felt in high dudgeon at the moment.

She gestured at his tray. "The dinner. Tell me what
you think." She said it for herself, for information, he
thought. There was no tension, no irritation in her
at the moment, but he took her for temperamental and
talked softly.

"I think I've never had cooking like this." He
smiled and rubbed his stomach, noting her eyes were
flint-hard slits watching his every move. Nothing
escaped her, except compliments.

"You think it's worse'n turkey shit, don't you?"
She indicated his dinner with her finger a second
time and he quickly took two bites.

"Yess'm, I think it's that bad, but only 'cause you
burned it and I guess that's 'cause of them old sloppy
stoves they got out here. Why I remember when . . ."

"Forget it," she said and walked back to the house.

He shrugged and watched her, smiling, noting she looked as good walking away, perhaps even better, and then thinking if he tried anything she'd be on him worse'n ugly on the lizard. Not worth the hassle anyhow. She's the meanest bitch I ever met and she's got nails for a heart, so don't give it another thought, my boy, he reminded himself. The door slammed behind her and there was only the sound of Dodger working on the guitar, the meadowlarks who still played their game of tag and the wind shoving the vanes of the windmill around loudly.

After a bit the old cowman stopped strumming and sauntered up to examine Frank's handiwork. "Thought you ought to know yer cattle've scattered. Horses too, but mostly they're on Ella's land." He waited but Frank only nodded and continued working the gravemarker. "I guess that's a pretty damned good job you done there." He gestured at the wood under Frank's fingers and nodded approvingly.

"I guess," Frank considered, "but damned if I know what to put on the thing but his name and date of birth and . . ." He avoided the words death and went back to work.

Dodger watched him, thought carefully, then asked, "You an' him ride together long?"

"Not long," came the terse reply, then Frank stopped and looked at the old man. "But he was a good friend, y'know?"

"I do."

"You understand why all this happened?" Frank's question was simple and sincere, but there was no way for Dodger to answer it so.

"You got in the middle of somethin' but it warn't yer fault," he said.

They were quiet a few moments, and during that time Frank finished all but his search for appropriate words to mark his friend's grave. His fingers played across the board as he thought. Somebody ought to fucking well know about Bill. "He saved my life once."

"That sure as hell counts for a lot," Dodger announced.

"We were gonna do right by this piece of land, though I guess Billy would've been happy enough just bein' a plain cowboy. I was the one with the jumped-up ideas. Not him."

"Well, you didn't shoot him, Buck." Dodger responded, fishing for and finding his old pipe.

Frank sat there, hands loosely holding the gravemarker, and looking off into the night. "You're right, it ain't my fault." He sobered darkly, looked at his hands. "But it don't help me to forget I let him down, and God that makes me wish it were me, rather than Bill."

Dodger waited, thoughtfully, until Frank stopped speaking, then he rose, mumbled that he'd be right back and he set the guitar down and walked back to his shed. In a few moments he reappeared and carried a long package under one arm. He paused near the lantern, and began unwrapping the oilskin like a carpet, gently rolling it out to reveal the two rifles carefully wrapped inside. He handed them both to Frank. "I picked them up with the rest of the gear. Thought I knew the big gun. Seen it before when I took part in the Johnson County War. Boy was kin to good people, Buck."

Frank took the gun that belonged to Billy and studied it, then Dodger. "You were there?" The old man nodded, but Frank knew better than to press. Still, he couldn't refuse the question he fought to hold back. "Which side?"

"Which one d'you think?" He spit, and grimaced, feeling his pipe sour in his mouth. "I ain't never been anything but a cowman my whole damned life, and I'll be damned if I'll ever take the side of the ranchers. . . . Save one, that is." He glanced at the house, then gathered up his guitar. Slinging it over his shoulder, he pointed at the gravemarker, then spoke again. "There's an old song about a dyin' cowboy. . . . Why'n't you jest write the words, 'I won't be home this fall.' Seems fittin' to me, don't you think?"

Frank remembered the verse and how it had been used on the graves of cowboys fighting for a place of their own a thousand times over. It was becoming a lament for the breed, a lament for the freedom that slipped away from them gradually and had been doing so for over fifty years. He watched as Dodger turned and walked back to his shed, going in and instantly blowing out the light. Frank used the lantern, moving it to see, then he took up his carving tools. He began to chisel the words bequeathed to him by an older cowboy, who'd never met the young man who was Frank's friend but knew him from a past feeling he'd never lost.

Ella sat in the darkness of her room, unable to sleep, but not at all willing to spend her time with Athearn. Still, she couldn't help but overhear all that he said to Dodger, and it made her feel worse than before when she'd known nothing about the boy who lay dead up in Wolf Creek meadows. She wondered if Dodger, who must have known she'd overhear them, had drawn the story out deliberately. He'd gotten on her earlier because she treated Frank so rudely, so abruptly, and then when she'd taken out his dinner and tried to talk to him, damn if he didn't up and act like a big horse prick.

But she was fair and remembered how uncomfortable she had been in his presence, and how the words hadn't come out as she wanted, and probably never would. It was not like her to be short of words, nor to have trouble expressing herself, but with him it became a thing she dreaded.

She wanted him gone, and yet she understood how

he felt and hoped that he'd stay now that he was here. She'd watched ranchers and small farmers give up so often, it frequently seemed as if she was a freak and that everyone was right in branding her so. That someone else would be so crazed as to stay in the face of death and slow destruction amazed and surprised her. She could hear the scraping of the chisels and knives and soon the sound lulled her to a half-sleep where she wondered if his determination was still with him—or had all that sentimental drivel turned him soft with thoughts about how it should be, not how it is. When the sounds ceased, and Frank moved into the shed, preparing for bed, she awoke, listened, and then rose, going downstairs and out the back door, drawing on a man's robe that was warm, but sizes too big and very old with signs of wear at the elbows and seat.

A light shone under his door and she assumed he was still up, so without knocking she opened the door as he was dropping his trousers, and stood there, unable to say anything, unable to turn away.

Frank could only turn and look at her, trying to hitch up his trousers, but missing a grip and the things slipped back down around his knees. He grinned foolishly, leaned on his crutch and said, "You got the advantage."

"I . . . wanted to know . . ." Her eyes moved down to his trousers and she shook her head. "Put yer pants on, will you?" She waited until he did as instructed and then continued, clearing her throat, making it as formal as she could.

"Heard what you said tonight. You still plannin' on stickin' it out here?" He nodded, and she could only shake her head. "Even if it means you might die like your partner?"

"I ain't runnin'," he replied, and then lowered himself to the bed. He jerked his thumb in the direction of Dodger's shed. "You got any more like the old man?" She didn't reply, but he hadn't expected her to. By now he had figured out there were only the two of them. It was the way he'd seen them walk together, and the way they made up a special unit. They were all alone and goin' strong. He studied her in the nightgown and bathrobe, noting she was not afraid to show how shabby things had become. Her pride was fierce, but not false and that he liked a lot. "Old man is one hell of a cowboy. You know that, of course."

"I do." Her answer was curt, for she wanted to hold her own thoughts and not follow his line of questioning. "You know, yer crazy for stickin' it out around here."

"I hear some folks think that way."

"But yer stayin' anyhow. Is that it?" She had expected he'd say he was thinking it over, but he was so matter of fact, she pressed further. "I suppose you expect you got some sort of friend and ally in me."

"No, matter of fact, I don't. I figure you hate my guts, and that's okay, but yer stuck with me, with too kind a heart to throw me out." His arm swept the room, "You can see I'm doin' my best to get on my way as soon as possible."

"I never give you no reason to think I hate your guts," she protested. "You got no right to say that."

"Okay."

She was fuming and had almost forgotten why she came down to speak to him but held fast to her thoughts and spoke quietly after a moment of staring tossed nails into his eyes. "Yer pretty smug with me, 'cause you got me pegged as jest a woman, but when you face up to the big guns in this basin, you won't be so damned simpleminded, nor so uppity either."

"If you say so, Miz Connors." He shifted his weight on the bed and lay back against the pillow. He closed his eyes and thought of the words he'd had with Ewing, deciding not to say he'd already met one of the big guns, and wishing she'd get the hell out and leave him to sleep. Maybe she was right. Maybe he was simpleminded for not throwing her out and right now, but it was her shed, and after all she had a right to her opinions.

"Well," she demanded. "What are you gonna do now?"

"Regards to what?" He said it wearily.

It was all coming out wrong and she felt stupid, standing there, carrying on this ridiculous conversation with a half-dressed cowboy. "It don't matter. Not tonight. But you go back to that piece of land, I'm gonna have to know yer intentions."

He wanted to ask what she was talking about, but couldn't and drifted away with the thought of what his intentions were about living.

Ella thought he might still be awake, but after some minutes when he didn't move, and finally emitted a snore, she sighed and studied his sleeping form. "You're gonna disappoint yerself and me, Athearn." She thought: He can't make a go of it, and neither can I, but I'll keep tryin' and he won't 'cause he don't understand. Not really.

When she walked back to the house, after blowing out his lantern and giving some late snacks to Patches, she thought that she could feel the shift in the weather she'd been hoping for. She studied the sky, noting it was clear and there were stars beyond stars. She thought: I wish he were the man to change the world, but that man ain't never been invented. Sorry, Lord.

Frank overslept and when he finally rose, it was far past 9:30. He found no sign of either Ella or Dodger, and the Model A was gone, leaving deep ruts in the night-moistened earth, indicating it carried a heavy load. Frank assumed they'd headed off to begin their roundup and took a spot by the door of the shed until he saw the note tacked to the door.

"You are on your own till Friday.
Help yourself to the kitchen if you can.
    Regards,
        Connors"

Couldn't even be friendly in a note, he thought.
His arms worked the crutch to fine efficiency and he
made the kitchen with little difficulty. He was beginning to realize he'd have to watch every word with
this woman, which made her like every other woman
as far as he was concerned, but the fact was that he
knew she was unlike any other woman he'd ever met,
in all the other ways.

He was curious how anyone so pigheaded could
still be alive in such a dog-eat-cat world. He decided
she was too tough to eat, so he nicknamed her ol'
Armadillo, for any cowboy knew no animal in his
right mind would eat an overgrown Texas lizard.
Too tough to eat.

He marveled at the kitchen, however, for it was a
place of order disturbed only by the frenzy of last-
minute preparations for heavier, more important
work. There were dirty dishes and pans, some he remembered having eaten off of earlier in the week. So
before preparing himself a meal, he cleaned the
kitchen, working not so much from knowledge of
kitchens and cooking but from endless hours of
Kitchen Police, well planned to frustrate and break
the most rebellious of spirits. Only when everything
seemed in its proper place did he cook for himself,
and when he finished, he returned everything to its
place and cleaned up his disorder. During the two
days he was alone at the ranch he only entered the
kitchen, though once he did glance into the living
room that lay just through the dining room. But that
was only long enough to peek, then he turned and
went back to his shed, and allowed her the privacy he
felt he'd like to have and knew he was losing each day
he remained here. Perhaps the sense of being trapped

here made him work harder, but the afternoon of the last day alone he walked for the first time without the crutch, and used a rope for the first time since the night attack a full eight days before.

The bitch with the ugly pups worried him, for in the days that Ella and Dodger were gone, there was no sign of the animal or her offspring. He hoped they were with Ella, but the last afternoon, about an hour before sunset, the bitch reappeared, crawling out from under the house, a little thinner than she had been a few days before, but otherwise about the same. The pups followed, rolling and lurching in a curious file that followed her scent until she came to a stop in the middle of the road that led off the ranch and sat down facing the mountains. She looked at Frank once, growled a warning, informing him that she knew he was a stranger, then waited patiently as the uppity pups mauled her teats and yelped when she shifted her weight, throwing their feed into disorder.

Her patience was rewarded a half hour after her reappearance when the Model A could be heard, then finally seen approaching the ranch.

Frank worked the rope, tossing the loop over two sticks protruding from a bale of hay, paying little attention to the truck or Ella when she stopped and began to unload the saddles that needed repair, the tack that needed stitching, after greeting the pups and the bitch. She only glanced at Frank, then continued with her work.

"Welcome home," he said quietly.

"See you're doin' a touch better yerself, now."

"Indeed I am, Miz Connors. Thanks to the use of the kitchen." He made a sluggish wave at the house but made no move to approach or help her, but here he was, on his feet and working a rope like a damned rodeo man.

She was about to say more, but hoisted the saddles and lugged them to the shed, tossing them just inside the door. She considered he might have some troubles negotiating the hunks of metal and leather, but decided the hell with the snotty bastard and tossed the tack on top of the saddles, then turned and trudged wearily into the house.

Frank watched her disappear, then reappear much faster, and cross the ground that separated them. She was fuming when she stood before him. She held a sheet of paper in her hand and waved it before him as she spoke.

"You tell me about this, Athearn, now."

"You can't read, huh?"

She studied him, mad enough to swing, determined not to give him the satisfaction. "Says 'Good stuff in the oven,' then you went and signed it 'Frank.'"

"Well, it shows you can read," he answered evenly. He whipped his loop into a coil, stood there a moment studying the ground before smiling at her calmly and continued, "An' if you was to look in the oven like the note says, you might jest find there's a casserole inside that might jest hit the spot."

"You think high on yourself."

He smiled warmly now, "Someone has to, I guess."

"Then you best think on this, mister cowboy." Ella shoved the note into her pants pocket, ignoring his eyes on her. "Since you are so damned able to be up an' around, and since yer able to clean my house and fix a meal, I guess yer just fit enough to git yerself gone right off my ranch." She hesitated a moment, then went on. "I told you I wasn't runnin' no hospital, well, I also ain't runnin' no hotel."

"And you don't take strangers into yer house."

"That's right."

"Mighty quick, ain't it?" he asked.

"You got here mighty quick, if I remember."

Frank glanced at the house and wished to hell he'd only fixed his meal and not tried to do her a favor. "Only tried to give you a hand. Saw how hard you been workin'."

"I don't need a cook or housekeeper, thank you, but I'm sure you'll be able to find work like that in town." She mused it for a moment, then said sarcastically, "Tell you what. I'll even give you a ride to town. Figure I can do that much. Got to go in tomorrow anyhow."

Frank studied her a bit through new eyes, wondering why she feared him. He nodded, and slung the rope over his shoulder. "Ain't goin' to town yet. Figure when I do, I won't need no chaufferrin', *thank you*."

He turned on his heel, walked to the shed and returned with two rough-shaped cowhide sections over his arm and he held them out to her, motioning with his head that she take them. "Lady, I don't want nothin' from you for free, so take these and with the work I done inside and in the shed, we ought to be about square. One thing, though, I figure to buy a horse off you, that is if you got one to spare."

As he spoke, she studied the leathers, unfolding them to reveal a fine handmade pair of chaps. She tried to hand them quickly back to Frank, but he declined with a shake of his head and took a step backward.

"I don't need no damned chaps," she said quickly.

"Seen them skunk skins you been wearin' and callin' chaps and it seemed that since I had the time, and you had some hides back there, I might do somethin' like this." He was kindly, but not overly so, watching as she held them up to her, considering the effort, appreciating the workmanship.

"I guess you expect me to thank you," she said, softly now, avoiding looking at him, "for the meals, for these things," and shook the chaps in his direction, "but I can't fawn after you in no way, nor can I say thanks for yer buttin' in when yer not wanted. Wish to hell I was the kind could do so, Athearn, but I ain't and it don't seem I ever will be." She held the chaps admiringly against her legs, and looked at them, then nodded. "It ain't at all bad workmanship, though."

"Why'd you ever sell me that land?"

She thought for a moment before responding, "I was narrow-bone-poor, desperate and foolish."

"You ain't changed all that much, I figure," said Athearn. And found the remark brought her anger to the surface quicker than he thought would have been possible.

"You got all the answers, cowboy," she retorted quickly, then retreating to the house, she muttered, "Yeah, cowboy, you kin borrow a horse." Then she slammed the door.

As night crept down from the mountain tops and across the ranch, Frank swung a last, slow loop, but never let go, and so it dropped down and he coiled it slowly once again, pondering the woman, wondering what it was that set it off between them whenever they crossed paths. He decided he'd never know, or that were he to know, he wouldn't care. "Well, I got a few answers, but you won't hear 'em," he said to no one in particular, before retiring for the night.

Ella stayed close to the ranch the following day. She lingered in order to undo some of the harm she might have done the night before, but found herself hiding from Frank rather than going out to him when he set foot in the ranch yard to add some finishing touches to the gravemarker.

She watched him from the kitchen window as she worked over a meaningless job, wishing she could find her way over the stumbling blocks that kept her from going to him in an easy manner and saying, "We got to stop this foolishness and try to get on an even footing if we're gonna be neighbors." But the thought itself made her fight talking to him all the more.

When he walked to the corral, carrying his rope, she knew what he was about to do and quickly finished up and walked to the corral as Frank mounted the larger of the two horses. He began moving the mare around the corral, getting to know her.

Ella climbed to the top rail of the fence as he backed the animal, tested her for reflexes and then gave her several quick turns around the corral and a short stop at the end. He looked at her quickly as he dismounted, but didn't say a word. As he patted the horse and spoke encouragingly to the animal, Ella dropped to the ground inside the corral and walked up to them.

"That the one you pickin'?"

He studied the animal and nodded, but still said nothing.

"Shoulda taken a gentler horse, though. Yer still too stove up for ol' Gus. That's her name, in case you wondered." She patted the mare affectionately and the animal nuzzled her in return. "She'll break you up in a day or so."

"Wouldn't think you'd be concerned about that." She noticed that when he spoke, his breathing was a bit labored and wondered if it was a wise idea for him to move at all, but she said, "Don't want you to fall off here an' sue me. Look like a sue-er to me."

He shook his head, grinned a wry short smile, then dug into his pocket and produced a few bills and some coins, dropping them into her hand immediately. "Count it, but there ought to be more than enough to cover the horse, the tack, and for some of the care you give me. I'll have to owe you for a saddle. Thought I'd take one of them old ones and repair it."

Before she could say anything he turned and walked into the barn, leaving her with the horse. She quickly followed only to meet him returning, carrying what he had of gear, including the two rifles.

"You ain't goin' back to that toilet you call a cabin, are you?" He nodded tersely, kept walking and moved back to the horse, forcing her to follow if she wanted to say more. She followed and stayed close to him as she spoke. "What the hell's the matter with you? You ain't got a root in the ground, not yet at least."

"Got me a partner planted here. Got a bullet wound says I got a share." He spoke quietly as he lashed his gear to the saddle.

"Then can't you see this just ain't the place to be?" There was concern in her voice that made him look at her for a while before speaking. "You're still here."

"Hell," her voice grew raspy, "I got roots like the mountains got roots. I got to stick it out."

He nodded in agreement, then looked at the shed, trying to remember if he had left anything behind. Then deciding he hadn't, turned and mounted the horse, wondering how she'd respond to being thanked. Not well, he quickly mused and looked at her with a granite face to hide the pain he felt. "Y'know," he said, "yer a damned fool. Anybody can see yer hangin' on and scared to let go. Seems to me a person in that situation might consider askin' an able-bodied man to come to work. We could've worked something out."

"You think yer able-bodied?"

He thought about it, nodded and spoke. "I'm up here, ain't I?" He raised a hand to his hat as he rode off. "I'll be back for my cattle and my horses."

As he rode through the main gates of the ranch, Ella left the corral, shutting and latching the gate behind her, then walked to the house, every once in a while glancing at him as he rode toward his ranch, sticking to the road.

Every minute that passed was filled with thoughts of the things she'd wanted to say, and she started up the stairs wanting to yell out for him to stay another day or so, that she was sorry for turning him out.

Ain't it wonderful how the rhythm of hooves that told me this was a good horse ten minutes ago is now a cursed thing that threatens to shake me apart at the seams, Frank thought as he rode Gus down the road. He tried to ignore the pain at first, admitting to himself that maybe he was pushing it a little, then cursing inwardly for being so foolish.

The sound of the approaching truck came slowly to him, and it hurt like tail flies on a canker sore to turn and see the black Model A come lurching up to him, raising a cloud of dust behind it. He pulled off the road to let the madwoman he'd named ol' Armadillo pass, but she slowed the truck, rolled down the window and drove parallel to the path he was taking.

She shouted over the noise of the clattering truck, "Thought about what you said. Guess I could use a hired man."

"Didn't say nothin' about no hired man, did I?"

"Said able-bodied man to work, is what you said."

"Don't mean hired man," he shouted back, still riding.

"Then what the hell are you?" She was getting hot all over again, irritated that he wouldn't stop moving. She felt rather foolish.

"Ma'am, I'm m'ownself, that's what. I'll work alongside you, but not for you. There's a difference."

She laughed at the thought, "You mean like a partner, don't you?"

"Not *like* . . . *as* a partner." He still kept moving.

She gunned the gas and the truck lurched ahead, forcing her to jam on the brakes and wait for him. "Oh, no, you won't!"

"Suit yerself," he said quietly as he passed and kept on going. The motor on the truck died from the start and stop, and Frank gained ten yards before the truck came parallel once again.

"I need a cowboy, not a partner." Ella waited for him to speak or stop, but he kept moving. "You owe me for the time and care spent on you."

As Frank reined in, she stopped the car.

"Lady, you got balls the size of grapefruits." He was quiet for a moment. "You call the time you spent on me *care*?" His voice rose slightly, indicating his anger. "More like torture I say." He seemed to be considering the proposition as he stared at her through snake-slit eyes. "Tell you what. I'll work a season for you. You can pay me any way you can at the end. But part of it has to be in stock. And if we find mine out there," he motioned at the mountains, "you an' the old man'll give me a hand gettin' 'em trapped."

It wasn't a partnership and she knew it, but it sounded dangerous and open and it seemed as if he could move in on her from a favorable position. She weighed the pros and cons quickly, then nodded. "Deal." She watched him nod, then she spoke again. "I'll start by givin' you some time off, cause any poor soul could see somethin's got to you." He grinned slightly, made a salute with his hand as she began to turn the Model A around. "Jee-zuz," she said overloud, "you sure are frail."

He dismounted and rested for a moment as the Model A trundled Ella Connors back to her ranch.

"Well, Gus," he murmured to her horse as she grazed at his feet, "looks like I went an' bought you when I didn't have to, now don't it?"

The horse raised her head at the sound of his voice and looked at him. "Yeah, I guess all you women think I'm some kinda sucker." He folded his arms behind his head and lay back for fifteen minutes before mounting and riding back to the ranch.

IV
JOBBING

April passed into May as wildflowers filled the basin, then died as they were trampled by cattle on the move. The roads were filled with cattle, horses and men all moving to a late summer deadline.

Ewing started an early roundup in the second week of May, one month behind the Connors Ranch who were already moving cattle from places of hiding high up among the peaks, and while he'd heard about this pitiful effort he worried not a bit, and continued on with his life, content he was working well and moving about as quickly as could be expected.

According to estimates, it was thought by Blocker they could harvest nearly ten thousand saleable head, and possibly a third more if they were to extend the roundup into late August. The beef of the Ewing spread were large, healthy, white-face range cattle that had been strengthened carefully over the years by select breeding. Grain feeding was a necessity and had been so for over ten years. Every man on the Ewing Ranch hated hand-feeding, but most of them were old hands and they saw the waning of the life they'd known on the range, saw the day would come when all the cattle could be tended by corraling them, feeding them and shipping them away, the result being a reduction in the number of hands. So there was grumbling and discontent for the first time on the Ewing Ranch, as the men who worked the land and cattle saw the twilight of their time on the horizon. The work slowed down, the cattle were allowed to drift, and when Blocker raised hell or went to Ewing about it, it seemed no matter which way he turned he got only apathy.

Ewing's eyes had turned south, toward the entrance of the basin, as more trucks moved into the region, red trucks marked ATKO OIL. It was rumored that a sizable pocket of black gold had been discovered at the mouth of the basin and the ranchers who lived there gladly sold leases to Atkinson on the hopes that they would be solvent enough to be able to last another year.

The few portions of government land in the Bear Paw Basin had been bored, tapped and blown to hell for oil, and every day of the spring and into the early summer it continued, each eruption of sand echoing across the basin floor, all of them heard by Ewing, who became daily more and more preoccupied by the flurry of activity.

When matters concerning the ranch were brought to him either by Blocker or Virgil Hoverton, the bank manager who handled the finances of the ranch as well, Ewing dismissed them with assurances that as soon as he had time, he'd take care of whatever the matter was. And at first they were satisfied. But when it became clear he was too preoccupied with the oil men, they tried to reason with him. When they did, he reacted with anger, accusing them of suspecting him of neglect, and when this happened, they went to all lengths to assure him it wasn't so. By June, when the bulk of the herd needed to be moved, the water on their route to the ranch had all but dried up and blown away in the strong winds. The herd was poised to move, ready to begin the long filtering journey to a place where they'd be treated for disease, branded if necessary, gelded when needed and eventually shipped when they'd been watered and fed to the bursting point. But the gigantic herd had no place to go unless Blocker and the Ewing men wanted to risk the chance of water stampede or even the loss of precious cattle due to starvation or thirst.

On the first anniversary of the landing at Normandy, Blocker went to the big house that resembled a castle and spoke calmly and patiently to Ewing for over and hour about how the ranch was suffering because there were things that needed doing, decisions that needing making, and at the end told Ewing that the water was gone and that it could only get worse in the next three months.

Ewing listened, said little except to ask a question every now and then, and finally when Blocker was through issued the following statement:

"We done it before. Didn't matter what the weather did, nor how hard the times was. We always done it, always. You, me, and the men. You gonna tell me after all these years you don't know how to conduct a roundup without me holdin' yer hand? I know you better'n that. Now I pay you more'n a fair wage 'cause yer a friend and the best man I ever knowed who worked a horse. Also, I pay you that sum because I trust you to make some decisions for me, to allow me to handle problems that concern the ranch that don't necessarily have anything to do with cattle. Now, you got a big herd out there without water, and you best figure out how to move them all on yer own. Now think on that, and if you can't do it alone, then come to me, Julie, and we'll just have to figure out how we're gonna get the work done. Any questions?"

Blocker rose, feeling very small in the enormous room. He pulled on his hat slowly, watching Ewing, and for the first time he hated the man before him, resented deeply the burden dropped so suddenly in his lap. "I know how to do it. You just may not like the results," the foreman replied slowly.

Ewing said nothing, his silence voicing the question. Blocker grew even more uncomfortable, more resentful, but searched for the right words to use.

"I might have to move 'em across that soldier boy's land."

Ewing smiled blandly and shifted his weight in the chair. "Don't know I've heard about him working the land."

Blocker spoke carefully. "He ain't moved on like we thought." Ewing waited for more and it dribbled out of the foreman in slow phrases. "Cole's been watching the Connors place from time to time. Had strays up there a month back." He felt sweat at his armpits. "Saw the soldier boy was up workin' with Ella and the old man. Seems they got more'n a few head up the line camp used to be ourn."

"That so?"

Blocker nodded.

"It don't mean nothin', Julie. She won't make the season and we'll have her place, and the soldier boy'll fall right along with her. Don't know shit from shine between the two of 'em when it comes to playin' the right game. You want to take the cattle over his land, you line 'em up, and on the day you move, I promise I'll lead you m'self."

Blocker knew it was an illusion. He'd known it for two seasons now. Something had changed in the old man. Like a light dimming, promising to return and finally dying. The thought made Blocker scared and confused. He knew the ranch better than Ewing. He knew he did, but when it came to management there were always the careful thoughts that backed Julie Blocker's forceful moves, and Blocker knew he needed the man who sat before him. But he was quite unsure how to reach across the gap that had grown between them.

"You think I don't give a shit no more, Julie?" The words, coming on his own thoughts as they did, chilled him. Blocker had a feeling Ewing could read his mind.

"Ranch needs you, J.W. There jest ain't no more to be said." Blocker felt some assurance as he studied his boss in the chair. "I do the best I can, but what really makes it work is you. Place this size takes a good general 'cause it's exactly like a damned army." Blocker's voice rose a bit. "And I ain't no general, no matter which way you look at it."

Ewing rose and moved to his foreman, clapping him on the shoulder. "I got a million hunnert things on my mind, Julie. You got to do what you can and give me time, and I promise you, we'll make this basin right."

Blocker's spirits fell at the words. "J.W., we don't need the Connors place this year. Next year neither." The stab of Ewing's eyes went right through Blocker, but he continued. "We do need to make a good sale this year or you'll be cattle poor, and you know as well as I do next year there won't be no market at all."

Ewing said nothing, his expression a mixture of anger and the hint of awareness of the truth in Blocker's words.

"You got the gift, J.W." Blocker shifted his weight, hating the words he knew he had to use. "You got it like yer grandaddy did. Don't make me carry failure when it ain't necessary."

"You make compliments sound like threats, Julie." Ewing spoke just above a whisper, his eyes riveting in on Blocker. "You're a good foreman, Julie, and a better friend, but for yourself, you are a bit of a damned fool." He softened and smiled. "Guess I'm only a couple years older'n you, but the fool in you makes me feel like yer damned daddy." He laughed softly and turned away, shaking his head.

"Yessir."

Ewing walked to the window and stared out at the ranch grounds. "Don't you yessir me. You already got yer point across."

Blocker read dismissal in the tone, but wasn't convinced he had made his point, or if he had, that it would be heeded. But he only nodded and jammed his hand deep into the Mackinaw he wore as he headed for the door. "I'll start 'em movin'."

"No matter what, Julie." Ewing didn't look at his foreman, but stared out the window. The words caused Blocker to look around as he spoke slowly.

"Yessir. No matter what it takes."

When the door shut behind Blocker, neither of the two men doubted that the last words were equivalent to an act of war.

The signs weren't good at all. The snow had vanished before April was gone and the lower plains and meadows were drying earlier than usual. Dodger missed the early morning drizzles that made it easier to move cattle, missed the sounds of soft rain and moving insects crawling beneath the leaf-mold forest floor. There was a difference in the light, he mused. When summer was on you, the light was long and friendly at first, then too long and deadly in the hottest spells, then dying off late in the summer, but fading like sunset in the north, quickly, with little compassion.

They should have been in the warm, friendly part of summer still, the happy time, and according to the calendar they were, but the fact was that the dead of summer was full on them with the daily threat of afternoon thunderstorms as warm wind met cold air. Damn but it bothered him as he moved through the forest and out onto a ridge where he could look down on the line camp and corrals below. He was the first one back, and though he'd come empty-handed, knew he'd be welcome to eat with Frank and Ella, who more than likely had a quite a few between them.

His eyes focused slowly on a thin stream of dust rising in the air, moving toward the town of Bear Paw, but by Dodger's reckoning they still had a piece to go. He tried to picture the herd that threw dust so high in the air, and made a quick guess they were about three miles away by crow-wing flight.

He saw in his mind the area where the dust came from and knew it was a low valley before you climbed into the lush foothills that marked Frank's land. "Humph." He muttered it, deciding to stay where he was for a moment or two before riding into the camp. Wasn't like he was late or something like that. His eyes shifted back to the dust again, but he made no judgments.

As if avoiding the thoughts that came with the dust cloud, Dodger forced himself to think about the ranch. He reflected that there weren't many men who had his pride at this moment. As he looked back over the last month and a half, Dodger had reason to be proud. If you'd asked him to explain, he couldn't, not in so many words, but you got the feeling good medicine had taken over this range and given it new life. While there'd been tension and friction in the ranks, as Frank would've put it, the three of them worked as a wonderful team. The miracle of it all was that in spite of tempers and exhaustion and all the other things that at first had them at each other's throats, they had managed to corral over sixty head so far and that was more than Dodger had really expected for the whole season.

He chuckled to himself as he thought about how strangely he had behaved when Ella drove into the line camp with Frank in tow. The boy looked near to dyin' from the ride, but was hangin' on even if he could jest barely fork that horse. And Ella of course never let up on him, pushin' him harder than she did Dodger. And while not ridiculing Frank, she talked to him in a tone that said, "I'm boss and yer help and help is kin to cowpie in my eyes, so keep out of sight."

It was strange how it worked. Ella was the boss. She made all the decisions, and they were good ones, but somehow along the way Frank would make a suggestion and if she listened and made good use of it, things went well. But then, she had a habit of telling him to mind his own business, and ignoring his advice. That was on days when he'd get uppity, as Ella would put it. It seemed that Frank had become the third part that the two-thirds known as the working team of Ella Connors and Dodger were looking for. They were a single unit, and there seemed nothing that couldn't be done among them. In Dodger's critical eyes, Ella Connors had been more than a match for any cowboy he'd ever known, with the possible exception of her father and J.W. Ewing, but Frank ranked beside her, though a shade under Dodger in his best days, he thought reservedly.

No brush was too thick and when they fanned out and combed the dense canyons that held three generations of fully wild cattle, those canyons were left barren of bovine life.

Each of them pulled long stretches at night with the cattle, singing to them, keeping them calm, for these wild creatures were so spooky anything could set them off, and fence or not, they'd be long gone for the hills. Yet when Athearn had worked a full day, grabbed an hour's rest after the evening meal, then stood guard for a full night watch and then some, he'd always be ready to go the next day just like they were, with no complaints, no grumbling and he never let up. It was as if this fight had become his fight, the land his land.

Dodger remembered the night they'd spent at the line camp while Ella guarded the growing herd. It had drizzled most of the day and neither of them felt much like sleeping, but there had been a bit of a distance between them so they said little other than what was necessary during the meal. Dodger had begun to act as if Frank were an outsider, and wished the first liking he'd felt for Frank would overcome the jealousy.

"Hope you don't go bad on us when we need you the most. Not now, not when it's goin' so well." There was the smallest hint of menace in the old man's voice.

"That's a helluva way to start, Dodger," Frank lazed.

"I don't get you."

Frank sat up and smiled, shaking his head. "Hell you don't. You been a regular shit heel and you know it, old fox. You been touchy as a teased snake and the woman's been salty as Lot's wife." His eyes rested on Dodger for a split second and there was understanding and compassion, then he looked away and spoke again. "I don't make a habit outta goin' bad on folks, Dodger, but I ain't gonna say it couldn't happen. It's all in the way you look at it and the view is kinda short in these parts."

It left Dodger without a response. The boy was smarter and better than he'd ever estimated. He reached for his pipe as his mind scurried over his emotions and he spoke straight to the man across the fire. "You got a place of yer own. You say you want to find yer cattle, but you ain't after them, yer pitchin' in like regular folk. Why'd you want to go an' throw in with us, boy?" He couldn't resist the jibe of "boy," but it went right past Frank who smiled warmly.

"How'd you get so old, bein' so damned nosy, Dodger?"

The old cowboy smiled as he struck a match on a fire-pit rock and lit his pipe. He held the smoke until the old burl was filled with a glowing burn, then slowly let the smoke flow out and watched it. "Jest luck and brains. You gonna answer me, Buck?"

"I guess you might say I like to weather the rough ones."

Dodger let out another cloud of smoke. "Well, Buck, you picked a lulu." He thought for a moment, "I guess I know yer stripe." And from that point forward the two men were inseparable, and if at first the shift went unnoticed by Ella, it soon became evident, for they had their own jokes and a few things they'd say that she'd be left out of, and it infuriated her, although she did her best not to show it. Secretly, she blamed Frank for forcing her out, and his presence alone drew harsh actions and words from Ella Connors.

It wasn't that she made him do the worst jobs, for that wasn't her way. It was the way she shunned any attempt at friendliness on his part, remaining cool and aloof and talking to him only when absolutely necessary.

In the month and a half of work the only time she'd been civil was when she and Frank returned from the line shack to the ranch. Frank had related the story one night when he and Dodger sat by the fire. They had gone back to the ranch, and Frank was supposed to go to town to ferret out what he could in the way of supplies, while Ella took care of taking canned and bottled goods she'd laid up in her root cellar the fall before, loading them in boxes so when Frank returned they could load everything on the truck and get quickly back to the line camp and the roundup. She had expected him before three, but he didn't return until an hour or so after sundown, and when she first met him, it seemed as though she'd summon hell itself to open up and swallow Frank for making her lose half a day. But before she could speak, she saw the mountain of supplies in the truck, and stood foolishly gaping at wire, rope, nails, posts, grain—the list went on and on. Everything they'd need for the full season. She turned on Frank in disbelief.

"You stole this."

"No."

She looked at the pile again, then shook her head. "You better tell me what this is gonna cost me."

He didn't say a thing for a few moments, then he let out a breath and spoke softly. "My credit's good, I found out."

"I don't need yer charity."

"No, Ma'am. You could probably do without it, but

I don't have yer particular insight, and if I'm in a fight then I'm in it to win."

"I can't take it," she said simply and quietly.

"If you say so." He turned quietly and got behind the wheel of the truck again.

"Where're you goin' now?" she said as she walked up to the cab.

"Thought I'd drop it off at my place."

"You mean you'd let goods like this rot at yer place?"

"The food's still the same as yer list, but the rest of the stuff'll keep all right. There's always next season. For me at least."

"Yer a damned fool, y'know."

"If it'll make you feel better, I'll keep the tab, and we'll take it outta the final split. I don't mind 'cause I don't have to pay until we've made the sale."

She studied him suspiciously. "How'n hell'd you drive a deal like that bein' new, when I can't an' I lived here all my damned life?"

"I guess I got a record that says I used to pay my bills."

It caught her short, but the simplicity of it floored her and she could only nod in agreement. "That will do it."

He climbed out of the truck and stood looking at her for a moment before he spoke, hoping she'd speak first, but when she didn't he ventured another question. "You not screamin' and throwin' bad thoughts at me right now a sign you'll keep this shit?" His use of the word *shit* in her presence for the first time surprised her, but she half-smiled, nodded and watched as he slapped the Model A on the fender and started off for the shed. He stopped and looked back for a bit. "I figured it was a little late to head back up."

"You figured right. We'll go out in the morning."

Frank nodded, gave her a little salute with his right hand and went back to the shed where he'd spent

time, which was how he thought of the invalid days.
He'd not been hungry in town, but now he was, and
since she was home he couldn't walk into the kitchen
and fend for himself, so he'd decided to tough it out
rather than ask her permission or get her thinking
he needed her. He could take it. When he couldn't
take it, he tried to sleep, telling himself he'd been
hungry before, but it didn't help the feeling in his
stomach.

Therefore, he'd said to Dodger when telling the
story, he was greatly relieved when she tapped on the
door, not throwing it open unannounced as she had
before, and invited him in to a late supper. Frank
quickly agreed and when she left him to clean up,
he did his best, and went to the big house not expecting much in the way of a meal, but perhaps an
insight into the woman, and a way to ease the strain
between them.

He was off on the wrong foot when he entered and
said, "I sure appreciate this. Thank you."

She was suddenly as cool as ever. "No need to
thank me."

Frank bobbed his head and thought that it was
going to be one of those nights and stood by the door,
hat in hands, waiting to be told to sit, or move into
the living room, or some such order, but while she
glanced at him, she seemed not to mind him near her.

"Yer workin' too hard. Gonna tear yerself up, you
keep at it. That sure ain't gonna do me a lot of good."
She spoke in time to the strokes with which she stirred
the soup.

"That mean you think I done a passable job?"

"Passable? Possibly." She smiled at the sound and
hoped he didn't see, but he did. Her voice dropped
and became softer. "Got to admit you are a fine cowman. Dodger keep pointin' it out like I ain't got eyes
for myself." She stared at him a moment. "I think
you'll probably go bad on us."

"You an' the old man really got me figured."

"Don't get me wrong now," she said quickly, "Dodger may have thought that once, but that's 'cause he spins off me, but my mind is set 'cause I can't figure out why you put up with what you do."

"Meanin' you been testin' me?" asked Frank laconically.

"Meanin' I don't believe in miracles."

He thought about it, then moved to a chair and straddled it, facing the chair back to the front, hands and hat dangling over the edge. She watched him go to the chair. "Beg pardon, Miz Connors, but with yer temper, you ought to start."

Nothing more was said until they had been at the table and well into the meal. Then Ella rose from her chair and went to a bookcase in the living room and returned to the table, sat down and began to read as Frank ate and watched her. She sensed his eyes on her and ignored them at first, then she lowered the book and said nicely, "Don't mind me, I always eat this way."

Frank nodded, gestured at the bookcase and rose from his chair. "You mind if I do likewise?"

She motioned at the living room and nodded her head, eating as she spoke. "Suit yerself."

Frank took his time moving to the bookcase and looked at the spot next to the shelves where a tall clock had once stood, its outline clearly defined by the faded wallpaper where the sun had etched the clock's solid shape.

Ella noticed him looking at the spot, but said nothing. Her eyes followed his fingers as they swept across the titles of the books. Then he selected one and swung it out from the shelf, but the book flopped open and envelopes holding unpaid bills tumbled to the floor. The yellow envelopes, the scrawl of "urgent" in pen across the faces, told Frank what the envelopes were, and her eyes watched his face and hands as he carefully placed them back in the book and looked over at her.

"It's my filin' system," she volunteered.

Frank read the title out loud. *"Shakespeare's Tragedies . . ."*

"Appropriate, ain't it?" she quipped quickly. Her eyes returned to the book, but when Frank turned back to the shelves her eyes were on him again. He selected Mallory's tedious version of the story of Arthur and he straightened, then curiously reached out and touched the spot where the clock had stood. He felt Ella looking at him and motioned questioningly at the spot.

"Was a clock my great-grandpa gave to my ma an' pa for their wedding." She thought about the clock, remembering how fond she'd always been of the husky ticking it made. "Like him, it was a noisy old thing. I never got a moment's rest."

He nodded and opened the book without comment, and the two of them read and ate for a few moments until he looked up at her and said quietly, "Sure is peaceful now."

She stared across the table, over her book, unsure of how he meant the last line, and finally she spoke. "Y'know, you push a little hard."

"If you say so."

It seemed he might go on forever with her like that, so she fell silent completely and smoldered, wondering why she'd given this damned time-robbing cowboy any kindness at all.

For his part, Frank had had a little fun with her, hoping to draw her out a bit, but when he left the house that evening he knew he'd gone too far and wanted to go back and apologize, but decided the next day would be a better time. Nevertheless, it took three and a half hours for him to drop off to sleep in the shed.

But she spoke to him the next morning only when she needed something, and gave him no chance for conversation before they left. As they started down the road, side by side in the Model A truck, heading back to the line shack, she turned to him and said the sentence that ended with a three day silence between them. "I don't want nothin' from you but work. Understand?" She waited for him to reply, but he merely gazed at her. "Gonna use these supplies 'cause you set the terms and if I don't make a profit, you'll get your money back and then some. Only thing is, I don't like you an awful lot, so stay the hell outta my way. I don't want to hear a word out of you."

She was serious, so silence it was the entire return trip to the line camp, and as Dodger helped unload, he couldn't help but notice the static stiffness that hovered around the camp when they were together. He watched them, knew something had gone wrong, but knowing them both now, wasn't too surprised, and made up his mind not to say a thing.

Now, confused and unsure of how to work with this woman, Frank finished his story, sat back, let Dodger digest what he'd heard, then looked across the fire.

"You'd better talk to me about the woman, old man," said Frank, and Dodger nodded, understanding instinctively what the younger man wanted to know. But no answer, no response came, and Frank shot him a bitter look. "You ain't gonna help me out a bit, are you?"

"Nope."

"Prick." Frank said it good-naturedly, then smiling, "Old Prick."

Dodger faced Frank with furrowed brows and a set to his jaw. And when nothing came from Dodger, Frank said, "I was tryin' to be a good neighbor, Dodger."

"I guess she takes it that you might be tryin' to buy a little piece of her like so many others've tried to do." Dodger said the words slowly and clearly.

"You think that's what I'm doin', Dodger?"

The old man studied the younger one sternly, then slowly shook his head.

"No, I don't. But what I think don't matter, understand?"

No more was said on the subject, but Dodger kept a casual eye on Frank and it was clear the younger man was trying to fit it all together, and having a bad time. Even if he'd been tempted, which he wasn't, nothing would have allowed Dodger to say a thing that could be used in any way against Ella, no matter what his instincts.

The next day, he heard the same story, though seen through different eyes, from Ella, and Dodger marveled that they were getting along as well as they did. It was clear she regretted the way she constantly lashed out at Frank, but was trapped by her own ways. She said as much and Dodger agreed with her, but try as they might, neither worked out a solution that satisfied her.

The one thing clear to Dodger was that she felt Frank was just too good to be true, and therefore trusted him little. It made the old cowboy wonder now just how she felt about him, but he quickly dismissed the thought with characteristic simplicity that belied his true feelings.

He quickly snapped his thoughts to the sounds of a horse picking its way through the woods and into the clearing below. Frank rode to the corral and turned two roped-together steers into the gate, removing the binds quickly with one hand. Dodger carefully urged his own horse down the slope and when Frank noticed him, Dodger gestured at the dust cloud.

"I saw it," Frank muttered, then dismounted and turned to study the cloud as Dodger swung to the ground and began to unsaddle beside Frank.

"Comin' from over yer way." Dodger spoke flatly.

"Yeah. It sure is." Frank turned back to his horse and swung his foot to the stirrup as his hand took reins and mane. As he swung into the saddle, Ella thundered into camp, skidding her horse to a painful stop beside Frank. The ride had jolted most of her wind out, and her words came in gasps.

"Ewing's movin' his commercial herd . . . onto your land. Wants to test passage rights. . . . Gonna go right straight across. . . ."

She whirled her horse and spurred off, then reined in at the edge of the line camp clearing and shouted back at him. "You comin'?"

Frank shot a curious glance at Dodger. "You want to keep an eye on our profits here?" He waved at the corralled cattle, and when Dodger nodded assent, Frank gave way and followed Ella at a trot that was built to a dead run across country.

The Ewing herd was only a shadow of what it once had been, but the shadow was still enormous. Without culling, nearly fifteen thousand head of range stock moved thirstily toward the lush meadows of Wolf Creek. The lead steers were cautious, and as they approached the creek, they bellowed to each other, then led the herd which stretched back over Ewing land for nearly five miles.

When the lead steers drank a bit, they were shoved across the stream from behind by the pressure of the herd, and once on the far side, were on the higher ground that belonged to Frank Athearn. Not one of the fifty-five men who guided the animals moved to stop the head of the column, and indeed, swiftly drove more and more of the once longhorn, now mostly white-face cattle into the stream and onto Athearn land.

The herd moved under Julie Blocker and Ralph Cole's orders, but they were under John Ewing's supervision, for good to his word to Blocker, he'd come out for the crossing and now sat on the flat slope that marked the edge of Athearn's land and waited with his head turned away from the herd, watching the back country that stretched up along Wolf Creek, high into the mountains.

It was much the same as the last time he saw it, though where Tom Connors had timbered the region, the forest had now grown back double in thickness and strength. It would be rich with game, he noted, then sadly thought there'd be no more of the fall hunts he and Matt used to go on. It was one of the few pleasant memories of Matt, but he passed quickly on as he sensed movement back in the trees and averted his attention, looking now at the herd with full proprietorship.

Frank and Ella weren't prepared for the number of hands, nor the quantity of cattle that filled the valley. They slowed their horses as they came out of the trees and rode up the rise to the spot where Ewing sat his horse and waited for them.

At they rode toward him, Ella leaned slightly in the saddle so Frank could hear her words over the noise of the cattle. "Look at the sonofabitch. Arrogant as hell."

Frank nodded, then spoke as he looked over at her, measuring his words. "I think the arrogant look is here to stay with J.W." He had the hint of a smile at the corners of his mouth. "Bloodlines."

"Fuck you," she muttered as they closed the last few yards and halted beside Ewing, who after a bit looked at them with a touch of scorn in his face that gave way to a cold smile.

"I think yer on my land." Frank spoke with no threat. It was a simple observation.

"You let him cross," Ella quickly interjected, "and it sets a precedent. It's a damned legal challenge." Frank looked at her a moment, then at Ewing, but she drew his attention again. "I know what I'm sayin', Athearn. You let him go, he'll walk all over you."

"You gonna mind my business for me?" The calmness in his voice was like a slap to Ella and she fell quiet, angry and shamed for this treatment in front of John Ewing. Frank looked at her a moment, then turned back to Ewing as the older rancher spoke.

"Athearn, I'm near out of water. You got the only route to water blocked by this here neck of land." Ewing watched the two of them through slitted eyes. "We had to move 'em around, we could lose maybe five, eight pounds or more and God knows how much water loss they'd suffer."

He waited as Frank looked the herd over, noting they were already attacking his grass in full force. "How many cattle you figure on bringin'?"

"Fifteen thousand head," said Ewing flatly. Frank whistled at the mention of the number.

"Well," Frank lazed, "seein' as yer about halfway across the creek . . ."

"The man is pissin' on you, Athearn." Ella spit out the words, ignoring the harsh looks from the two men.

Frank calmly turned back to Ewing. "As I said . . ."

"No!" She shouted it at him, then spurred her horse toward the cattle, a free hand swinging the 30-30 carbine into the air, using the lever action, chambering the first shot all in one action.

The two men watched, stunned as she charged the herd with a yell and fired once, then levered another shell into the chamber and fired a second, then a third time. The mass of reddish, white-face, somewhat long-horn cattle wavered, moved, then broke in all directions, all semblance of control out of the hands of the cowboys as the Ewing men found themselves faced with a violent stampede.

To Ella, it seemed a lifetime before the herd scattered, and she found herself lucky not to be engulfed by the panicked animals. As the herd broke in all directions, she ceased her yelling, stopped her firing and turned her horse, swiveling her head, looking for and finding Frank as Ewing rode off quickly after the cattle and his men. She angled her horse to where

Frank still sat, faced him contemptuously, about to speak, but he cut her off with a sweeping motion of his right hand. There was no doubting his anger.

"I would've handled it, dammit!" he shouted as he fought now to control his horse.

"You were gonna let him go right on across."

But there was no answer from Frank. Instead, he set his spurs into the horse's flanks and rode quickly off in pursuit of Ewing's fleeing herd, leaving Ella sitting in stunned silence, watching him go until all the men and cattle were only a haze in the distance and a fading sound of rumbling. The disappointment, then the anger took turns racing through her, then she turned her horse and rode slowly back toward the line camp.

As she rode a chill took her as she wondered what the act of retaliation would be from Ewing. He'd probably "handle it personally himself," as he liked to say. And as she thought that, she knew that she wanted him to come, that this time she'd be ready. But she'd said that before, she reminded herself, and remembered how Ewing had reacted to her threats, and recalled the moments of shame at his hands.

"It's down to the two of us, J.W.," she said aloud and startled herself, then wondered quietly which one of them would be left alive when it was all over. The image of two elks fighting for control of a herd flashed through her head, and she remembered when she'd last seen such a battle and how she'd marveled at the match of the two bulls, and in that second realized she felt she was more than a match for John Ewing, and rode straighter, prouder, the illusion sheltering her mind in broken silence.

The Ewing herd was used to shots fired at coyotes and snakes, and to being confronted by men on horseback, but their thirst this day blurred their reason and they bolted at Ella's charge. After a half mile or so, however, they slowed to a walk and allowed themselves to be contained by the Ewing men, John Ewing and to everyone's surprise, Frank Athearn. Frank worked beside Ewing and Blocker, keeping a cautious eye on the herd and keeping a cautious ear turned toward Ewing, waiting for the word that would mark injury or possibly death for him. But the word never came.

When the herd milled and lowed at being run away from the water, Ewing edged his horse to Frank and indicated with a motion of his head that they ride off out of earshot of the men and foreman. Frank glanced about him, noticed the number of unfriendly faces, and the hostile stares, then quietly followed Ewing to the selected spot and stayed his horse, waiting for Ewing to speak. The rancher's face was stern and righteous, but there was something in his eyes as he stared at Frank. "I appreciate the gesture of helpin' out."

"Better'n finding dead Connors cattle shot down in pastures or worse," Frank said slowly with no hint of warmth.

Ewing studied him again, puzzled at the attitude. "It still took guts, boy. I suppose you think helpin' me out a bit buys out her act?" Ewing's voice was cold, distant.

"It could."

"Yes, it could," said Ewing, then he hesitated and chose his words carefully. "I hear yer quite a cowman. Word's out about you. Seems you seen now what she's like. You still dead set on workin' with her?"

"Don't put me in the middle, Ewing."

"You put yourself in the middle, boy."

Frank bit back a response, and sat rigidly, staring at the herd, then glancing at Ewing.

The old rancher made a motion with his hand to indicate the basin between the mountains. "Indians called this part of the mountains, 'I am my past . . .' Nothin' but Blackfoot and buffalo in those days, days when my grandpa first set foot in this place." He was absorbed by his own words and his voice, while quiet, was passionate, compelling. "He fought like hell for every inch of this place. Took it in the end from the Blackfoot, but he had their blessing. Ran his cattle with the buffalo, never tried to spoil the land, never wanted to change a thing. But time took the buffalo and the Injuns too, and pretty soon my grandpa owned it all, from mountain to mountain. It was like that when I was born and stayed like that until he died." His eyes held some bitter memory, his voice held the pain as he continued. "Then the scavengers set in. Small ranchers first, then homesteaders and farmers. It warn't the damned sheep that spoiled Montana, it was all the damned people. It's taken me twenty-five years or so, but I've almost built it back the way it was. Only thing tougher than starting fresh is tryin' to bring a dyin' thing back to life." He softened a bit, his manner warm, encouraging. "Well, look around you, Frank, 'cause I done that very thing."

Frank glanced down the basin and bobbed his head as if someone had just shown him a new species of lizard. If the lack of interest disturbed Ewing, he didn't show it.

"Only a matter of time, boy. Just a matter of time. She can't hold out and yer smart enough to know that."

"I guess I ain't that smart at all, 'cause I guess that everyone deserves a fair chance."

"Fair chance?" Ewing exploded in laughter, then sobered. "She's had more'n a fair chance. You seen how she's laid waste to a fine ranch, yet here you are helpin' her out, sealin' yer own fate as well. Don't be a fool, boy."

"That's twice you called me fool, Ewing." Frank's voice was barely audible but dangerously steady. "I know a bit of range law. I'm givin' you crossin' rights this time, but don't make it no habit. I don't ever want to see you on my land again, and I'm sure the same applies for Miz Connors."

He started to turn his horse, but Ewing's voice

stopped him. It was quiet and rational, and there was respect in the words. "I guess if I was you, and I was younger without a care, I'd be caught the same way. But I think yer worth more than you do, I bet."

"You'd lose," said Frank as he rode off.

Ella had returned to the line camp in silence, said nothing to Dodger, but calmly went to work about the camp as if nothing had happened. When she spoke to Dodger it was in short, abrupt sentences. In this way she let him know something was wrong and she was not about to be pressed. He tended the horses as she prepared the evening meal.

It was the last of twilight when Frank emerged from the aspens that ringed the line camp and rode to where his gear was neatly stored with the rest. Ella ignored his hostile look, but when he went past she studied him, waiting for him to turn and call her down or say something that would enable her to call him down for his own part in the afternoon's activities. But he never spoke to her or to Dodger, choosing instead to show his intentions by packing and sorting his belongings.

One look at Dodger's sinking face gave her second thoughts but Frank had piled everything he wasn't taking right away, wrapped it and tossed it in a wood tool shed that leaned against the line shack cabin. He quickly caught the reins of his horse and came up to where she and Dodger stood. "I want you to know why I'm leavin'."

She spoke quickly, but meant it. "Just so's you go."

Frank nodded, frustrated that she saw no error in her act, that she felt no remorse. "I am, but yer gonna hear." She started away but his words followed. "I knew what I was doin' but you didn't trust me. It was my land, and you'd fire my ass for meddlin' in yer business, but you got yer own cute ways. Well lady, yer welcome to yer whole damned mess. You made it, you clean it up."

Dodger looked from one to the other, but so far had learned nothing from the words that passed.

"Babysister, you best tell me what happened."

She turned, looked at Dodger, but before she could speak, Frank chuckled and spoke sarcastically. "Hell, old sage, she just stampeded Ewing's herd, that's all. Christ, I thought you knew everything, Dodger." Frank shook his head bitterly and led his horse off a few paces, mounting up and riding off quickly into the gloom that had settled first in the forests and now swept across the clearing.

Ella continued to work but felt Dodger's eyes on her until she couldn't stand it anymore and faced the old man, speaking clearly and firmly. "I ain't sorry about what I did, Dodger."

"You oughta be." Dodger spit into the fire. "Ol' J.W. couldn't've split you an Frank better if'n he'd used a axe."

She shook her head firmly and glanced into the forest, still listening to the fading sounds of Frank's horse as he headed away. "Can't trust Athearn."

A full minute passed with Dodger never taking his eyes off her. "Yeah, Babysister, he sure is sneaky. Always talkin' up like he does an' showin' common sense. Bad stuff."

He knew her eyes were cutting him down as he walked to the fire and poured himself a cup of coffee and wondered what the hell they'd ever do now. If they had a chance it had just been shot to hell. Damn, he thought, I know you got ways, Lord. Just don't show me all yer tricks at one time in my life.

I know I'm in love with you, dammit, and I know as well I really oughtn't be. God knows, it's a complication I don't need and neither do you, but the truth is, I'm hooked and I wish to hell I could tell you how much, Miz Connors, he thought as he rode toward his ranch on Wolf Creek. The sun was gone, and the night was straggling in through the low mountain passes.

He'd come to admire so much about Ella Connors, found so much to respect, that he wasn't aware he was in love until the moment he'd returned to the line camp and seen her face. She fought to conceal the distrust, but it was clear in the intensity of her quick glance. And in that one look she said she felt betrayed and he realized how deeply he felt for her. A quick-witted man would have found a way to win her in that moment; a sly man could have duped her. But Frank could only turn his back and walk away from her. No matter what he did at this moment, he would have been wrong in her eyes, so he naturally chose the one that hurt him the most. It wasn't her problem. Damn if she didn't have enough of those already.

I don't like startin' something, then backin' off without pullin' my share, he thought, but lady, you don't trust me and ain't about to try, so goodbye for now and good luck to you. He wanted to say he understood she was alone and taking it in the head from start to finish and he'd be there if she needed him, but it just came out wrong when he saw her look, and now it was over. He was running out and hating himself for it. Maybe I don't love her as much as I think I do, he mused inwardly. If I did, wouldn't I do everything to stay with her?

"Not unless yer a total fool, Athearn," he said aloud to the night.

At first he had thought she smiled little, and in the days when he was recuperating, she spoke even less, but as they began to work he noticed that many things pleased her and caused her to smile. Her sense of humor was fine, though she was fussy about sharing. Then there were the times when she would force a smile, and the memory was unpleasant to him. But when she smiled for real, it came from deep inside, and with it came a warmth that was shut off and controlled the moment it emerged.

An hour of such thoughts brought him to his ruined ranch and for the first time he saw Billy's grave in the shadows at the base of a cluster of aspens. Dodger had picked the best spot, but Frank merely studied the ranch and the grave quietly from horseback. Instead of dismounting and making camp for the night, he pushed on, past the ranch and down the narrow road through the aspens to the highway that wound through the basin to the town of Bear Paw.

He'd already cursed himself for getting involved to the point where he felt foolish no matter which way he turned. He felt bound to stay and finish what he'd started, but there was no way to deal with the Connors woman. If he was open, she doubted the sincerity; if he was withdrawn and quiet in her presence, it only added to her suspicion and distrust, and to his sense of alienation. He didn't blame her, for it was clear she was up against terrible odds, and one could only take so many head shots before getting a bit scrambled. But there was something more to her lack of trust and whatever it was nagged at him.

He damned himself for even considering anything as foolish as a relationship between the two of them. No way a match like that could ever work, and he doubted if there was a gambler in the world who'd take odds on the teaming being successful.

It took Frank over two hours to reach Bear Paw, but it wasn't nearly enough time to sort out his thoughts. For a moment he reined in within sight of the town. He considered his foul mood, which had grown worse instead of better for all his hard thinking, and was almost tempted to turn around and head back to his ranch. But the promise of a beer and a sandwich overrode any objections he might have, so he urged the horse into Bear Paw, stopping and dismounting before the Lime House Saloon and Cafe.

He noticed a black Model A truck down the street as he clumped up the steps of the saloon and wondered if it was hers. Then, deciding there must be at least ten trucks like that in these parts, he shoved through the doors of the once busy, now ghostly Lime House.

The building had been remodeled over the years to the point that the original clapboard construction no longer existed, but various experimental walls and supports took their place tenuously. The latest of styles affected by the Lime House were due to the efforts of a traveling salesman anxious to unload a shipment of glass bricks. Tourists heading for the park and stopping for a quick meal labeled the place Neo-Quartz Decor, and the glass bricks that dominated the windows and the area behind the bar reflected the lights of three beer distributors.

Frank noted three men he hadn't seen at the back table near the rest room, and moved to the bar to discover Dodger sitting quietly, sipping a beer.

"Howdy, Buck," said the old man.

Dodger smiled into the mirror, watching Frank suppress a grin and slide onto the next stool.

"Guess you sure licked that roundup pretty damned quick, old man."

"Yeah," drawled Dodger, sipping his beer, smacking his lips, "We're jest hell on wheels. You probably saw," he added with a wry jab.

Frank nodded and signaled the girl serving as bar dog for a beer and she turned to pull the draught. It was hard to avoid looking at Dodger in the mirror, and Frank finally turned to him, stared for a moment and quietly shook his head without a smile.

"You still looking for a dog to kick, Frank?"

No response.

"I took the truck. Went to yer place, followed yer sign, Buck . . ."

"I know why yer here, Dodger. Might as well look for hair on a damned frog."

Dodger thought for a moment, then nodded. "Damn if'n she wouldn't flay me alive with her tongue if she knew I was talking to you."

Frank received his beer, paid for it and looked into the deep foam as he spoke. "Then don't."

Dodger signaled the girl and she came up to him. Dodger gestured to his empty beer glass, "Take another one, please, Holly." He tapped Frank on the arm. "Don't she look pretty as a spotted dog under a red wagon?"

The girl reddened slightly and Frank gave her a quiet, reassuring smile. "Yeah, she does."

"You sure are the one to jump without knowin' the right direction." Dodger knew he got Frank's attention and continued on. "Thing about the Connors is they's tough. Ella, her pa, Tom, even her ma, God rest her soul. Any one of 'em'd fight a rattler and git in the first bite." He smiled and reflected on how things had been as Frank waited patiently. "Course it all goes back a bit in time before the whole picture seems to fit . . ."

"I suppose I'm gonna hear it." There was a sarcastic edge to Frank's voice.

"Matter of fact, you are. About sixty years ago, her grandpa, John Connors, was top hand for Jacob Ewing, J.W.'s grandpap. Married himself to Jacob's daughter. To their way of thinkin' he warn't nothin' but a jumped-up, common cowboy and a Irish Catholic to boot." He paused and took a breath, expelling it slowly, noisily. "Old man did right, though, and give them what's now the Connors Ranch for a weddin' present. It was a decent and common thing to do, and probably woulda worked had ol' Jake lived forever. Guess the old man figured he had himself a

top hand and more control over the cowboys, but
shows you how things work out." He reached for his
pipe and began to fill it as he spoke, his eyes lifting
to watch Ralph Cole come through the Lime House
doors and move to the three cowboys at the back table, shooting Frank and Dodger a harsh glare as he
passed.

Cole spoke to the cowboys at the table and two of
them turned around to look at Frank as Cole slid
his chair in and poured himself a drink from the
bottle on the table. Dodger watched him in the mirror with one cautious eye.

"Connors and his wife started up his own place
and while old Jake Ewing didn't much like it, his
rule was never to hurt kin. Swore and made his men
swear as well. Ignored his daughter and her cowboy
husband, though, and lavished everything on her
younger brother, who was J.W.'s father. You followin'
this, Buck?"

"Oh yeah."

"Hope so. I may not have all that much wind left
and I hate like hell to waste it." He squinted and
lit the old pipe. "So, couple years later, Jake's boy's
wife give birth to J.W., and John Connors and his
wife had Tom not too long afterward. Old Jake, sly
fox he was, thought it'd be best for the family to
put the old hate away and so Tom and J.W. was
raised like brothers, with the old man jest waitin' so's
somethin' would allow him to gobble back the Connors Ranch. I guess legal-like it could have been his,
but it woulda made him look bad, so he decided to
wait it out."

"It never happened."

"You ain't dumb for one so young, now are you?"

Frank said nothing, but noticed the men at the
back table watching him and Dodger.

Dodger continued with his story. "Tom Connors
and Johnny Ewing. Quite a pair. Grew up closer'n
any two friends I ever knowed. Then something hap-

pened. Tom's dad died and Tom was left with the Connors Ranch. Couldn'ta been more'n fifteen or so." He drifted a moment, then blinked something back. "Ewings tried to get Tom to give it up and throw in with them, but Tom toughed it out and sooner or later he and J.W. had words over it."

"How you know all this, Dodger?"

"I ain't sweet sixteen, you know."

Frank nodded and sipped his beer as Dodger puffed on his pipe and got back to the story.

"J.W. went off to the first war and whilst gone, his grandpap died and afore J.W. was discharged his own father had pissed away most of the basin they had left. J.W. made up his mind to get it back and not just the ranch, but the whole basin, just like it was when Jacob first settled here. Far as I know he ain't never give up on the idea, and I don't expect him to." He relit the pipe, then continued, "Kinda feels anyone won't bend to him is scum. Like so much crap that can be swept from the land. He finally moved on Tom Connors, but Tom never bent, never give in, and that's why Ella is the way she is. . . . Hell, she was weaned on war. Never knew nothin' but fightin'."

Frank nodded, the words having some effect, but he shook his head. "It won't work, Dodger."

The old cowboy considered his drinking companion, then tamped his pipe and relit the cone. "Y'know, Buck, down in Texas, where they'd ruther eat a horse'n ride him, they got a old-timey word. Stargazer. That's a horse that's had the bit jerked so hard when it slows up or is in corral, it's always alookin' at the skies."

Dodger wondered to himself if he should continue, for he'd talked far more than he ever expected to, and he didn't care for the sounds that came from the table where Ralph Cole and the three cowboys sat.

Still though, he'd started it and knew better than Ella how much they needed Frank. "John W. Almighty Goddamn Ewing ain't never once let up on her reins."

Frank let it settle in and studied his beer. "Ain't no way that woman's ever gonna trust me. You know that."

"You only been readin' the easy signs, Frank. With her, it just takes more time."

"Don't know many men live to be three hunnert years old, an' I figure it'd take that long with her."

Dodger found himself nodding, though he didn't really agree with Frank's estimate. "I know it ain't easy, Buck."

"Easy? Runnin' full speed against a brick wall or a herd of buffalo is easy!"

"Yeah." Dodger watched in the mirror as Ralph Cole rose and walked toward them. "But there's a side to her that's worth all the trouble."

Frank's eyes looked over the edge of his glass, at Cole's reflection in the mirror as he spoke. "Yeah, I seen it." He still watched Cole who stood behind Dodger, looking back at Frank in the mirror. Dodger turned to look at Cole, and jerked a thumb disdainfully at him.

"This here's Ralph Cole, Frank, and Ewing mostly keeps him around to keep his windmill agoin' with all the big talk."

Cole reached out, took Frank's beer and emptied it on the floor, then slammed the empty glass back on the bar and slid it away from the two men.

"Dodger," Frank said softly, "I hope he has a very good reason for the prod."

Cole was a large and powerful man, and if too heavy for the finer side of cattle work, he was valued for his strength and a tough nature that forever had him in trouble in one of the three counties that ran through the area. He was the survivor, and the youngest of three Cole brothers of no relationship to anyone as far as was known. And being the youngest, Ralph was the smartest of the three brothers, which it was said was the reason why he was still alive. It was rumored that Cole once killed a man, but it was Cole who started the rumor and no one believed it much anymore or if they did, were beyond caring. Ralph Cole was a bully and the leading delinquent of the basin at forty-one years of age.

"Got reason enough, Athearn," Cole said. "Emil Kroegh was my bunkie." Frank merely looked at Cole and examined him, the name of Kroegh being linked in his mind to the killing of Billy. Cole motioned to Dodger in disgust. "Understand how this ol' windbag'd work for Ella Connors, 'cause he ain't good fer nothin' but sugar-tittin', but they say yer one helluva cowman, though I don't believe it. Figured the man'd take down Emil Kroegh'd be a whopper, but shit, you ain't nothin' but a paperback who couldn't lick his upper lip." He smiled, looked pitifully at the two cowboys. It was a bitter smile but it still improved him a bit. "Horse's ass'd live off a woman don't deserve nothin' better'n road apple pie. Boss knows her for a whore. Guess we know how she's been payin' you."

Cole couldn't remember afterward if nine or ten men had hit him. He felt where Frank had exploded into his midsection, doubling him, and his forehead was cracked and swollen from where it had been driven into the bar. He was conscious but going when he hit the floor, and when he opened his eyes Dodger was standing over him, pouring beer on him to bring him back. Cole saw Blocker enter the Lime House as Frank started out.

"Want you to see this, Ralph," Dodger's voice was bitter and deep. "It's for Ella." Dodger swung his boot and planted the toe full force under Cole's chin.

Everything in the room stopped but the coffee machine, the juke box and the screen door which swung back and forth. Blocker was just inside the door, facing Frank. The three cowboys were on their feet at the table, but not moving. Dodger stood over Cole, and the waitress, Holly, who was more than used to such goings on, continued cleaning up behind the bar, satisfied no damage had been done in the scuffle.

Blocker studied the scene, then stepped up to Frank, took his arm gently and whispered to him. "I ain't in this, son. And you oughtn' to be."

Frank spoke a bit louder. "I guess I heard enough of yer advice, ain't I?" He twisted away, but Blocker held fast and jerked him back. "Boy, you . . ."

The blows that dropped him were as savage and quick as the ones that felled Cole and the two lead Ewing men were down, and still the cowboys at the table never moved. Frank motioned to Dodger to come with him, but waited until Dodger cleared the door before following the old cowboy into the night.

The night had cooled considerably, and the men buttoned their jackets against the cold as Frank led his horse and followed Dodger to the truck. The old man swung the door wide, smiled and bobbed his head. "That was plain skookum back there, Buck."

Frank said nothing in reply, but smiled at the word, once Indian, now thought of as old-time Montana. It could have meant anything, but coming from Dodger it was special praise.

"You comin' back with me, Frank?"

Frank studied the almost deserted street, then looked back at the light spilling out of the Lime House. He shook his head firmly as he spoke. "Like to, but it won't work, Dodger. Not as long as she thinks I'm some kinda woods-pussy."

They stood there a bit longer, then Dodger extended his hand, they shook and then turned and parted, Dodger starting the truck, Frank mounting his horse. Each was more than content to allow the night to swallow his thoughts and actions.

V

THE TALLY

There were no reprisals. No jests. Nothing. Dodger worked as he did before, Frank left with no sign that anything had happened, and except for the fact that the work was not as enjoyable nor as profitable, it might have been that Frank had never been there at all.

Profitable. Ella considered the word and laughed bitterly to herself. It might just as well be over right now. In the six days since Frank had been gone, the two of them, working harder than they had ever worked before, located and trapped only nine head and those were rank steers that were too old to sell.

She watched Dodger rigging a finger trap, a fine effort, but how many would it corral? Five, six? Not enough and not fast enough. He had reminded her that anything was better than nothing. It was clear the work was getting to Dodger. It took him longer to mount and dismount and when he worked with his fingers she could see the arthritic joints that must hurt and certainly slowed him, but about which he never complained. They ought to quit now, and if she were smart, she would. But she knew she never would. Dodger finished up, moved to his horse and mounted, then followed her as they headed for the upper meadows where they discussed the possibility of finding a large batch of cows and calves.

An hour of climbing winded their horses and brought them out under the shelter of peaks, but above the tree line. A wide meadow fell down into the trees and there, fenced in a makeshift pen, were about fifteen cows and a large, ugly bull that Ella had never seen.

"They ain't mine." She let the wind carry her words.

"No, they ain't. Fact is, they're Frank's and I kinda hid 'em out on him. Figured at first if he found 'em, he'd be gone to his own place. I kinda thought we needed him."

Ella's look could have frozen the ocean, then she gave the cattle a long, careful inspection. "Not bad stuff, y'know?" Dodger said nothing but nodded to her phrasing. "Got to give 'em back, Dodger. Son-ofabitch jest might say we rustled 'em."

He gave her a wry grin, then shook his head, chuckling. "Yeah, Babysister, he jest might." Dodger ignored her harsh look at him and moved to drop the wire gate he'd made for the cattle.

Damn you, Dodger, she thought. I ain't about to take them cattle back. Yer gonna go instead. I know what yer tryin' to do, you old reprobate, and I ain't about to be shoved into workin' with him. She watched Dodger drive the cattle out as the cows and calves followed the lead bull, Buster. She waited for him to start them down the meadow, but Dodger reined off to one side. "Well, take 'em on back," she said.

"It ain't no business of mine, Babysister. You take 'em back."

Frank had only briefly considered going for his cattle, but since it was late in the season and there wasn't much he could do with them other than water and feed, he decided they were probably fine right where they were. Instead, he went to work righting the wrongs of the buildings, stripping away all good wood that could be salvaged and starting with the old, but sturdy frames. He'd cleared a spot for a spring garden and late one evening turned the soil over and made neat furrows, but did not seed.

He admitted to himself he enjoyed working in the garden far more than hanging the gate or working on the structures, though he could use his hands quite well and was competent as a carpenter. He had a limited idea of design and therefore decided to stick with the basic structure as it was, though what use some of the rooms were for was beyond him.

By the fourth day he'd made a list of the supplies he'd need to make the cabin habitable, and yet he held off going to town and ordering. There seemed no urgency to anything he was doing, so he lazed along, enjoying what he could of the work, not slacking, but not pushing himself either.

After six days of work, he was rather surprised with the results on the morning of the seventh. All he had to do was order up about fifty dollars of lumber, about twenty-five dollars worth of hardware, and he'd be right in business. He had just a bit more than that amount in mind anyhow, and had laid the money aside, but something still kept him from using it. This morning, however, he'd risen, stirred the last of the coffee and made some more, for this was shaping up to be a five-cup day, and set right in stacking the wood he'd salvaged to reassemble the cabin.

He was paused for his fourth cup of tar-black coffee, made with old grounds and salt, when the sound of cattle echoed out of the double meadows. It was hard to tell where they were coming from, for the sound was distorted, but in moments his well-trained eyes detected movement where the aspens met jack pine. He watched the flashes of red and white moving through blackberry and scrub oak until Frank's own bull, Buster, trotted into the meadow. There was no mistaking Buster.

The herd followed, cautiously trailing some ten to fifteen yards after the bull, and bringing up the rear, urging them angrily forward, was Ella Connors.

That she'd drive his cattle in was a surprise in its own right and should have been enough, but he wondered if she hadn't brought the beef back just to add a little more to his discomfort. But as she rode closer, she seemed tense, but not particularly angry. He was determined not to say much, and definitely not to start anything, or even come close to arousing her, and since almost anything but hello seemed to elicit a rise from her, he figured out way before she reined in that they were due to have a short time together, if any at all. He rather anticipated her dropping off the cattle and then riding away without a word. He found that he was wrong, and watched as she dismounted, tied up her horses, then busied her hands and eyes by tightening the cinch, then the bridle, and finally checking the saddlebag ties. Everything that could be worked by her fingers was manipulated as she spoke tersely to Frank.

"Didn't want you sneakin' back for yer beef."

"Obliged." Frank stood still, coffee cup in one hand, one knee bent as he leaned on a pile of rough-cut one by twelves. "Where'd you find 'em?"

She glanced up at the mountains, nodded in the general direction of the peaks. "Ain't so bad, you know where to look."

He checked his motions and held all curiosity out of his voice. "How's it been goin'?"

"Fine." She was hoping to give one word replies, but it was getting harder.

Frank walked to her finally, uncorking his canteen as he swung it from the post where he'd hung it that morning. He offered her the bottle but she declined with a swift shake of her head and looked at the work that he'd done. "It's gonna be nice."

"Yeah, it is!" he said, then gestured at the watering

trough. "I guess you been a ways. Could be yer horse needs a drink."

She merely looked at him and spoke quickly. "We hid yer cattle out on you. Thought it might stretch some more work outta you."

"It don't matter now."

She was adamant in the tone of her voice, her hand movements. "Yes, it does so matter. Ain't never cheated a soul in my life. Even had you stayed, I would've given them back." Ella waited for a calling down, but it never came.

"You want that water or is that horse really a camel?"

She shook her head stubbornly.

Frank's patience was even. His words came easily. "I ain't gonna consider no horseful or mouthful of water no debt, y'know."

Their eyes met and held, then she reached out for the canteen and wiped it clean as she led her horse to the trough and let him drink. She raised the canteen to her lips and drank deeply, but kept an eye on Frank, watching him watch her.

"Wish to hell you wouldn't watch me that way."

"Hard to watch you with my eyes shut."

"Don't watch me at all," she said with finality.

Frank took the canteen back when it was offered. "What the hell is wrong with you?" The anger in him, even if quiet, caused her to look at him and say nothing. "Figured you for tough before prideful when the chips are down."

She'd been resolved to say little and stay cool, but his words brought her own quick temper alive. "And what the hell is that supposed to mean?"

Well, he thought, I'm in for it now. "Meanin' you don't fool me none. You ain't gonna make it, jest you an' the old man. Oh, he's good and so are you, but you jest ain't enough hands."

She turned and swung her horse so she could mount,

ride off and not have to listen to this. She didn't come here for this.

"Forget any deadlines." His voice stopped her, but only for a second as she swung into the saddle. "Maybe you don't care, but I figure it's 'cause yer damned near punch-drunk." Ella merely looked down at him, her face rigid with anger at being called down so. This wasn't what she'd expected, nor was it anything Frank intended to say. It just continued to spill out. "I ain't comin' back to work for you as no hired hand, this time." Her look said, "Who asked you?" but she didn't say a word. "It's gonna be fair-share partners or nothin' and for the season. Truth is, you need me." That's right, she thought. I do need you, dammit. The next words he spoke surprised her. "And I guess I need you as much, maybe more. . . . I could hang on for one year alone, but then I'd have to pack it in." There was nothing she could say. "I figure the same for you."

"You really like to figure, Athearn."

He nodded, but his face showed no humor now. His eyes held her and made her uncomfortable. "It helps," he said simply.

Ella took a breath, then let it out with a soft, "Oh Jesus."

"I ain't out to take over yer ranch. Don't want nothin' but fair and equal treatment. . . . But I do need the help and so do you. Only difference is, I ain't too proud to admit it."

What he said made sense, and though she was angry, she held her temper in check long enough to weigh his words thoughtfully as she watched Frank move to the watering trough and refill his canteen.

"I'll think on it." Her voice was barely audible. A breeze drove the aspen leaves to a chattering frenzy, but Frank did hear and turned to look at her.

"Ain't nothin' to think about. It's a straight deal."

She nodded. "Maybe. But I ain't never had no partners before."

"Sure as hell kin understand why." He hoped his jest wouldn't cause her to bolt or explode in one of her fine rages. She took a deep breath, then nodded again, but reluctantly.

"Jest for the season, Athearn. One season, then it's over."

Frank held back the relief he felt. "I'll be by in the mornin'."

She turned her horse, but he detained her further by walking up to her and speaking in a more personal tone. "Just one more thing."

"What is it?" There was icy impatience and little tolerance.

Frank wiped the inside of his hat brim with his scarf and looked at her as he worked. "You say my name all terrible-like. Make a good enough name sound like horse pucky. Could call each other Frank and Ella like civilized people."

"Oh Jesus." She stared at him in disbelief, then relented. "All right."

"All right what?"

"All right . . . *Frank* . . . Jesus Christ!"

If she hadn't been in agreement with him, or if the self-control she exhibited had broken, he would have been cut short early on. But she was surprised to find that she was beginning to have to work at being angry at him, and recognized in herself that what had passed between them before led to now, and now would lead her on a different path for the future. And while something gnawed at her, telling her to hold back, she felt more now than resentment. She smiled quickly, shyly, then turned and started her horse off, building to a trot, then a canter as she headed back to the line camp.

Frank watched her until she reached the trees, then turned and scanned his under-construction ranch, and made a promise he'd get the place done as soon as possible. Then he moved to pack up his gear, still a bit stunned that he'd said what he did, even more

surprised that she'd agreed and floored totally by
the smile she'd tossed at him as she left.

Well, he thought. That's fine for today, but tomorrow it could all blow up in my face. He hoped not,
but decided to prepare for the worst, just in case.

The fact that work had stopped, or almost stopped,
on the Connors Ranch for a week seemed to make no
difference, for the three-person team worked like ten,
and by skill and planning more than made up for
the time lost.

As the summer drove ahead, and the war in the
Pacific drew to its finale, the mountains rang with
shouts and yells as the three forced more cattle than
Ella knew she had down toward the corrals in the
highland meadows. There was no snow above them,
and by August only a tiny glacier that never saw the
sun continued to feed the Connors and Athearn
streams, but the water was gone before it reached the
flats and the Ewing cattle began to suffer. There was
no time to drill wells to fill the dying holes, and each
day that went by passed without the usual summer
showers that brought relief.

They took turns waking and working, sometimes
going for days without any sleep at all, but never
slowing, never flagging. There was laughter when the
three of them worked together, though it was heard
only by Dodger, Ella and Frank. The work was good.
The rewards and promises grew before their eyes.
They were invincible.

Utilizing old traps and corrals, building new ones
when they had to and using bulls to call the scattered cows and calves from dense cover, they amassed
over three hundred head by the first of August, and
on the tenth they made a windfall discovery of a
cluster of cattle on the north slopes of a wide canyon
numbering over one hundred animals in all.

When the herd reached five hundred head and they decided they would start the job of cutting, branding and culling the herd, they had their first sit-down, hard and hot-cooked meal together.

Each one took a part of the preparation and the meal was the most lavish any of them had experienced in some time. And when it was over, before they began the nightly job of rotating watches to keep an eye on the herd scattered over eight corrals in three adjoining upper meadows, Dodger indulged them with a song.

He was aware that each was keenly watchful of the other, though they thought themselves quite clever in that they were never caught looking or staring. Ella and Frank kept their thoughts about each other to themselves. But Dodger was ignored by them, so he could stand back and watch them slowly adapt to each other. His age gave him wisdom that enabled him to live with them and never discuss this thing that was happening. A word would spook either one, and plunge a whole damned day into a stream of denials and ruffled feathers. At his age Dodger felt he scarcely needed to waste a day. So he kept the banter going and watched them relax in each other's company. By this night they seemed like three old-time cowhands with no age or sexual difference between them. They were a circle of friends by the fire.

The talk was light, about cattle and horses and men they'd known over the years, and it was at times like this that Ella always surprised Dodger, for she continually contributed a story that even Dodger with all his age and windy ways had never encountered. He wondered if she made the stories up, and then decided they must've come with all her readin' and such, for while he'd taught her to spin a yarn he was sure he was still the champion liar. But she was sure good at it. Frank had a different way with a story, and Dodger assumed that his background was one mixed with packers and hunters, for those men spoke slowly and savored words. Frank spoke in phrases that were his alone but sounded as if they'd been sung by bards and minstrels of the old country. Dodger placed great store in what he heard, and was glad he still had most of his faculties.

When the conversation at last died away and Dodger's arthritic fingers fumbled on the guitar strings, he put the instrument in its broken case and slung it over his shoulder as he rose and tipped his hat to them. "First watch's mine." They nodded but looked into the fire, stuck there, they were so relaxed. "Y'know . . . nights like this're sure a lot better'n standin' on some ol' nasty street corner, chewin' tobacco, spittin' and tryin' to make a slick spot so's you kin git some old lady down."

"Uh huh." Frank, then Ella murmured it.

"Well then," he tried to think of something clever to add, "don't take no wooden organs." And he strode off into the night, the guitar case slapping against his leg. They could hear him mount his horse and ride off but it was some time before Ella could look up from the fire and stare in the direction she knew he took, then she looked over at Frank and queried, "What'd he say?"

Frank looked up from the fire, thought back over what he'd heard, then shook his head. "Ask him when you see him. I ain't gonna say it."

Ella smiled. "You're afraid to say it."

He shrugged and settled back against his saddle. Interesting, he thought. She's fine as long as we ain't alone, but she sure gits right down to it when we are. He made up his mind not to be drawn into a fight.

Ella drifted for a moment and was soon caught by the fire again, and it held her until she forced herself to look over at Frank again. She felt a bit drowsy and stifled a yawn, then asked, "How come you ain't never married?"

"What makes you so sure I ain't never?"

"You don't know how to talk to a woman, that's how I'm sure."

"I do all right."

"Shit." She thought about it. "You git all stiff if I go an' even open my mouth. You can't even answer a simple question."

"I don't guess you ever asked a simple question in your life, Ella."

Her eyes smiled. "I guess yer right there."

He sat up and tipped back his hat. "Y'know, if I was to ask you about why you ain't never married, you'd get all ugly and start fat lippin' me to death." Her mouth moved in protest but he held up his hand. "Gimme a break, will you? You know *damn well* that's what you'd do."

She looked into the fire again and noticed little flame people and knew it was time to turn in. "Trouble is, you have some way to figure me out; damned how you always do it, but you do. Ain't comfortable with somebody lookin' over my shoulder so to speak." There was a long pause and Frank got to his feet and began to remove the pans and dishes to a garbage tub that stood near the line shack.

"It's only for a season," he said sympathetically.

"Yeah."

"You don't have to sound so overjoyed."

Ella looked at him lifting the dishes and rose to carry her share. "I ain't no fool child. I know what we're doin' here an' I know how much is yer doin'. Guess I'll always be grateful, but I said for the season and the season it is." He stood motionless, and she mistook this for obstinacy. "It ain't enough for you, is it?"

He was a touch confused. "I don't think I understand." He fought for something to say that made sense. "I . . ." He shrugged and walked away to the garbage tub and after scraping the dishes into a refuse pile, dropped the dishes into the cool, soapy water. He came back to her, some of his thoughts in perfect order. "You keep lookin' for the rough spots in me an' you'll find more'n enough. Get it through your head I don't want a thing from you. You ain't gonna force me to give you any reasons not to trust me no more. There ain't time for it, in case you hadn't noticed." He paused, knowing he was a bit out of control. "I figure in time we could be friends, but I guess you don't need no friends."

"That ain't fair." She was very calm and quiet.

"No, I guess it ain't, but I'm tired of bein' fair and havin' you jest kick the livin' shit out of my soul for it, lady."

He looked levelly at her, robbing her of the will to deny his accusation, then walked to where he'd spread his blankets and calmly turned in for the night, ignoring her as he undressed as if she didn't matter in the least.

Ella scraped her dishes, rinsed, then washed and rubbed them dry. She dripped a handful of water into a worn towel and with no words and the shyest glance over at Frank, entered the line shack for eight hours until it was her turn to rise and take over the last watch. She slept for only ten minutes the whole time, and spent the rest of the night wondering what it was that made her keep him constantly at an arm's length. The more she pondered the question the more it twisted and snaked and came back to haunt her in a thousand tiny demons that represented every wrong, real or imaginary, she caused or experienced in her entire life. She was actually grateful for Frank's rap on the door at two in the morning, relieved to be able to put her mind to better use.

At any time of the year Virgil Hoverton had more than a few reasons to visit the Connors Ranch. He liked Ella genuinely, though he knew she distrusted him, and he knew it wouldn't matter if it were he or someone else. A banker was a banker and that was that. He thought of himself as *her* banker, though their relationship had strong adversary aspects to it and he often felt more like he was tying her to the tracks and wearing a black cape. There was always some offer for Ella's land that he could take to her if he so desired, but knowing her feelings on the matter he never did, but refused every offer outright.

Because he liked Ella, held her note and was the only banker in the region, Virgil Hoverton deeply wanted her to like him in return, and if she couldn't bring herself to like him, at least to respect him for what he did. But the closest Ella would get to acknowledging him as human was to occasionally call him Virg and not banker, or that banker, or that damned banker.

"How much longer, Virgil?" Neal Atkinson's quiet voice startled him. He had assumed the man was asleep and marveled that anyone could sleep when they were twisting and wrenching steadily uphill over a deeply rutted, poorly maintained road in Hoverton's car.

"Maybe ten minutes. Fifteen possibly."

Atkinson nodded and leaned his head back against the seat and closed his eyes. He'd said only a few words to Hoverton as they drove into the Bear Paw from Lewistown. He realized that while he had to deal with Hoverton, he found the man totally uninspired and dull. No wonder his wife left him, even though the woman was a bit of a toad. Neal Atkinson tried to nap and couldn't, in fact he'd been having troubles sleeping for about three weeks. The pressure on him was tremendous. His ownership of Atko Oil was in peril, or at least his working control. Too much had gone out in a short period for exploration without results. Stockholders, sometimes even the smallest ones, demanded results or they sold and your company died.

His family railroads were dead and dying. That

much was clear. He was damned if he'd let it happen
to Atko, for it was *his*, built from the ground up, and
he was proud of his single achievement in life. Since
he couldn't sleep he straightened and looked into the
narrow rear seat of the car where George Bascomb
lanked about trying to get comfortable in the
cramped space.

"Where's the main area that you suspect?"

Bascomb motioned vaguely in the direction they
were heading as he spoke. "It's back and west of here.
You can see the faults and the depressions, but its
tricky. I walked the area for about a week before I
saw it, and I was following trace at the time."

"Any road for the equipment?"

Bascomb considered. "I wouldn't consider it a
road. It's more like a cut, but we could doze it wider
in about three days and if there's enough equipment
over the road before winter, in the spring you could
be in action."

"Spring?"

Bascomb smiled and bobbed his head twice. "It's
terribly late in the year to get many results now, and
you won't be able to work rigs or much else in eighty
below weather."

Atkinson turned back and faced out the front window, aware that Hoverton was absorbing it all like
the moss on the rocks soaked up the sun. He shut his
eyes and took a deep breath, but knew it would do
no good whatsoever.

Just to cull through the five hundred head they'd
gathered, and to cut, brand and notch the calves
took the three of them over two weeks of bone-break-
ing work. But it was done and after they turned out
the calves and cows retained to build the herd, they
had space to spare. The bulls that had been gathered
and turned out were doctored and babied during the

time of their captivity. And perhaps it was the number of bulls sprinkled about the meadow corrals that drew more stock, for every morning would find a fresh batch of mooning cows who had come miles to answer the bellows of the handsome brutes. Ella, Frank or Dodger, whichever discovered the animals each morning, would gladly oblige the cows by opening the gates and allowing the lovesick bovines admission to what Frank began to term "The Connors Passion Pits." With the cows came steers, who normally stayed close to the mothers and calves, some instinct saying that that was the place to be. So the act of having to physically round up the cattle was greatly aided by the increasing number of cattle in the pens. The more they got, and the more noise, the more the animals that for years had been wild as African Cape Buffaloes were compelled by curiosity toward the lush lower meadows and the pens that would catch them, changing their wild ways.

At first, the three-man team was at a loss, but soon they worked out a system where one of them would scout the foothills and drive in loose animals during the day, while two of them would doctor, cut, brand, notch and generally pull the animals into a small but fine commercial herd. It was awkward, but it worked, and soon became almost factory-like so *well* did it work.

The terrible work of castrating bull calves was done with black humor bandied like halloween treats on a dark night. When it was the three of them working it was never serious, but when it was any two of them, the discussions were about things that mattered deeply, though in the case of Frank and Ella, they were scrupulous to avoid going too deep. It was as if neither seemed to want to know much about the other, but in fact wanted the knowledge desperately, and the way they talked was in great circles, covering the matters they wanted to know about with lofty

phrases and high ideals. Frank recalled that his father
called it "Injun Play," for he'd seen the Crow and
Blackfoot talk for hours without ever getting to the
point and yet be understood.

This particular morning Dodger took to the hills
and his sweep kept him out of camp all day, so the
two of them worked feverishly and quietly until
noon, accomplished a lot, then slowed the pace as
they went about roping calves and dropping them
near the branding fire. While Ella would hold the
head of the calf and notch the ear, Frank would hold
the hot iron until it sizzled through the hair and into
the hide, then he would put the iron on the fire, and
with a knife kept sterile in hot water, would de-ball
the stunned calf. The sounds and smells that offended
outsiders were something they'd grown used to, but
neither could really handle the stunned horror of the
calf when the act was done, so they went easy and
coddled the animals, trying their best to ease the
shock.

They could hear the sound of a vehicle far below
but each knew it could only be approaching the line
camp, so they waited and worked, content to see whoever it was whenever he arrived without worrying
about it in advance. At length Hoverton's car lurched
ruggedly into the clearing near the line shack cabin
and stopped.

Hoverton and Atkinson clambered out, then un-
winding slowly and following them came Bascomb,
unknown to Ella, but not to Frank. The cutting and
branding continued as the three men approached the
corral, Atkinson walking beside Hoverton, Bascomb
hanging a few feet behind.

The banker and Neal Atkinson quickly scanned the
cattle in the pens. "Virgil." Atkinson's voice was soft,
hard to hear and Hoverton turned to look at him. "It
doesn't exactly look like she's washed up and ready
to fold, does it?"

Hoverton could only shrug, a bit dismayed, but he knew a lot could happen regardless of the number of cattle they had penned up here. The three of them drew up to the edge of the area where the branding was being done and stopped, allowing space for the strenuous and dusty work. Bascomb's nose wrinkled at the odor of burnt hair and hide. Only Atkinson seemed at home, moving closer. His eyes watched them work, his interest high apparently, a smile on his lips when he caught their eyes.

"Ella . . . Athearn . . . how are you?"

Ella straightened and dropped her iron back into the fire. "I guess you kin see we're jest about fit as hell." She grimaced a bit. "But I don't guess you came all the way up here to ask on our health."

Atkinson smiled, chuckled and edged a bit closer, nodding a greeting again at Frank as the cowboy looked at him. He spoke to Ella. "It doesn't mean I'm not interested in how you're doing." She just studied him, noting what his idea of outdoor clothing was—a tweed jacket, sweater underneath, with open collar although it was three degrees past ninety in the shade. "Ella, you evaded talking to me a long time. I thought maybe coming here, seeing you on your home ground, you might just be a bit more amenable to talking a little business."

"I ain't never run from you like you make it sound, Atkinson, but I jest don't see we got a whole lot in common." Her eyes ranged over to Bascomb, who'd moved closer, and she nodded at him. "Who's he?"

"This is George Bascomb, our chief geologist in charge of explorations."

The man looked like a tall weevil in Ella's eyes and was probably just about as useful, but the geologist stepped forward and spoke.

"Miss Connors . . ."

"I guess I know already what it's all about." She turned away from Bascomb, to speak to Neal Atkin-

son. "Seen yer trucks in the next basin, watched 'em
come closer and closer. Figured it'd only be a matter
of time till you up and come into our place."

"It's a rich basin," Bascomb interjected. "There's
a lot of wealth in here."

Ella made a sweep of the landscape that lay before
them with her arm. "Already got m'wealth. Ain't
particularly interested in anything could wreck it."

"You don't understand," Bascomb moved into her
line of sight, "somewhere out there is an enormous
deposit of oil, or at least we think there is. All the
geology leads us to think it's back against the mountains, or up at the entrance of the basin."

Even if he had been telling her there was gold at
the entrance of the basin, her reaction would have
been the same. She looked at Atkinson, then Bascomb
and smiled wickedly, pegging that they were after
something for little or nothing if they could get away
with it. She shook her head, spit on the iron and
watched it sizzle, then she ground the iron down
against the calf's hide and said nothing. Frank made
his cut, then she notched the ears and the calf was
let loose.

"Ella." Atkinson's tone caused them to look up.
He was almost stern, but still a bit cautious. "All
we're after is a short-term lease so we can get on with
the testing. The cattle business hasn't been right in
thirty years, except for the war. There was no market
after World War One and the same thing could happen again." He gestured at the cattle. "You could
survive quite well with oil money, and you know it.
You could certainly do without this sort of work each
year."

"I like this sort of work," she said levelly.

"This ranch'll kill you in the end."

"Way I hear it, everything'll kill you in the end,
you ain't careful." She glanced at the three men,
swept her eyes over Frank and then looked down the
basin, taking in the stretch of plain that fell south

and east. There were dust devils on the flat, and thunderheads were forming to drop rain on the mountains, to attack the plains with lightning. "Been through bad times before. Drought, blizzards, depression, tick fever, hell . . . I seen it all. Seen Ewing's viciousness as much as my . . ." She looked over at Frank pointedly. . . . "partner." He continued with his work, did not look at her, but listened carefully. "But he's still here, and so am I and I ain't never changed the land exceptin' the few fences I put in." She sniffed the wind. "Can't see no reason for me to go oil."

Hoverton had to speak up, and he spoke without feeling, just laying out a few simply facts. "I'd say you had reason enough. What happens if the war ends tomorrow? What happens to the price of beef opposed to the cost of your mortgage? Ella, listen to Mr. Atkinson. You could lose this place in a month and this could be the one way you can be sure to keep it." She said nothing, but listened. "It's just a lease he wants. He doesn't want to own the land."

"You heard what I think, Virgil. But I guess you'll want to talk to Frank as well." She motioned to Atkinson. "Well, go on ahead. Better'n talkin' behind a person's back."

Atkinson looked to Frank who said simply, "Got nothin' against oil personally, but I sure as hell like the smell of cows and cowshit a whole lot better. Nothin' personal."

Before Atkinson could reply Ella walked closer, spoke to him quietly, making it tough for Hoverton to hear. "By the way. Ewing know you come up here with this offer?"

"He will."

She shrugged. "Probably be better for you if he didn't."

"I'm not worried about J.W., Ella."

"You oughta be, Atkinson. You really oughta be." She moved back to the fire and selected a new, hotter

iron. "Get another calf over here . . ." She hesitated.
. . . "Please."

Frank rose and turned to rope another calf.

Atkinson raised his voice slightly to be heard. "I've
done this a few times, you know. It always begins the
same way, but sooner or later it turns around."

Frank glanced over. "Could be things is different
here."

"You could be right," Atkinson agreed. "But I
think you're making a big mistake." They said nothing, but continued with the work. "I can't force you."
Atkinson stopped abruptly. It was over. There was
no appeal to this jury. "Good luck with the roundup.
Hard work deserves its own rewards."

They jerked their heads to indicate their thanks,
and to acknowledge they'd heard him. And with that
the three men turned back to the car, wondering to
themselves why they'd even bothered.

When the car disappeared out of sight, Frank and
Ella dropped their tools, finished their last animal,
then moved off to the line camp shack.

Though they weren't at all tired from work, the
strain of the meeting had exhausted them, and without saying so much, knew they needed the break and
moved off together.

"Y'know," Frank drawled, "what Atkinson said is
right. About the oil I mean. If you were to agree to a
lease, and they was to find oil, you'd be home free."
They removed their chaps and gloves and draped
them near the shack, on a pole. Ella washed in the
trickle of water that flowed in an old stream bed
beside the shack, then scooped water to her lips.

"You could be free of Ewing . . . an' me, an' everything else that bothers you so damned much." He
knelt and washed his hands carefully.

Ella shook her hands and arms dry, then went for
a towel to dry her face and when she finished, politely
handed it to Frank. "My father fought like hell to
hold this ranch. I'll be damned if I'll let them make

a shit pile out of the paradise it is by letting Atkinson and his kind rape it and turn it into a stinking oil field." Her voice was deep and brooding. Not at all filled with her usual passion. Frank watched her talk. "Day ain't been marked on the calendar when that'll happen and I doubt to God it ever will." She turned a gentle look in his direction and her voice changed to understanding. "I guess I can figure how you feel, and if you want to sell yer piece to 'em then go ahead. But I don't want to know about it. You understand?"

Frank hung the towel to dry, and they moved around the firepit, absently stirring it to life, adding new wood to the flame as the fire gained new life. They fastened a rig into place and hung the coffeepot to warm, then they moved away from the heat and stood looking down at the cattle below them.

"You expect me to cut an' run so easy after all this?" His hand motioned to the cattle.

"You're the one tellin' me I ought to sell, that they're so damned right."

Frank shook his head. "Didn't say you ought to, said *if* you was to sell. Guess there's a difference." He waited for her to agree, but when she didn't protest, he accepted that as good enough. "They were right about the kinda money you could get, though, and about how chancy the markets are an' all, and I was just makin' sure."

She looked over at him and wiped her hands on her levis. "Of what?"

"Well," he sucked air for a second, "you don't always look on both sides of things."

I like this man, she thought, I like the way he thinks. "I ain't about to start now." She smiled, and watched him grin down into the fire as he checked the coffee. She knew some retort flashed through his mind, but he seldom gave her harsh digs anymore.

He sobered when he looked up at her, though his eyes said the thought was still there. "Well, you

might consider that with all that 'damned' oil money
you could go anyplace in the world, see anything, and
like a caterpillar turn right into a butterfly of a fine
lady. A *fine* and *fancy* lady."

"Now ain't that jest some picture," she laughed.

"I think it could be," Frank said, rising with the
coffeepot and cups. "But it depends on whose eyes
you look through."

"I don't understand," she said, meaning she did but
didn't really want to discuss it. But she was curious
enough about him to find out if she had him pegged
correctly.

"I think you do," he said, but added quickly, "but
just in case, it's that some folks look at you and see
good things, but you only see the ugly ones, and so
you picturin' you must be one helluva sight." He
thought he'd said it a bit harshly, and scanned his
mind for something to ease his words.

"I guess that's true." Well, she thought, he certainly has my number, but she found that she did
not resent it at this moment.

"Of course," he said quietly, tipping his hat down
so she couldn't see his eyes, "I'm one of the ones who
see a beautiful lady with promise for even better in
the years to come."

His sudden lyricism made her stare at him. Before
he'd been clever, but mostly when attacking or jest-
ing, and with cowboys it was easy. But his words fitted
with the gentleness that both attracted her and
bothered her at the same time.

"I've known some ladies in my years on earth." He
looked apologetic, boyish. "Not many." He blushed
a bit. "Not even by a preacher's standard." He
dropped his voice and dug at the ground with his toe.
He wished desperately that he'd never started on this
course, but he had, and cursed his own honesty.
"This ain't the thing to admit to a soul, let alone
you, but you got to know, that while there ain't been
many, and few of them that mattered more'n a few

seconds of my life, but . . ." He was losing his train of thought, and his voice failed him. God, not now when I need you, Lord. Please don't let me down. "But the one that did, left me with the knowledge of what a woman is about, leastways the good things. Ella, you got all them things and more. I'm pleased to call you more than a partner." He saw her tense slightly at the corners of her mouth and added, "You may not like it, but I consider you a friend. A damned good one."

"Frank." She stopped and sighed. She'd heard everything in spite of her efforts of the last six months, and knew how happy she was now contrasted with back then, and then she had an image of Ewing and a desperate sinking feeling went through her. When she tried to speak, she almost gagged and it took everything to control her stomach, which seemed to grow smaller and press against her backbone. Her voice finally found the words, forced them out calmly. "There are a lot of things I like about you. I guess you are one of the best folks I've known. Not too sure I believe all I see an' hear sometimes, but discounting half, what's left ain't bad at all. Glad to have you for a neighbor." Now, she thought, here's the tough part, pard. "But I said for the season, and I meant it. After that, yer on yer own, and so am I." Frank nodded, and she thought, You damned fool, you don't even know what yer noddin' into. Her voice quivered in her chest and she hoped it wasn't too obvious. "Now I guess that I got enough of you, and carry enough of your thoughts and feelin's that I don't need any more. You understand, I can't carry anything you want to dump onto me." Her voice toughened as she saw his angry expression. "See, I think up until about a minute ago, we been just about good enough friends for me. Any more, we might not like what we find."

"Meanin' you don't want to give it a chance."

She looked at him and nodded flatly, exactly, and

then averted her eyes to the cup in her hands. "It's good enough."

No it isn't, Frank wanted to yell, but muttered, "I guess." He considered the fact that he'd blown it now, but shrugged if off in favor of a deep hurt inside he'd never experienced before, and didn't understand at all. How do you put a closed end on friendship? Pretty tough to me, he mused and looked at Ella. Her face showed nothing and he wondered how to reach her. He changed the subject. "Y'know, long before I was a full cowman I worked remudas for my family and I guess you could say I got to be an expert on horses. Been meanin' to tell you what fine animals you got, but then I guess you know that." He finished his coffee and reached for the pot again.

"Nez Percé originally." Ella nodded north to the mountains above them. "Part of the horses lost by Joseph when he was hit by the army at Big Hole. Folks say they's some sorta figment, that they never existed and they're a legend, but let me tell you, yer ridin' a legend then whenever you set astride one of my horses."

There was a very long silence between them now and they watched the shadows lengthen, and listened to the wind in the aspens. Suddenly they both heard the sounds of Dodger driving more cattle into the clearing, and they stood watching as Dodger maneuvered six adult steers to where others like them waited and watched.

Dodger called up to Ella, "I found a place where you got coulees you never knew you had. Found you a batch more, then found these suckers you call steers when I was comin' in." He pointed at the steers as he let them into the corral. "These here are just hardy siwash, y'know, but they'll cut the mustard I guess." He started toward them, but Ella merely gave Frank a strange, distant look of appraisal, then turned and went into the line shack as Dodger dropped off his horse and stepped up to the fire, ready for the coffee already poured and handed to him by Frank. The old cowboy glanced at the shut door of the shack, then eyed Frank.

"Hope I didn't disturb you none," he ventured and waited until Frank shook his head. "In my youth, I was known to cut a big gut myself, Buck."

"You think that's all I ever do with her? You think I jest play the fool?" Frank's face was angry, tense, and he fought not to explode at the old man. "It ain't that, Dodger. It ain't that." He turned and walked to where the horses, still saddled, stood in shade, and he began loosening the saddle cinch. Dodger led his horse over, began the same process, and watched Frank from the corner of his eye.

"You hollerin' calf rope, Buck?"

"I'm still here, ain't I?"

"More or less," drawled Dodger. "But I been watchin' you and when you ought to be more outspoken, you tend to whistle on it with yer breath." Dodger sucked air. "Never known that to do anything but give you brown-nose fever."

Frank stopped working on his horse and came around the animal to stand facing Dodger. "Old man, I figure you got some of the answers, but you ain't givin' me nothin' but garbage an' you know it. You want to play matchmaker, you best look to half yer investment."

Dodger glanced at the cabin as Frank looked over there, but the door was still shut and no noise came from inside.

"It's more than just pride, Dodger. I can see that."

"Good eyes."

"I ain't stupid. My heart and my eyes always agree, but my mind tells me to forget it. You understand?" Frank almost whispered, so quiet was his voice and Dodger leaned forward with his head bowed to hear him. "It's Ewing. I can tell as much, 'cause I can't even mention the man." Dodger said nothing and Frank understood that for an admission of fact. "Tell me about her an' Ewing."

"Told you once, didn't I, Buck? He's her enemy." He spoke with brick-like tones to his voice.

"There's more to it, old man." Frank grew dark, intense, and looked in the direction of Ewing's land, then back to Dodger, his eyes almost pleading for an answer.

Dodger felt sorry for him, was tempted to say something, but his duty was deeper than he thought and he could only shake his head. "Guess I said all I'm about to that night at the Lime House, Buck. That ought to be all that matters."

Frank was hurt, he thought the kinship between them was just a bit stronger than it actually was, and now felt foolish. He wanted to resaddle, mount and ride off, but he stayed where he was and thought for nearly two full minutes before even taking a breath.

"Yer right, Dodger." Frank folded his saddle blanket, when he'd normally bunch it and carry it loosely, but he was stalling and was suddenly conscious that he had no idea why. "It ought to be."

"I figure you need my advice on the matter like them steers need saddle blankets."

"I need some help, I think."

Dodger spit out his entire chaw and covered it up with some quickly scuffed dirt. "Hell you do." The old cowboy's eyes were ballbearings and he didn't smile. "But sometimes I think yer thicker'n seven men on a cot. Use yer noggin, boy."

The heat on the basin floor climbed to one hundred and three degrees and lingered, stagnant for five days early in August, and the Ewing herd dropped another two thousand animals as a result. Animal carcasses littered the prairie but lay only on the Ewing land.

People started to talk of the basin in the past tense, aware that the last act had been designed by fate and nature. J.W. Ewing was seen less and less away from his ranch. An attitude of despair and gloom hung in the passes, descending heavily from time to time, and then it would go back up high in the mountains, waiting.

The storms still hit the mountains and the upper meadows, the great stacks of clouds a mocking reminder to the people below of their plight.

To minimize his losses, Ewing sold calves for baby beef or veal before they were ready and took a beating on price. He sold the older steers next, but they were underweight and bony, and were scooping bottom penny for sure. But they were sold rather than left to die, and Ewing realized there was nothing he could do to save the herd. If winter were even normal, it would still cripple whatever animals survived this plague of deprivation. And with the grass destroyed, what about next spring and summer?

He looked to the mountains and knew she was up there someplace. More than likely all the activity was centered at the line camp, for there'd been no sign of the three of them for over a month. He hated the feeling that he'd been shunned by God, while Ella'd been blessed this year. He blamed God. He blamed Ella, for if he had her land he wouldn't be faced with losing his herd. He blamed Frank Athearn for upsetting the balance of things. For robbing the Ewing family. For robbing J.W. Ewing.

While Ewing studied the mountains and watched the clouds, the clock struck seven. He'd been aware of the sunset but it seemed some time back. The rancher turned from the window and moved to the bar to pour a drink for himself. He'd seldom had more than one or two drinks a day, because he wished not to break the pattern of working. But he found he was sleeping only two or three hours a night, and the rest of his hours were spent in a curious mixture of reality and nightmare. He felt assured that no one saw through his calm exterior, for he was careful with his facade.

He glanced at the clock again, then looked at the stairs as if he could will Neal Atkinson out of this continual tardiness. He'd heard the man's feet moving overhead for some time, but he never left the room. Half-past six, the agreed time for them to meet, slipped by unnoticed and when Atkinson came down the stairs at last, it was almost half-past seven. "Sorry I'm late, J.W.," was all he said.

"Drink?" Ewing moved to the bar.

"A neat Scotch, please."

The two men took chairs facing each other and sipped their drinks. Few lights were on, and as darkness grew outside the room grew long in shadows, and where it was impressive when lit, it was gloomy and foreboding in the dimness. The great bear in the corner rose to terrifying heights. It was as menacing as Ewing seemed himself this night.

Neal Atkinson found himself strangely uncomfortable and off balance and wasn't sure what it was that made him so. "In case you don't know, I visited Ella Connors today," he volunteered.

Ewing smiled slightly. "I know." He took a long sip, then, "Ain't much goes on hereabouts I don't know." In fact, he only thought they might have been there. He'd seen Hoverton, spoken to the man and noticed his agitation, and surmised this trip they were going on had deviousness behind it. He held his curiosity in check, assured Atkinson would fill in all the details.

"Might interest you to know she's not interested a whit in oil."

Ewing bobbed his head. "Ain't surprised. She's cattle folk."

"I thought her being a different generation might have some bearing. That it might give her some nsight, but she's as stubborn as any dyed-in-the-wool hellback-homesteader."

"It's pride, boy. Surprised you don't recognize it."

"I do!" said Atkinson, then added, "I just don't put much value in pride. I've never seen it turn a profit."

Atkinson studied his Scotch, holding it up to the light. "Well, it looks like she's going to have a good year, so it'll be a while before she'll even be ready to listen again." He smiled reassuringly at Ewing.

"It don't matter how many half-wild cattle she and that damned two-bit cowboy corral. Come summer's end I'll have that land. No matter what. I don't intend to go through what I'm goin' through one more year."

"I'm sorry about your herd. Tragic."

"Yes. Tragic." Ewing's voice mimicked him. "But t ain't stopping me. I ain't come this far to quit."

Atkinson was forming his thoughts, looking for an opening, politely listening as Ewing continued.

"The oil's why you been fired to see me, ain't it?"

Atkinson was a bit uncomfortable. He set his glass down and folded his hands in his lap. "It's very important. We have to talk about it."

"What the hell d'you know about anything, Neal? What's important to you ain't but fly shit to me, or don't you know that?" Ewing perched near the fireplace which was dark, and stared at the hole in the stone as he spoke. "You ain't got no value but money and stocks and such, and why hell, that ain't much o value if you think on it. You got a big and fancy home in Long Island, but you don't value it."

"Rhode Island."

"Whatever," growled Ewing. "You ain't never had o earn a thing, never had to do real work a day in your life and that's the fault of yer family. But you ought to get out on yer own, do real work and you might understand what it is that yer doin' to the world."

"J.W. . . ." Atkinson began.

Ewing continued, ignoring the interruption. "You're gonna know what yer doing, or trying to do, from my point of view. You're a guest under my roof and by God you'll listen. You want to take out the oil been layin' in the ground for years and you don' give a shit what happens to the basin. I seen the sumps that fill up the low spots. You know what I call 'em? Nigger Sloughs. Not to mention the stink. It may work in Texas, for what those people know about cattle could fill a flea's skull and you'd still have room for the Bible and the flea's brain. Besides, they don't seem to care if they look out on all that metal and garbage, but that's a Texan. . . . But this's one Montanan who'll fight as long as possible rather'n see you kill off the very thing I love."

"Oh J.W.," Atkinson said with a hint of despair, "you've looked to the horizon so long you've lost sight of the land under your feet. You're one of the last of the great empire builders." He sounded as if he didn't truly like the word he'd used. "I admire that, but frankly, I never heard of an empire running without capital. You've spent all you had and more just building up to now. You have no reserves, and you're still talking growth when you can't even make it one more season as far as I can see and from all I hear."

"Don't believe all you hear and see."

Atkinson reached into his jacket and produced an envelope, opened it, slid out a piece of paper and unfolded it before handing it to Ewing. "Would you say that's an accurate statement of your net worth? And debts?"

Ewing read a statement that itemized every cent he'd spent for fifteen years and showed to any reader that he was financially in the worst possible condition. He was steps from bankruptcy.

"Where'd you get this, Neal?" he said in quiet disbelief.

"You own everything but the bank." There was no apology in him.

"And if I remember, those notes with interest would come to nearly one million."

"Yes."

Ewing handed back the paper and rose to look out the window, but his face grinned as if he were part of some great joke. "I'd say you had it figured pretty slick, Neal." He chuckled. "Heard of this happening a few times to bigger men'n me, even been known to use the trick m'self once or twice, but I never thought I'd be had the same damned way, 'cause damn . . ." He chuckled again.

Atkinson watched the rancher, surprised at the reaction. He'd been prepared for anything but this. He was pleased, but still annoyed by a sensation which he interpreted as fear. He chose every word. "I understand how you feel, J.W. But it doesn't have to be as bad as you think. The war has made it more than possible to find oil and not ruin the land."

Ewing merely looked at him, nodded and walked back to the bar.

"You're going to see that it's not so bad."

"I'm gonna have to see that, or be a bitter man the rest of my life. Wouldn't want to have a bitter Ewing on your hands now, would you?" He laughed, making a threat a joke, but the point was clear to Atkinson who laughed slightly. When neither man could think of anything more to say, Atkinson broke the silence with his goodnight to Ewing. He went upstairs, leaving the rancher alone in the great room.

Ewing remained motionless in his living room for over an hour before Blocker came in and spoke to him. The two men discussed the ranch until the talk turned to Ella Connors and Ewing fell silent, brooding intensely.

"Oughtn' to worry about her, J.W." Blocker wa
reassuring. "Just 'cause she's got cattle penned don'
mean she's gonna make market. Truth is, she can b
stopped and easy."

Ewing thought, go on, Julie. You blunder yer wa
into it and then we'll hear you be the one to com
plain when the going gets hot. He said, "Long a
there's been Ewings there's been a Blocker at his side
Been like thieves in everything and the Blockers ain'
never let me down."

"No sir."

"We got something precious here, Julie. Could g
quickly if we ain't careful. . . . I remember I was
boy an' saw a bulldog take a bull by the nose an
wrestle him to the ground. Never saw that before an
I was impressed, but the dog was a fool and bit to
hard, and damn if'n the bull didn't stomp that do
to death. Bull'll only take so much, y'know."

Blocker nodded.

"Got us a whole pack of dogs to deal with, Julie.

Japan had surrendered, and there were some cele
brations, but there was too much work, too much t
be done before sale time, and the basin was a flurr
of activity.

The activity on the Ewing Ranch was directed no
toward sale but survival. As the drought continue
each day brought more deaths, and the carcasses pile
up faster than they could be skinned and the mea
stored or dried or destroyed, and disease spread quick
ly as a result. The Ewing herd fell to ten percent o
its one-time size.

Huge columns of stinking smoke hung over th
basin as thousands of dead cattle were piled to
gether, covered with wood and doused with kerosene
then cremated. It was faster and cheaper than buria

which would not have been so splendid nor so public as these towering symbols of failure.

People looked at the clouds and shook their heads, but the talk had shifted away from the Ewing Ranch. Attention was focused on the red trucks with the ATKO OIL logo, as more and more of them arrived in Bear Paw.

And Ewing could only stand and watch as the end of his ranch loomed first on the horizon, then crept right under his nose, though to the few who came in contact with him he seemed even more alive, more filled with drive, than he had earlier in his life. They came away from him totally convinced they'd see the day when John Ewing ruled the Bear Paw once again.

The aspens in the high country turned on the first cold snap, and they were glorious, though the reds and oranges and yellows were a bitch for they camouflaged the cattle who were still sought by Ella, Frank and Dodger as they made a final sweep through the hills. They were in search of the wilder, more intelligent of the cows and the older calves who'd earned their wild ways well.

Frank had spied a cow leading several steers through a thicket, had separated the steers and moved them off, letting Dodger rope the cow and drag her off in another direction. She was wild and unruly and it took over an hour before Dodger was calmly allowing her to drift beside him as they swept back to the line camp along a strip of grass that bordered the Ewing and the Connors land.

The land rose, then fell away to the north and when Dodger reached the high point he could see the line camp above him. It was, perhaps, a hundred yards up, and about a half mile across the shallow valley. He waved to Frank who was below him, mov-

ing the steers, and as he turned his horse along the
rim of a sharp cliff about ten feet high, he kept an
anxious eye on the cow who was maneuvering away
at the end of the rope, nosing curiously toward a
thicket where she spied a possible cover for her
escape. Dodger let her pull at the rope, then jerked
her slightly off balance and she bellowed in protest.
The old cowboy seemed to anticipate her every move
and increased the speed of movement, jerking the
rope hard, then allowing his horse to work the cow
in the same fashion until they were brisking along the
rim rock cliff.

An explosion ruptured the grass and aspen silence
and the ground to Dodger's right erupted in a gusher
of water and sand that rose fifty feet in the air. His
horse bolted in a panic, the cow ran in the opposite
direction, and as Dodger fought to control both, the
line went taut, and the cow, horse and Dodger went
down in a tangle of rope, horns and legs, falling the
ten-foot drop down the cliff, then rolling over and
over down the long, stump-laden slope, the two animals and the old cowboy stopping in a dusty tangle
halfway down the hill.

From the line camp, Ella had heard the explosion,
seen the gusher across the valley, and when she saw
the hints of men and animals falling and rolling she
knew there was trouble, though she couldn't be sure
exactly who it was. She ran for her horse, which stood
nearby, and mounted, riding quickly out of the camp
toward the site of the accident.

The first explosion made Frank look up, and the
steers he was moving spooked a bit and ran off, but
they were ignored by Frank who was already urging
his horse up the slope to where the horse, cow and
Dodger had come to a halt.

A second explosion made the animals struggle in
panic, and Frank could hear Dodger wincing and
gasping for air. The cow struggled to her feet and

jumped away, still snarled in the rope. The horse lay across Dodger, both forelegs broken, and yet the animal was terrified and trying to get away, trying to rise, each move grinding Dodger into the earth beneath her.

As Frank slid to a halt, dropping to the ground, he'd already assessed the problem and his hand held a carbine and his fingers tightened on the lever. He quickly swung the rifle to his shoulder, took a fast aim and pulled the trigger. The shot took the horse between the eyes, and she stopped her struggles, dying instantly. But her body was still wrenched forward and backward by the frantic moves of the cow. Frank stepped across the taut rope and quickly cut it, allowing the cow to break free and run back to the hills.

A third explosion made Frank flinch as he used all his strength to move the horse's body from Dodger's. The old cowboy did his best to help, but they could only budge the animal a bit.

"No good, old fella." He bent beside Dodger and wiped dirt and sand from the old man's eyes. "Hold on, Dodger." Frank rose and walked to his horse, and taking his rope and making sure it was tied around the horn, walked back and slipped the loop around the horse's carcass. He glanced down at Dodger. "It ain't gonna be easy."

"Didn't expect so, Buck."

The old blue eyes twinkled through pain.

Frank walked to his horse, spoke a few gentle words and then forced her to pull the other horse from the body of his friend. For his part, Dodger used his remaining strength to shove the horse clear, and when the job was done, found he had neither the strength nor the will to rise, but gave it a shot. He was only to his knees before Frank stopped him and forced him to lie still.

"It might be bad."

Dodger knew it was and nodded and smiled. "Might not, and wouldn't I look a fool lyin' around if it was just m'breath."

When Ella thundered up moments later, he tried again, but she angered when she watched him and badgered him into staying put until Frank could ride back and get the truck, to take him down to the ranch.

Dodger reluctantly agreed, saying, "Ruther ride or walk, for you know I hate that contraption worse'n death itself."

But it was done, and he was taken with love and care back to Ella's ranch.

The old man would not allow himself to be housed in her bedroom or any other room of her place, but insisted that they take him to his small cabin. It was his home and he felt if he had to be under a roof, it might as well be his own. They backed the truck to the door and half-carried the cowboy to his bunk where he sat in great pain and allowed himself to be skinned to the red-handles he'd bought only a month before from Sears.

"Not m'underwear, Babysister. I still got my pride."

"You still got bull-headed stupidity, old wind." She spoke the words with affection but he wouldn't allow her to remove the underwear.

Frank stayed with Dodger, as Ella went for Doc McGowan over the old man's protests. The doctor spent a long period alone with Dodger, and when he came out his words to Ella were grim. "He's never going to be able to ride again. Not like he'd want to. He's stove up pretty bad, few broken ribs, lots of torn cartilage, possibly some internal bleeding, but I can't tell here and he won't let me get him to town or the hospital or anything else."

"If we was to get him to the hospital, he ever be

able to work again?" she asked, already fearful of the answer.

"No."

"Is he going to live?"

"I can't tell." He hated the expression on her face. "I'm sorry, but there's only so much I can do, here." He gestured deploringly at the cabin and began shoving things into his car as they stood there. "I've given him something for the pain and tomorrow I'll come back and we'll see how he is." He eased up a bit more. "There are no major bones broken. He just might be all right, Ella."

"All right." She waited until he backed the car away and drove off before walking to where Frank stood quietly waiting.

"He gonna be all right?" He indicated the cabin with a nod of his head.

"Yes," she lied. "He's gonna be okay in a day or so." And Ella thought that Frank knew better already and was prepared to spare her by not pressing the fact. They entered the cabin together, and moved to the chairs facing the bed where Dodger lay, propped up by pillows, looking funny, she thought, in that old candy-striped nightshirt he'd love forever. "Ain't you a pretty picture, though?" She spoke quietly, but with humor.

"Thought mebbe I was a horror picture from first light on you, Babysister."

"Doctor says yer limbs are fine but you oughtn' to move around for a while." Then she added, "Jest in case."

"In case what?" he asked suspiciously.

"In case you fall down and hurt yerself. You know, you are not only a clumsy but nosy old man, and for the life of me I have no idea how you ever got so old, bein' that way." She smiled, though, to show she wasn't really angry.

"Well," Dodger started, "I ain't all that sick, and there's still one helluva lot of work to do."

Frank chimed in with, "Man's just fallen down a cliff, pulled his horse down over him and he's tellin' us he's straight as a skeeter's peeter in matin' season."

"I ain't exactly all that well," Dodger grinned. "You gonna give me a chew, Buck?"

Frank nodded and reached for his tobacco pouch and handed it over to Dodger who took it, shoved it under his pillow and lay back with a smile. "You kin claim it later, but I guess you got yer own and I ain't, so I'm sayin' squatter's rights fer now if'n you don't mind."

Frank touched his hat brim and eyed Dodger as he rose and turned to the door. "Yer an old thief, Dodger. A horse thief and a chaw thief." He turned at the door and winked once before going out. "Take care, old-timer."

"Take keer yerself, Buck."

Then it was Ella and Dodger alone.

"I ain't gonna be aworkin' no more, am I?"

"Who said?" Ella demanded.

Dodger wouldn't look at her for a bit. And when he did, he was withdrawn and quiet. "You don't have to tell me. I guess I know what's goin' on inside."

She wanted to shout at him and tell him to get his damned ass to the hospital, then. Don't just let yerself die, old friend. "You're tough as Mexican leather. Hell, you'll be fit in no time at all."

"I midwived you." He had indeed. "Damn near raised you, too." Truth again, and right in this room. "And since you've spent hours with me areadin' an' ateachin' you right here, you ought to know that I don't allow no lies under my roof."

She could find no words to answer him beyond a simple yes, that she just couldn't speak.

" 'Course, you know, my old tall tales were not always the total truth, but there was a side to it. You never believed all them stories anyhow, did you?" She shook her head. "Ella, my ridin' and ropin' days are over. Now you gonna tell me who's top dog?"

She couldn't answer, remembering the game they'd played whenever she was low or miserable.

"Well . . . ?" He was waiting for her.

"One that fights the hardest."

"Remember it," Dodger advised.

"How'd I ever forget it, old buzzard?"

"I mightn't always be around to remind you how it is." He smiled and then settled back against the pillow, trying to close his eyes and sleep. Ella remained a few minutes, then when his breathing showed sleep had overtaken him, she rose and left.

Frank had slept from just past eight that night, waking only once and glancing at the old windup clock that showed him it was just a little past 1:30. He thought he'd heard a noise, but assumed it was the dog Patches, who'd come back from wherever she'd been while they were working. It was just a small sound and when nothing followed it, he went back to sleep.

Dodger had risen carefully at 12:30 and began to dress, each effort a major one, and it took nearly three-quarters of an hour before he had finally pulled on his boots and buckled on his spurs. He had to sit, and he was surprised to find he was totally winded. At 1:10, he rose and walked outside moving to the corral. He quietly selected one of the few horses there, saddled the mare and led her back to his cabin.

It took him another half hour to pack his bedroll and warbag, then he looked around the room, blew out the candle and went out carrying all of his possessions in the world that mattered. It hurt to leave the photographs behind, and he had to remind himself that he wouldn't be missing them all that long. He walked to the door, swung it wide and labored his goods out into the morning darkness.

He couldn't remember this particular horse's name and just clucked softly to move her away from his home, away from the Connors Ranch, toward the mountains.

Ella rose first, a half hour before dawn, dressed quickly and went to see to Dodger. Upon discovering him gone, and surmising what he intended to do, she ran to the shed, shouting for Frank, telling him what had happened and then she dashed to saddle the horses and Frank rose, dressed in a flash and washed in the watering trough just as she led his horse up, handing him the reins and swinging herself aboard the other horse.

With Frank following Dodger's sign and leading the way they covered the distance to the line camp in a third the time taken by Dodger.

When they reached the line camp, there was no sign of him, and they were a bit puzzled for the sign had led there. They'd lost the track on rocky ground but continued on, and now they sat their horses, trying to figure out where he could be, what and where and how and why, but they kept their thoughts private and finally Frank started up, realizing something, with Ella following along, knowing he was back on the trail again without saying so.

Their horses carried them to the spot where Dodger had fallen and beyond that to the grassy no-man's-land that separated her land from Ewing's and there, surrounded by the same cows and steers, they found Dodger's horse calmly grazing among the cattle.

Near at hand was what they thought at first was his camp, but as they drew even closer they realized the old man had made his bedroll, placed all of his possessions near it on the ground, tethered the horse, then come back to the bedroll and gone to bed alone and quietly and just an hour or so before they'd arrived had passed on quietly in his sleep, his last chore done to perfection.

Together they got down, moved to his body and wrapped the bedroll around it tightly, Frank using a rope to bind the wrappings. As they drew the canvas around his white-haired, peaceful face, Ella bent gently and kissed the old man goodbye for the only time in her life. She had never touched him even once in all the time she'd known him, she thought in sudden anguish.

They closed him off from the sun, then lifted him between them and carried him to his horse and gently laid him across the saddle and tied him there. Ella took his horse and Frank drove the cattle as they moved back to the line camp and finally back down to the ranch itself.

Ella dressed the body in Dodger's best clothing, which wasn't much, and she shaved the face of the stubble, making him look more than simply fitting, and while she tended to that, Frank built a simple pine coffin of planks and nails, carving a quick semblance of Dodger's name on the lid as a finishing touch.

When all was ready, they loaded the coffin containing the body into the bed of the Model A truck and drove to a neatly dug grave alongside that of Ella's father. They buried him in a late afternoon windstorm that swept across the dry basin floor and said quiet prayers together. A rough slab of wood was the marker and in crayon, for the time being, Ella wrote in nice script letters:

> DODGER . . . "He was the reward of
> friendship, and it was the best reward of
> all."

"Didn't he have no other name, I mean other than Dodger?"

Ella shook her head and then nodded. "He didn't want it known. I guess it don't really matter now, but if that's the way he wanted it, that's the way it'll be."

Later, they couldn't say how long it was they stayed at the grave in total silence, but the sun went down, the wind came up and the stars were twinkling before they left and drove back to the ranch.

They hardly spoke to each other. Ella was in pain with grief, and Frank kept his distance, did not intrude on her privacy, for he knew how much the old man'd meant to her. He knew how much he had felt for Dodger, how drawn he'd been to him even in a short time, and realized it must be so much worse for Ella.

They ate together but in silence, and several times Frank had been sorely tempted to reach out, take her and hold her, but something in him kept him from doing so, and he was glad.

After dinner, each went his own way, Ella heading upstairs to bed, and Frank reluctantly going back to his shed to bed down for the night.

The next morning they loaded the Model A and were kept constant company by the sound of oil explosions going off down the basin in their dull, booming groups of three. Ella began to speak loudly, the words turning to a shout as she called down the wrath of God on the men who'd come to break the tranquility of her beloved Bear Paw Basin, the men who unknowingly had killed her Dodger. She shook with rage that welled up into massive sobs as she sank to her knees on the windmill platform and cried piteously as Frank looked on, stricken by something in her he hadn't expected ever to see. He reached out to touch her shoulder, then dropped beside her and held her awkwardly in his arms until the crying subsided. They rose after a bit, and though the explosions continued they ignored them as they went down the ladder. Frank walked Ella to the back porch and watched as she went inside without a word before he turned toward the shed.

He thought about what had happened and found to his surprise his own sense of commitment was total now. He was hooked worse than a fifty-cent matador by a five-dollar bull.

"Sonofabitch!" was all he said.

The plane banked for the final approach to town and Atkinson looked down where Ewing's car waited beside the Bear Paw Milk Products building, and checked his watch. They were all right on time.

Moments later he was in the car after a cold, incisive greeting from Blocker that bothered Atkinson a bit. The trip to the ranch was made in complete silence.

Blocker could scarcely help but notice Atkinson as he pored through the papers, linking Ewing land with Atko Oil. He hated this oily little fly fart beside him, for he saw in the man's hands the end of his life, and for all his country pragmatism Julie Blocker was a passionate man with strong instincts for self-preservation. He wondered at this moment how he could direct this righteousness to Atkinson. How could he lay their case before this man who he knew had no understanding of the claim Ewing and men like Blocker and others had on this basin? There should be a way, Blocker felt, to reach out to this oil man, to shake him to his roots, to show him he can't just have his way in this matter. But try as he might, there was no ability left in Blocker to deal with it at all, so he drove on to the ranch in silence.

When they reached the ranch and Blocker had stopped the car, he turned and looked Neal Atkinson in the eyes, and said softly and without a hint of emotion, "Oughta think about what yer doin', Mr.

Atkinson. In good faith you ought to keep faith."

"It's none of your business, Julie. Sorry, but it just isn't."

Blocker nodded once and thought, then it serves you right, you bastard, it serves you right.

A storm was building in the mountains and it promised to be a terrifying monster as cloud piled onto cloud against the mountain passes, and while it seemed to be the one that would bring relief to the Ewing lands, Ewing was not particularly moved as he stood at his living room window and watched the clouds swallow the sun. He smiled wryly as he thought, it's just too late. Far too late. His ranch was devoid of cattle save a few hundred head out of thousands, including his breed stock. The parched earth was green only where the few inadequate wells drew small amounts of moisture from the depths.

He stood with his back to the room, trying his best to ignore the men who spoke to him and Neal Atkinson. George Bascomb had taken almost a half hour setting up the aerial photograph and maps on a portable stand he'd brought along. It was his life, they told Ewing, and it was his future, but to his way of thinking it was no future at all and he did his best to drive them out of his mind. Only a bit of data leaked in at first, but little by little Ewing found himself drawn into the discussion that turned from the presentation of facts to the sounds of speculation. He was a bit surprised to find they were talking with a sense of concern, which meant that something was wrong and out of their control.

He didn't understand the technical jargon, but the photographs drew his attention and while Bascomb explained anticlines and alluvial fans and such, Ewing studied the photographs he knew to be of his land.

"You got one of these for every hole you blew in my land?" He asked the question in general, but it was Bascomb who answered dryly, though with a smile.

"Those and several sheets of paper as well." He motioned to stacks of notebooks he'd carried into the room, and smiled again.

"I guess you know what yer doin'," said Ewing as he turned to face the two oil men. "You really love all yer paper, don't you?" He smiled bitterly and listened as Bascomb glanced at the paper, nodded absently and spoke.

"You can see for yourself, Mr. Ewing." He pointed at one large photo, then the map with the index marks. "We tested everywhere, up to and all around the edge of the Connors land. We completely covered your land." He pointed to several places on the map and Ewing watched him with interest now. "You have traces, some very good indications, but this . . ." He pointed to one spot that was covered with marks and symbols and numbers. "This is where the oil that's fit for pumping is located."

Ewing was cautious with his words now, structuring the thoughts, but he couldn't resist a smile at the obvious. "That's Connors land, boys."

"There's still a way to get to the oil, J.W." Atkinson watched Ewing with fascination now for the smile never diminished. "We can drill diagonally under her land from the edge of the creek."

Ewing figured they'd have some solution, but he played out his hand anyhow. "Know a bit about mineral rights, and I guess you won't have a chance in hell of drilling without her permission and I doubt she'll ever give you that. You ain't got no oil unless I kin get that land."

"I'm sure she could be convinced in time," speculated George Bascomb, drumming his fingers absently on the map surface.

"You don't know Ella Connors, Bascomb," said Ewing tensely. He looked over at Atkinson and noted the detached air of the man as he looked on.

Atkinson broke the tension with a swift move toward the maps and photos, sweeping them up and handing them to Bascomb for removal. "Thank you, George." Bascomb nodded and placed the papers and notebooks, photos and maps into two satchels and bid goodbye to the two men.

When Bascomb had left, Atkinson found it difficult to control the surge of anxiety over being alone with Ewing and having to say what he was about to say. Atkinson was a man obsessed with personal power, and therefore he recognized Ewing's power. He knew his safety at this point, as well as his future, might depend on how he played this match. The thought amused and calmed him. He considered this matter of real danger in the same way that he considered a tennis match or a match race. When he spoke, his voice was soothing. At first.

"J.W., I know how difficult it was for you to give us permission to test." He watched Ewing circle the room until he came to the window where he stopped to watch and listen to the storm that swept through the passes and crashed against the mountains and lit the meadows with lightning. "I suppose the ranch is beyond recovery for the year," he continued. Ewing glanced at him.

"You got a shoulder in the bank door. I guess you seen all the books by now, Neal." He was quite pleasant but for the meaning of his words. "Was a time, however, you'd not be here with all the knowledge you got." He shrugged. "When a man draws a better hand, losin' an' winnin' ain't got no kin with feelings. You jest take the loss and say next time." He smiled. "Next time, I won't be so foolish. There won't be no loose ends to git caught up on."

Atkinson felt his palms and wiped a trace of moisture on his pants discreetly. "I have to protect my family's investment."

Ewing moved toward him slightly. "With the losses, and all the winter could bring, it might be five years before I can make a dent in the debt." He studied Atkinson, watched the uneasiness spread across the gentle features. "Me not havin' the oil ain't gonna help you none."

"No."

Ewing settled against a chair and watched Atkinson sit across the room and casually cross his legs, making an effort to appear relaxed. "Then what do you plan to do, boy?"

The matter-of-fact phrasing startled Atkinson and he had no trouble at all saying it straight out. The challenge was just too tempting. "I'm going to try to pull the ranch back on a paying basis at least."

"And jest how do you plan to do that?"

Atkinson shifted his weight and leaned forward, folding his hands. "I'm going to take over the operation. Bring in a management team that can do whatever it takes to bring back the herd and the land. And while that's being done, I can wait and watch Ella. I've always thought that you were right. She can't hold out forever, but I'm going to be here when she folds, or at least someone who can act without passion."

The words sliced through Ewing, but he never showed that they affected him at all. He nodded and continued to lounge against the chair.

"In the long run, it's for your own good." Atkinson was soothing again. "You won't be out. You'll be guaranteed a fine salary for as long as you live. You won't have to take another risk. You can travel or you can stay at home. You'll still have the ranch house and of course a say in everything. It will still be the Ewing Ranch, and no one but you and I have to know otherwise."

Ewing smiled and his eyes narrowed as he exam ined the oil man from head to toe. "An' when yo turn me out, you gonna give me a gold watch, Neal?

"It's not that bad, J.W."

"Know what yer doin'?" He gestured at the stuffe grizzly bear in the corner. "Makin' me no better' that damned stuffed bear."

Atkinson rose, uncomfortable beyond his abilitie and yet soured by the way this meeting had gone He'd been prepared to be tough, but sensed the con trol Ewing used to hold down the anticipated anger and knew it was time to leave. "I'd better stay i town tonight."

Ewing moved to him, still smiling, but warmer now more friendly. "Hell, she's good as yer house now Might jest as well make yerself at home." He clappe the younger man on the shoulder and guided hin gently to the stairs. "It ain't like yer no stranger."

"I'm sorry it had to be this way, J.W."

Ewing thought, bobbed his head, and spoke. "We'r different breeds, both doin' what we think best." H considered everything, and patted Atkinson's arm a fectionately. "I do appreciate you not tellin' anyon about this. Like doin' things my own way."

"You'll have every consideration, J.W." Atkinso shook the rancher's hand, then turned and went up stairs to bed, feeling little triumph and a consider able amount of concern.

The storm brought rain to the basin of the Bea Paw Mountains, drenching the entire flatland bottom dropping over two inches in four hours.

Snow fell high on the peaks, but melted quickl and ran into needy stream beds. But it was the light ning which was the villain. Trees and undergrowt dry from the long parched summer flew into flames i seconds as electricity flashed along the ground an the clouds rumbled and crashed high above the meadows and peaks.

In the Connors line camp, as John Ewing heard the death sentence for the Ewing Ranch spoken by Neal Atkinson, Frank and Ella sat in the small cabin and wondered when the next roll of thunder would hit, when the next spark of electricity would light the skies so they could see the cattle. A ruckus had started down in the corrals, and they hoped the animals would quiet before the storm compounded the frustration and fear, and drove the cattle against the fences that held them.

A small flicker of static electricity flashed over the horns of the cattle and they knew it for St. Elmo's fire, and as they watched the fairy-like flickering, there was a second flicker, followed instantly by a blinding flash and a resounding roll of thunder that swept down on the Connors Ranch from granite mountaintops and echoed back again. It was the breaking point for the Connors cattle.

The older cows who had been penned in storms fought for control, but were knocked aside in panic by the younger ones who pressed and were in turn pressed by more from the rear, and in moments the entire herd was bearing down on the lower fence that was the portion of the corral heading downhill. It had been hit by surges before, and had held well, for it was built for heavy use and intended to last forever. But it had been tampered with. A simple matter. Two cowboys, one of them Ralph Cole of the Ewing Ranch, had neatly roped the main poles, the supporting poles, and wobbled them in the earth one afternoon when Frank and Ella were off working the hills and certain to be gone for some time. The footings were loosened and the fence was rendered nearly useless. Ralph Cole and the other cowboy then disguised their work so no one would be the wiser. It was simple but effective sabotage. Now the work paid off, for the fence went on the second try, and like a river breaking a dam, the cattle trickled out at first, then the stream grew wider as the panic and fear built, and the animals poured across the jumble of logs and poles and rails, racing away from the storm that terrified them, plummeting downhill in unified flight.

It stunned the pair at the line shack window. They were prepared for almost anything, but they had no idea of what had been done to the corral, and felt secure that the fence would hold. Now they watched it go down, the cattle stream away, and they couldn't move for seconds. Every bit of work was going down the drain before their eyes. Then the shock gave way to better instincts that drove them into the storm, to the horses, kept saddled just in case. They mounted without words, made tight loops in their ropes, and tying on their hats, were off in moments after the rampaging herd that crashed noisily below them in a thicket of aspens.

The land favored Frank and Ella and fate did the rest, for the cattle were flanked by dense woods and steep embankments, so the animals were funneled from one meadow to another and so on down the side of the mountains, racing under control despite the panic that drove them, and reacting to a more basic instinct by remaining a herd as they ran. Had any one animal broken off, one group veered away it would have been over indeed, but Frank and Ella flanked the cattle and badgered them into line, using the stampede, allowing the cattle to run their panic and using the force to bring them onto the flats where they could be headed and turned and eventually stopped.

And then it occurred to them that this might be the chance they needed. If they could keep them together and running, they could bring them to the ranch. They'd thought it impossible before, at least for the two of them, to do such a thing. But now by accident . . . they saw what was happening and knew at the same time what they could do. Frank waved once, finding a single gesture that meant, keep them going, and got an instant reply showing she'd thought the same thing. They raced ahead of the lead animals, taking terrible risks and miraculously staying up. The horses were prime, kept for the possibility of such work and the animals acted as if they knew their masters' minds, nipping furiously at the lead steers and cows, turning them back when they veered out of line, and in time the herd was brought to a gradually slowing run.

The storm swept past, angrily hurling its wrath up and down the basin, but by now the herd had exhausted its panic, and if they felt any fear they were too tired to respond. They allowed themselves to be driven by Frank and Ella who kept at them, head and tail, until they were in sight of the ranch. As they looked over the herd and knew they'd come through without a loss, they couldn't hide the pleasure each felt. They'd been helped along just a bit further, and this time by nature. Frank grinned as the first sign of dawn lit his face and Ella laughed aloud as she saw the boyish pleasure in what they'd done, and her laugh brought a high pitched yell of pure joy from the cowboy who was her partner.

Their victory brought them closer. Each was strongly aware of the other's desire now, and it became a waiting game to see which one would be the one to make the first move.

On her part, Ella was just a bit too shy, while Frank was terrified of another rejection, though if you had asked him he would have denied it.

They stood at the edge of the large receiving corral and looked at the animals they'd fought so hard to save and felt not only pride, but a special unity that they hadn't had before. There were no words for what they felt at that moment, so they could only stand and admire what they had done.

Frank glanced at her once, caught her eye and saw the look of "well, we done it, pard" and it was too late for him. He reached out and tenderly took her hand in his. For once, she didn't draw away, but tightened her hand around his and it gave him a second's more security. He took her other hand and she gave that one a tender squeeze, but she could only look at him now with a flat, unyielding stare that shook him. As he tried to force himself to bend to kiss her, she quickly raised up on her toes and kissed him. It would have seemed to an onlooker that it was the first time either had kissed in their lives, for they were awkward with their hands, awkward with their bodies. It was the kiss of two curious, exploring children.

When Ella stepped back and drew her hands away, all the months of tension and anticipation over this moment showed in her eyes, but her voice was calm and steady.

"Yer gonna think I'm terrible."

"I am?"

It was easier than she thought it would be. "I want to be with you."

"Uh huh." Frank wasn't too sure he'd heard her correctly. And if he had, he wasn't sure he believed what he heard. He smiled and felt himself blush at the ears.

"You don't understand. I want to be in bed with you. Now." She felt herself start to redden as she saw the look of astonishment give way to understanding. "Never mind. I see it's a problem."

"No, ma'am," he said politely, his mind reeling. "No problem, just a little surprised is all." He glanced at the house and felt the need to clear his throat. "I guess I don't know quite what to say."

"Don't say anything." She began to walk to the house, and while Frank followed, he was disturbed and he lagged behind a bit, deep in thought, his eyes on the ground. "One thing, Ella."

She turned and looked at him, her voice rising, the anger building quickly as she spoke. "God, but you get me crazy, Athearn."

"No crazier than you make me, dammit!" he suddenly shouted at her. "I ain't never had a woman do the askin' is all, and it kinda surprised me. You mind if some things in life surprise me?"

She smiled gently. "You about through?"

"Yes."

"You coming?" she asked nicely.

"Yes."

She reached out and tenderly took his hand and led the way into the house and upstairs to the bedroom.

Frank awoke and it was dark. It took moments to place that he was in Ella's bedroom and moments more before he was aware that she was gone from the bed beside him. He sat up and listened, for he could hear her downstairs, moving in the kitchen.

Their lovemaking had been as unsteady and awkward as their first kiss and just as touching. Each could feel the need of the other and responded to it as best they could. When it was finished, neither was satisfied, but they held each other tightly and were secure in that closeness. No words were spoken at all, and when they made their wishes known it was with their bodies and hands.

When he had first known her, Frank had not expected the degree of skill that Ella showed as a cowhand, but it pleased him. Now the same pleasure came with the discovery that she was more sensuous than he would have believed. It was clear he wasn't the first man to have made love to her, and he wondered how he stood against the others. Something in him made him change others to the singular other, and it bothered him. He felt a twinge of jealousy he quickly dismissed and then rose and dressed.

The radio forecast more bad weather for the remainder of the week and as Ella sat quietly shelling peas at the kitchen table she wondered if they'd be able to get a buyer out to the ranch before the weather closed them off. The prices were already beginning to fluctuate.

The sound of footsteps overhead startled her, and she felt herself slide into remembering what had driven her downstairs when she wished more than anything to be back in his arms.

He had been tender and gentle with her, forcing her to control her impatience with him. She'd never been touched with this sort of affection and found it moved and disturbed her, robbing her of pleasure and strangely substituting something she couldn't identify, but a thing that drove her to need him all the more. She resented it, for it robbed her of control and she fought him without letting him know.

When it was over the first time, she curled into him and hoped he couldn't feel the despair. When his hands brushed her to life again, she went to him a bit more eagerly, with more openness and curiosity. It was as if this was the first time she saw or felt him. She felt things that hadn't touched her since she was barely sixteen years old. What she felt with him the second time frightened her and she knew he was more in love with her from his touch than from the fact that he whispered the words to her. Ella was frightened of him and for him, and had no words to explain her fears, so she held him and fought tears and felt no joy from her passion. When he finally slept, she rose and dressed and came down to the kitchen to lose herself in work. But she went over and over what she knew she must do until she thought she'd scream the words the moment she saw him. As he came downstairs and into the kitchen she looked up, saw him smile, and then she forced a quick smile and went back to her work with a diligence that defied words. Frank slid onto a chair with one motion and watched her hands, her face.

"Hello," he murmured.

"Hello."

He pointed to the peas. "That ain't the answer to whatever's botherin' you."

She looked up sharply. "Nothing's botherin' me."

"Oh." He fiddled with a pea pod that lay near his boot, picking it up, examining it. He tried to change the subject, more than used to the mood changes and flashes of temperament, and this evening desirous of neither. "I bet we might jest clear five cents a pound with these babies." She said nothing. "Gonna more than make yer loan, y'know?" She nodded, biting her lip ferociously, eyes on her work. "I know we said one season an' all," he continued, "but I was thinkin' we was to combine my animals with yers we'd get new blood with no outlay and . . ."

"I ain't been fair with you, Frank."

"Beg pardon." He watched her now, but she kept her eyes down.

"You got to know why it is I am the way I am." Her voice was shakier than he'd ever heard and it was as if she fought back tears.

"You don't have to tell me a thing, you don't want to," he volunteered, hating to see the pain in her.

"You have to know this, or there won't never be anything right between us." She had to force the words now. "There's more between J.W. an' me than I let on." She groped for words now. "Was a time I didn't hate J.W. Ewing like I do now. I guess I hated him always 'cause I was raised to, but there was a time I forgot to hate." She thought back on how it had been and formed the words in her mind carefully, taking care with the pictures she drew. She watched Frank suspiciously now and tears welled in her eyes.

"My pa an' J.W. was at it off an' on afore I was born. Long as I can remember, any an' all Ewings was forbid to me. Even when I was a child. Even though Matt Ewing an' me were the same age and went to school together an' all that, it didn't make no difference. They was just all bad to my pa's way of thinkin'." She found it hurt to swallow and she had trouble getting her breath. "When I was about fifteen, I would come from school, mount up and go right out to work the herd. Wasn't much different in those days except we kept them bunched up the meadows way. I used to work the bunch over Wolf Creek way. Near where your place stands. An' Ewing, well, he'd come out there and just watch me. Then he'd watch me in town. And watch me in school and around school. Got so he was always there . . . watchin'. Waitin' an' watchin'. And, I suppose, as is the way with young girls, I became fascinated by him the way a bird is fixed by a snake. He was handsome and dashing in those days." She thought suddenly that Ewing was still a handsome and dashing man, though it had been years since she'd thought of him that way, and the fact that she did now, even in remembering, bothered her. "I started sneakin' out to watch him with his herd when he'd bored with watchin' me all the time."

"There's a big water hole, stream fed ceptin' this year, and one day he spied me out there watchin' him and before I thought to ride off, he'd cornered me and told me I ought to git, and that if my pa found out, he'd wallop me, big girl or not. You know how I am. I was worse then and twice as sassy. Told him I had a mind of my own. Did what I wanted. And . . . I guess he pretty well had me figured."

She found she couldn't continue and looked down

at the pea pods in her lap and swept them onto the floor in a disgusted motion. "God, but I was a fool." She looked at him now and forced out the rest, trying in vain to hold back tears that flowed freely with the words. "I spent every moment I could with him."

"You slept with him?" Frank placed the question gently before her, and the violence of her reply startled him.

"Yes!" She sobbed and shuddered. "He had me all he wanted and I couldn't get enough of him. You understand?" Frank only looked at her with compassion and love. "We did things I never knew people did, and in time I grew to think that was all there was to it." The next sentence was the hardest for her. "I loved the things he did to me. I was ashamed of it, but I loved it." She took a deep breath and let it slowly out before continuing. "All the while, he was fightin' Pa. There was a lawsuit and Pa won. Pa fenced the land. Your land now. And Ewing went crazy. That's where the Ewing Ranch began an' he's always wanted it."

She remembered how it had been. "One night, Pa, Dodger an' me was eatin' supper and J.W. rode up, yellin' like crazy for Pa to come outside. He did, and I went with him. Stood right beside Pa as J.W. told him about us. Told him we'd slept together. Told him every damned thing we did." She choked back a rush of tears. "Pa looked to me for a denial which I just couldn't give. After that, Pa just gave up. Never was the same."

Frank waited for more, but she sat quietly, then began to shell peas once again. The abruptness of it all, coupled with the revelation, made his already tender senses reel and he tried to find the right words to comfort her. He could only think of, "It don't matter to me, if that's what yer thinkin'." He added, "I love you for what you are, not what you been, though I don't rightly know how to split one from the other. I guess ain't a person alive don't carry some such secret, but it don't matter to me as far as you're concerned."

His frankness comforted her a bit, but she shook her head. He hadn't quite understood. "It don't stop then. Ewing still came, and I tell you, I can't stop him, an' I ain't all that sure I want to. Now do you understand what's wrong?"

He smiled gently. "It really don't matter. I'm willin' to give it a try. Might be things'll work out, but anybody could find reason for it not to work. Swear to God, yer tougher on yerself than you are on your animals."

If anyone had told her a man could feel that way, she'd have called the speaker a liar to his face, but she believed Frank now and nodded, then said quietly, "I want to try."

Julie Blocker wondered if the sugar would take effect quickly. He'd heard about the trick but wasn't sure. He had difficulty locating the gas tank, but did, unscrewed the cap and added the cup of sugar quickly. Then making sure he wasn't seen, he screwed on the gas cap and moved quickly away from the machine he'd just sabotaged.

As he turned the corner of the Bear Paw Milk Products building, he tossed the paper envelope that held the sugar into a pile of rubbish and brushed off his hands, as if that cleansed the deed. He quickly remembered that he'd done the same thing in the past. If not the actual deed, then a thousand similar deeds, and those old deeds bothered him more than this one move for survival. He felt the need for a drink and his long strides carried him toward the Lime House. He checked his watch and figured he had just enough time before the dance began.

He felt a strong wave of righteousness as he thought

about how he'd gone to the great house three mornings back, rapped on the living room door and entered to take one glance at the haggard, unshaven face of Ewing who'd sat up all night after a meeting with that damned Atkinson.

A quick look about revealed further that there'd been no heavy drinking. No glasses, no bottles.

"Sit down, Julie."

"It's almost 8:30, J.W. Want to move them Angus, but you said you wanted to go along. A sit on my part might make it a bit too late."

This is when I will find out how tough you are, old friend, thought Ewing. I will give you the test to find out if I have a man left to my credit.

"You can go in a moment." Ewing paused, and eyed the stairs, then fixed Blocker with an uncomforting look of authority. "You better know it ain't my ranch any more. I got no say in things."

Blocker waited a moment, hoping for a clarification that would say this was a might be, and not a definitely is.

"It's as simple as I owe Atkinson money I ain't never gonna have unless the ranch makes a profit. He knows it, but he ain't about to treat us fair." He thought the use of "us" a nice, spontaneous touch, while Blocker was clearly moved.

"He's gonna make it a regular corporation and turn us over to the poor farm. I'm sorry it's like this, Julie, but I wanted you to hear it from me. Not him." Ewing gestured angrily toward the stairs.

"I'm sorry, Julie. I let you an' the boys down."

"No sir. I don't see it that way." Blocker spoke simply, but was deep in a mire of confusion. "I see it that you give yer life to this place and now, when you stand right on the edge of holdin' it all, that bastard . . ." He lowered his voice under the sharp glance of Ewing. . . . "That bastard would cheat you without a fair chance." He thought. "I remember when you got that money from ol' man Atkinson, and I damn sure remember the terms, for I witnessed the paper."

"Well, that paper is what gives Mr. Atkinson the ranch."

"That money was like a gift." Blocker couldn't believe what he was hearing.

"Julie, he's using it like a note. He says I ain't fit to run this place, and I guess to a young man it might seem that way. . . . Hell . . ." Ewing merely shook his head and glanced at the clock. "You better see to those Angus. Storm didn't help 'em none, I guess."

"Yessir." Blocker thought a moment. "The note was personal."

That's it, thought Ewing. Mull it over. You'll get it.

"It was just between the Atkinsons and you."

Ewing nodded. "Go on, Julie. Talkin' on it ain't gonna make it better."

Blocker nodded, and left, but he moved like a man suffering a massive heart attack. His breath came in angry bursts as he worked throughout the day, thinking of the injustice around him.

He only had one moment of regret. He passed the young pilot as he walked toward the Lime House. Blocker shot him a pleasant greeting, and watched the young man walk down the street, then went into the Lime House and had three drinks when he thought one would suffice and didn't.

The barbecue and dance were called the Four Basins Celebration, but those who came were not only from the basins that adjoined the Bear Paw, but were farmers and ranchers and townsfolk from places as far away as Lavina, Musselshell and Roundup with even a few of the low-lifers from Lewistown drifting in for a bit of free food and drink.

Tables and an outdoor dance floor had been erected

on a sunny hillside, for the weather, while pleasantly warm in the day, was nippy late in the afternoon.

Ewing and Atkinson stood by a solitary aspen talking quietly, with Atkinson speaking and Ewing nodding in response from time to time. But Ewing heard little the oil man said. His attention was on Ella Connors, who had arrived late, eaten quickly and was now dancing with Frank Athearn under lights that had been turned on in anticipation of early sunset.

She looked prettier than he could ever remember, and he realized he'd never seen her in a dress before in his life and the dress, which was a peasant skirt and blouse, gave her a soft and feminine look. He could tell she was happy with this cowboy, and resented the happiness. She laughed when they missed the cues and the squares dissolved in confusion. She greeted people she'd avoided for years with an enthusiasm he knew came from the fact that they'd made their sale, delivered their cattle, and now all that remained for indefinite security was that they pay the note and continue to work as well as they had. Ewing gave them credit; they'd done a fine job. But it didn't matter, for he'd already made plans for the future and the plans included them.

He wished that Kroegh had succeeded and had killed Frank and then regretted not doing it himself when it would have been so easy. He thought, I'll be damned if I'll see her with this man. If I can't have her, nobody else will. And the thought blurred with his desire for their joint lands, and he saw only that they'd united to spite him. It wasn't right for her to be with that cowboy, and he certainly couldn't be man enough for her.

"When the changes come, they'll be gradual and it will seem to the world you've done it on your own." Atkinson gestured at the people eating, the people dancing, and smiled. "There might even be a way to work Ella around to our way of thinking."

Ewing had only half-heard, and nodded absently.

He saw his car turn into the picnic grounds and saw Blocker get out and help himself to a drink. He noted his foreman seemed a bit shaky. There was only one look exchanged between them and it said that Blocker had done as was expected of him.

Ewing checked his watch and glanced at the sky. "Yeah." He clapped Atkinson on the shoulder and spoke with concern. "It's getting late. I don't want to rush you, Neal, but you said you wanted out before dark."

Something in the attitude bothered Atkinson but he waved it aside and placed his dish on a table close at hand. He carefully wiped his hands with a paper napkin and Ewing looked on.

"I appreciate it's only you and me and Virg Hoverton that knows about this, Neal." Ewing's voice was soothing and gentle, but his eyes watched for a sign on Atkinson's face that said he might suspect what was coming. The oil man's gentle features changed little.

"It won't be so when I get back to Omaha. It's only fair to tell you I'll have to involve my attorney in the matter. Virgil is good, but he can't handle it all alone."

"Yes." Ewing's eyes were hooded and lazy. He sensed but did not see Blocker come up behind him and stand waiting.

"It's about time, Mr. Atkinson," said the foreman.

"I'll be back in about a month, J.W." He extended a hand to Ewing and pumped it.

Ewing merely looked at him and turned to Blocker. "You seen to it Mister Atkinson an' his pilot got food and drink for the flight? Long trip ahead."

"Yessir," said Blocker. "Seen to everything."

Atkinson clambered into the front seat of the Packard, and rolled down the window.

"You'll see, J.W. Everything's going to be all right," Atkinson said cheerfully. Ewing smiled in return and patted him fondly on the arm.

"I'm beginning to believe you're right. So long, Neal."

Blocker shoved the Packard into gear and whisked Neal Atkinson the fifteen miles back to where his plane stood gassed and waiting, in Bear Paw City.

Ewing turned back to watch the dance and his eyes caught Ella's and held them for a split second, but he saw the fear rise behind the fading smile, and then she quickly was danced away and out of sight. He was content to know she still feared him at least.

The long shadows obscured Ewing from God and the world as the rancher made his solitary way to the fortress-like house. He'd been riding only an hour when he heard the sound of the Atko plane as it taxied for a takeoff far down the basin floor. Then the sound changed as the plane became airborne and began its steep climb. He raised his eyes and tried to see it, but the sun was gone, and there was no light to catch the metallic surface. He thought he glimpsed a running light, but wasn't sure, so his ears followed the sound as the plane banked toward the mountains.

Darker patches of blue-black showed the plane was heading into a storm, and Ewing wondered if they would even make it that far. The sugar would be forming a gum on the pistons that the cold air would solidify. The plane would drop like a stone in those mountains.

Now, thought Ewing, there's just the banker. And Frank Athearn. And Ella Connors. He rode peacefully to the ranch.

As Frank drove them back to the ranch, he tried not to think about Ewing and Ella and what could possibly lie in store for them, but found it difficult.

He tried to replay the moment when they'd trumped the buyer the day before, getting the price to six and a half cents a pound, even if they had to deliver to the shipping point, in this case a railhead close to the mouth of the basin. The delivery was no problem for there were men out of work now and grateful for anything that might come their way. Some of them were Ewing men, but since they'd been recently released from Ewing's employ, they bore Frank and Ella no grudges. Three men agreed to work a quick drive to the railhead and the morning of the dance saw the cattle safely packed and shipped off, the three cowboys paid well and paid off. It was a fine moment and Frank could savor it. But when he glanced at Ella and saw the worried set of her face, the joy was reduced to the anger he had tried to obliterate.

He brought the truck to a halt on the road that led to the ranch and turned off the motor and they sat in silence listening to the wind as it cut across the sage and broom-willow, giving an eerie night sound to the basin. The equinox had brought a new set of stars to the sky, with Orion's belt noticed and pointed out by Frank. She only glanced out the window.

"It's Ewing, ain't it?" Frank reached for her shoulder at the touch.

"He's going to kill us. Or one of us." Her voice dropped and Frank recognized the depths of her fear and didn't doubt her words in the least. "I saw it on his face tonight. And he knows I saw it." She shook as she talked. "I've seen him like that before. I was small but I saw his eyes and I never forgot it." There was no hysteria, but her fear of Ewing and her understanding of the ruthlessness of the man made her sense the possibilities in horrifying clarity. "I saw him burn people alive just because they held the land and I seen him gun cattle in corrals, shoot prize horses just to get his way."

"It's 1945." They sat in silence but his logic could

not outweigh hers. No matter how many times he told himself no man would be so brutal in this day and age, he remembered he'd only just been spared Ewing's wrath once before and he began to feel that what she believed would happen could in fact happen soon. "There ought to be something we can do."

She spoke very calmly now, her mind working. "We can move on and give in to him or we can stay and fight."

He shook his head, not satisfied with the answers. "There must be some law."

"Not in Bear Paw. There's just Ewing's law. You ought to know." She studied Frank now, wondering what it was that made him look for the most logical answer when there was no logic in what was happening.

"State police," he said, simply.

"You don't think Ewing's got their ear as well? I tell you, Frank, we can run or fight and there ain't no more choices." She continued to watch him, and felt relief as the movements of his jaw and mouth and head said he was accepting the possibility that they were indeed cut off with no place to turn.

It was Frank's turn now to study Ella and he did so intently. She was uncomfortable under the scrutiny. "What happens if you have to pull the trigger on Ewing, it comes to that?"

"I don't know." She pondered the matter deeply now. "I just don't know if I could do it. I've thought about it before, but I still don't know."

"You got to know. One way or the other. *I* got to know. You understand?" His voice was rasping with the pain this questioning caused him.

She said, finally, with difficulty, "Yes. I can do it." And she waited for him to say, "Are you sure?" but it never came. Frank merely reached over and gently touched her arm and said, "Good." He started the car and shoved it into gear, swinging them down the road to the darkened ranch. "It may come down to it, but I hope to God it don't." The autumn night swallowed the tiny truck, as Orion's belt rose higher in the heavens.

Virgil Hoverton was shocked when the word reached him the next day that Atkinson's plane was overdue in Omaha and no one had heard from either the pilot or Atkinson. There'd been a stop in Billings scheduled and cleared, but they never landed, nor had they filed a new flight plan. Lewistown, Helena and Great Falls reported no sign of the small plane. Neither had any of the South Dakota or Wyoming towns large enough to warrant a landing strip.

Two days later a search party flying over the Bear Paws returned with aerial photographs of the wreckage of the Atko plane high on the side of a peak and already covered by a thin powder of snow. There was no sign of life and it was assumed that if they'd survived the crash, exposure to near zero and subzero temperatures would have done in the oil man and his pilot.

Four days later a search party reached the wreckage after packing in as far as they could and continuing the rest of the way on foot. The news was grim. Atkinson and the pilot had both survived the crash, but had been injured, and the cold had killed them within the first three hours. The bodies of the men were brought out, but the plane was abandoned until the spring when it might be possible to conduct an investigation. But the truth was, the crash was attributed to engine failure and the storm they'd flown into. The plane was forgotten and left to rot on the peak. The matter of Neal Atkinson was over for all but his closest relatives and friends, and for Virgil Hoverton.

The accident alone would never have worried Hoverton, but the affair over the Ewing Ranch made him edgy at best, and now with word of Atkinson's fate he wondered if there might not be some remote connection. He knew nothing about airplanes, but Atkinson had boasted of this plane and how he'd acquired it when the military went begging for as good a craft. He remembered that the young pilot was superb, to use Atkinson's own words. He knew of the meeting between Atkinson and Ewing and how concerned Neal had been over the lack of anger or resentment on Ewing's part, or so it seemed.

What added to his worry was the telephone call from Ewing demanding to see him, and now. It wasn't the demand. He was used to that. It was the cold, distant tone that reached through him and almost sucked his life through the telephone wire. He had some vague notion that the notes he held in his safe were tied to this call, and both of them somehow linked with Atkinson's death, and he wished he could heed what the message was, but the connections he made frightened him so he blotted them out, thought how foolish he was being and made ready to see Ewing as ordered.

He assumed that Ewing knew of Atkinson's death, for it was the talk since the wreckage had been spotted and two members of the rescue team were Ewing men, Ralph Cole among them. He'd have the opportunity of telling J.W. what had to be done with the ranch now, but he wasn't too sure he'd be able to bring the matter up this night.

He packed his briefcase, and as an afterthought stuffed in the note on Ella's ranch which had been payed in full and needed only delivery. He felt pretty good about the two of them being able to make payment and was cheered that they found a special sort of happiness together. He'd seen them when they came in with the check from the buyer and felt himself knowledgeable enough about people to know that, under the banter, they were deeply in love.

He left the bank with mixed feelings. Joy for Ella,

and fear mingled with curiosity about Ewing and the ranch. He locked the bank, bidding good night to the tellers, then crossed the street and stopped by Stadt-lehoffer's for a bottle of inexpensive Scotch to take to Ella's. He knew they most likely wouldn't do it for themselves and thought they might even let him linger a while and enjoy their company.

Frank and Ella were, perhaps, the only ones in the basin who knew nothing of Atkinson's disappearance and who, if they had, would have made the connection with Ewing in an instant. If they had heard, they would never have made the decision to split up, Ella taking horses that had grown lean and bony during the months of work to some low meadows where they could water and graze. Frank went to Musselshell in the Model A truck for a load of wire urgently needed and left behind by an apologetic Stadtlehoffer. The German volunteered to go back in two days, but they were taking advantage of mild weather to repair fences they would need before the heavy snows made it impossible to work fence.

There were so few days before winter would come, they found they could not stick together for all the work. But they went about within easy reach of a rifle that if on horse, would be under the left leg, butt forward, and if on foot, within a yard or so at all times. It was a rule they hated, but enforced, and when one would be lax, the other would remind him of it and the guard would be solid once again.

They discussed this move that would split them, and in discussing things, somehow tried their best to convince themselves they were being a bit foolish. Perhaps Frank was right, and because it was a time when such things no longer happened, there would be no concerted effort to remove them from the land

Ewing thought his. But if they thought they were foolish for anticipating trouble, inner voices told them contrary. They were aware of every sound, every movement.

Only when she was above the ranch and hidden from the world by the mountains did Ella Connors let down her guard and ride with the horses until they reached the spot she'd selected for them. She dropped to the ground and removed the hackamores and leads, dropping them into a gunny sack, and remounted, leaving the horses to a few weeks of romping and feasting without the burden of man.

When she started back to the ranch, she reflected that it would be dark in a few hours and wondered if this would be another night they'd spend waiting for Hoverton to come by with the note, and decided in the light of things that they could wait for that.

Ralph Cole seemed to have taken over the running of the house, for it was he who met Hoverton at the door and showed him to the living room. Hoverton had never been comfortable in Cole's presence and felt the man a bit too far over on the vicious side. Now he felt overt dislike on Cole's part and wondered the reason. After Cole withdrew, he paced the room until Ewing came down the stairs slowly, not speaking, his face stern and forbidding. Ewing was a larger man than Hoverton, and he remained on the bottom step, emphasizing the difference, by that much.

"Yer lookin' quite prosperous, Virg."

"Thank you, J.W." Hoverton showed his nervousness and always had around Ewing.

"You wanted to see me, J.W.?"

Ewing motioned to a chair but never moved from the step. "Take a seat, Virg." It was imperative, and Hoverton sat after a slight hesitation. Ewing watched

the banker fold and unfold his hands over his briefcase. "You got to be gettin' along, Virg? Seems to me
you just got here."

Hoverton nodded and breathed shallowly. "I was
at Ella's. Left her a quick note to say I'd be by a bit
later."

"I hear she paid the note."

"Yes," said Hoverton and hoped the matter would
be left to drop. Ewing only nodded and stayed on the
step looking down at the man in the chair. Hoverton
wondered if he was sweating openly or if he was
clammy only under his clothes.

"You heard Neal Atkinson planned to take me
over?" Ewing waved the question aside as he spoke
it, but his manner was cold and arrogant, his eyes
those of a wolverine. "Of course you did, and he
come close, didn't he, Virg?" Hoverton looked at the
floor and said nothing. "But that don't matter now.
. . . The man stole from me, and you know how I
feel about thieves." Hoverton looked steadily at the
floor, then raised his eyes to protest, but Ewing's look
made him freeze and swallow air. "I know how to
handle thieves, don't I?"

Hoverton was drawn to nod in spite of himself.
"J.W. . . ." He began the sentence, but Ewing cut him
off by continuing.

"If Atkinson'd been stalled, I might have gotten
Ella's land, and I wouldn't've had no problem." He
came down and stood over Hoverton and gently
gripped the man's shoulder and shook him in a
friendly fashion. Ewing smiled coldly.

"But I ain't got Ella's and it looks as if I might've
lost the only chance I'll ever have, don't it?" Hoverton
couldn't and wouldn't answer. He blinked at the
rancher. "You understand what I'm sayin', Virg?"
He waited for only a moment. "You could've stopped
it, but you abandoned me."

"I didn't have a thing to do with it. She whipped

her problem and while she didn't come out rich, she's set for another year or two. But that wasn't me."

Ewing ignored him. "I suppose you'll head on out there and have a little celebration. Bet you even went and bought a bottle for the occasion so's the three of you can sit around and whoop it up like you an' Neal Atkinson did when you went through my books. That right, Virgil?"

Hoverton spoke up now, angry that he could be considered a traitor. "It wasn't like you think, J.W. I didn't have a choice in the matter."

"I figure you did."

Hoverton knew he had to go on with it, but could barely force himself. "I have to do what I'm going to do. I have stockholders and board members to deal with."

"That's the excuse everyone gives these days. Ain't my fault. It's the stockholders or the unions or the commies or some such drivel. Like to know why you can't be a man and admit you done wrong by the Ewings and face the music."

Calmly, Hoverton went on with what he had prepared to say in the near future, and was saying now when he wished himself a hundred thousand miles away.

"I have Neal Atkinson's instructions and I have your note to his family. I'm sorry, J.W., I really am, but I have to put the takeover into work. The bank . . ."

"You gonna tell me about the bank?" Ewing thundered at the man. "My grandpa built that bank, and I loaned you the money to stay open in '29, and you who'd be a clerk but for the Ewings is gonna tell me about the damned bank?"

Hoverton heard a door swing open and saw Cole enter, followed by Blocker, and they stood to one side, watching and listening as Ewing continued.

"You ought to remember them days, Virg. I never

failed you once. I trusted you. Put everything in yer hands, I did." He shook his head sadly, but there was vicious anger under the sadness and Hoverton felt it with every cell. "You tried to sell me out, Virg. Got to rank you with the vultures and scavengers."

Hoverton could hear only fragments of the statement as his heart threatened to explode in his chest. He felt Cole and Blocker come up to him, and tried to listen to Ewing as the rancher leaned closer and said, "You really disappoint me, Virg." Ewing nodded to Cole and Blocker, then turned and went upstairs, ignoring the banker as Hoverton screamed Ewing's name and begged for mercy.

Ella came in sight of the ranch just before sundown and thought that it had been years since she'd run on these flats that eased slightly downhill to the ranch house. Her mount was a favorite gelding named Parsons and she only had to ease up on the reins and speak the horse's name and he was off with the slightest touch of her spurs to his flanks, running for the ranch and still not pushing himself. She remembered how Parsons had always been a runner and knew him for a fine, surefooted beast, and therefore had no reason to hold him back. She gave him his head, but stayed ready for a problem and they flattened out the mile, the half mile, the quarter mile and slowed as they came through the gate.

Something made her study the ranch house as she rode up, but knew it for her own panic. She was alone, and Frank might not be back for several hours, and she remembered the time she'd spent alone in this house and laughed at herself for being overcautious.

Parsons waited patiently as Ella unsaddled him, but he was not through running and showed his desire by pawing the ground. When she turned him into the corral, the horse came to the rail and watched her every move as she gathered the saddle and carried it into the shed, then returned for the rifle in its scabbard and walked into the house, pausing at the back porch to turn a dripping faucet and scan the horizon for some sign of the truck, only to find none. She kicked the screen door open, shoved the wood and glass inner door and stepped into the kitchen, resting the rifle just inside the door, against the table. On the table was a note from Hoverton, which she read, stating he'd stop back in the evening.

Ella washed her hands at the kitchen sink, checked her appearance in the hall mirror and took the stairs one at a time, allowing herself to relax. Her hands and eyes brushed the photographs that hung in the stairwell and she thought how happy she was now, and how many years she'd climbed these stairs with no feeling to sustain her but the comfort of times past . . . her mother, her father, the early days with Dodger and some of the other hands that worked the spread in days gone by. Her world was a world of men, and she realized as she drew near her own room that she was glad she'd kept it soft and feminine. There was a warmth she felt each time she crossed that threshold, and in a way she was glad Frank wasn't with her. Just for a moment, at least. A moment of privacy made her conscious how great a part of her were the house and its contents. She turned the handle of the door to her bedroom, stepped inside and stopped short, her breath caught in her throat.

A shotgun barrel pressed against her throat above the collarbone. Ewing's voice was flat and lifeless as he looked down at her face. He watched the eyes. "Big time for you, ain't it? Cattle to market. Debts paid. New man in yer life. Quite a time."

She knew better than to move, and didn't have to look to know he had the hammers back and cocked, a finger resting on the double triggers. She was quiet and controlled. "J.W. This is crazy." When he said nothing, she continued. "Frank's on his way back."

"He ain't nothin' but a boy. You ought to know I wasn't about to let you be shed of me so easy. You ain't gonna block me no more. Not on the land, or on us."

"There ain't no *us*, J.W."

"Yes there is. It's jest you can't see for that boy." His eyes ranged around the room, taking in for her benefit the things he'd been looking at for over an hour while he waited—Frank's clothing, Ella's clothing, thrown loosely across the bed they'd slept in the night before and hadn't made. "He ain't the one for you, Ella. You know that. Boy's gonna gentle you to death." His hand came up and caressed her arm through the flannel of her shirt, and she stiffened.

"You're wrong, Jack."

He held her arm, studied her face and shook his head. "I know every inch of you inside out. I ain't wrong and you know it."

She fought to keep from running, fought to keep her voice calm. "I know you ain't no part of my life, Jack. And if you want this land, you'll have to kill me for it."

"I've given you all the leeway—"

"You don't give nothin'." Her calm was real. "All the years you been pretendin' to everyone that you been the one leavin' me alone, an' I been the one defyin' you. But you call what you been doin' to me, leavin' me alone?" She made no effort to conceal her disgust with him. "You talk honor, but you don't have the vaguest idea what it is. Virg Hoverton has more honor than you, though I been late in discovering it."

Ewing said nothing, but drew a veil over whatever feelings he might have had left for her. It was the tone that affected him as much as the things she said.

Ella sensed what she'd done, and instantly dropped the contemptuous harshness. She spoke logically. "Virg is on his way over here, by the way, J.W." The words had no effect. "You can kill me, but you'll have a tough time explaining the body to Hoverton."

He looked at her as if he didn't understand what she was saying. There was distance behind the expressionless face.

He turned, and reached for the closet door, saying quietly, "He's already here."

Ella's eyes dropped to his hand on the doorknob, not understanding, and then moved up to see bare feet hanging on the clothes hook. Her eyes dropped the length of Hoverton's body. The throat had been cut and not here, for the blood that covered his horrified face left only traces on the floor. "My God, Jack," she said at barely a whisper.

"He was a scavenger. I cut him like a pig." Her heart sank as she fought the sickness brought on by a new level of fear.

The Model A had stalled a mile outside of Bear Paw, and it had taken Frank an hour to make the return trip with a borrowed set of a tools necessary to repair the broken carburetor. He prayed he was doing it right, and damned the sun for setting when he needed it.

But the repair went well, and the truck started up, though he had little but common sense to sustain him through the repair. He never trusted his luck on things he knew nothing about, and prayed to whoever would listen. He hoped he could make it to the ranch where Ella, who seemed to have a mechanical mind, could fix the damned thing.

He lost power once, but the Model A restarted and he kept up his prayer to the truck, to the God of things mechanical, and to whatever had allowed the strange truck to exist as long as it had. He also had the good sense to thank the spirit of Henry Ford for building a tough and durable car, and felt relieved

when he could give up this litany, for the lights of
the ranch shone warm and friendly in the distance.

It felt good to be coming home to someone, and he
thought how he'd never thought about that before.
But then, he decided, I been thinkin' on things I
never knew existed, let alone never thought on before.

He rolled the truck right up to the porch, and
sprang out, his spirits high. He left the roll of barbed
wire in the bed of the truck, but took his rifle, then
decided against that and tossed it on the front seat.
His good mood carried him right through the kitchen
where the radio was playing soft western swing. He
smiled and took the steps two at a time, pausing only
to knock for a second at the bedroom door, and he
shoved it open with an expectant smile on his face
as he stepped inside and was plunged into uncon-
sciousness as something came across the back of his
head and dropped him to the floor.

John Ewing took his time, but moved with planned
actions. He heaped Frank and Ella's clothing on the
bed, carefully lifted the oil lamp on the nightstand
and unscrewed the cap and chimney. He poured the
contents of the lamp onto the clothes and bed, then
splashed what remained on the curtains and chairs.
He replaced the chimney of the lamp and set it back
on the nightstand, then fished in his pocket, found a
match and struck it, letting it take hold until it could
be dropped onto the clothing.

The clothing and bed burned slowly, then caught
and flared in the middle of the room, until the flames
spread to the windows and chairs. He swung the door
open and stepped out into the stairwell, closing off
the fire. He waited a moment, listening to the crack-
ling of the flames and then walked quickly downstairs, through the kitchen and out into the night air

where Blocker and Cole waited for him, holding the reins of his horse. He spoke loudly to be heard as flames rushed up through the roof.

"Shame, ain't it?" He glanced at the house. "Three of 'em, havin' such a good time an' all. Celebratin' their note payin'. Too bad. Little bit too much to drink, knocked over a lamp and the whole place went right up. Just like that." He smiled at the two men. "It's just that easy, boys." He turned his horse and led them from the Connors Ranch as the roof burned quickly and the flames spread through the house, even showing in the downstairs windows. He could hear it crack and groan as he rode away and knew in seconds it would all be over, and he'd have no worries, ever again. He felt certain of it, and held the desire to turn and look back until they'd reached the gate.

In darkness, and aware he was in pain, Frank's senses told him of the fire. He could hear it and smell it and a sense of survival brought him through the grayness and up from the floor of a cramped closet to his knees. He could feel another body, and his hands discovered Hoverton and the gaping mouth that hung beneath his chin. He recoiled, and groped to find Ella propped against the other wall of the closet, bound at her wrists and ankles, already choking on the smoke that filtered in through her nostrils and was blocked from escaping by a gag. His hands felt her, found the bonds and clumsily undid them. He was finding it almost impossible to breathe and he pulled the gag from Ella's mouth and shook her until she looked at him through smoke-damaged eyes. She nodded in the gloom of the closet, though she could barely make him out.

Frank shoved against the closet door, but heat

made him draw back. "Can't get out there." His words were punctuated by a crash as part of the roof collapsed beyond the door.

Ella was kicking at a small panel in the rear of the closet and as Frank turned, he saw her break it open and begin to crawl through. He slithered over Hoverton's body and followed her into the narrow opening.

The crawlspace led to the narrow attic behind the fireplace, and there was the small window of the attic that led to the outside back porch. She led him to that, not even pausing to kick it out. They went out, dropped to the roof of the back porch and poised for the jump to the ground.

The house began to crumble from the west, for the fire was driven by a wind from the east, and that freak of nature was all that saved Frank and Ella.

It must have seemed to Ewing that nature thwarted him at every turn this year, but his sense of irony failed him now as he turned to watch the house die and saw, in addition, Frank, followed by Ella, jump from the roof and run from the burning house.

In that second, Ewing panicked when he had never done so in his life before. He'd never lost his head, even in the worst of circumstances but this time he could not restrain himself. He clawed at the shotgun, dug in his spurs and charged them, screaming oaths at God for letting them live. He closed the distance with his horse reaching maximum velocity as he came thundering down on Ella, who'd seen and heard him, and was racing for any cover. The horse hit her and knocked her to one side as Ewing fired first one barrel, then the other at Frank, who had seen him at the same time as Ella, and yelled a warning as he dove for the Model A. The truck was hot beyond endurance from the fire, so Frank had broken a window to grab the rifle. But before he could lever in a round, he saw Ella hit by the horse and go flying.

Ewing leveled the shotgun at Frank and fired. But when the animal hit Ella, it stumbled slightly so the shotgun aim was off. One charge took the remaining windows from the Model A and showered Frank with slivers of glass. The second charge caught Frank in the leg and knocked him to the ground in pain.

Ella was dazed, but tried to shake it off as she got to her feet and ran for the kitchen. She remembered her rifle and was going for it even though the kitchen was hardly standing and filled with flames. She threw herself through the screen, grabbed the rifle and stepped back onto the porch. She could see Frank beyond the truck, crawling, reaching for his rifle, which he'd dropped, as Ewing pivoted his horse.

For a second, it was unreal. There was no sound. No movement. Blocker and Cole had not moved from the gate, stunned by Ewing's action. Ella stood on the back porch, rifle at the ready on her shoulder, and aiming at Ewing's head. Ewing had reined in his horse, and was shoving two more shells into the shotgun he'd broken open to reload. Frank had reached his rifle and was levering a shell into the chamber. Only seconds for all of it, but to Ella it was nightmarishly long. The heat behind her made her dart suddenly into the open, and a shot rang out as Cole broke the calm and fired at Frank, who was on one knee, bringing his rifle to bear. Ella turned, ignoring Ewing for a second, and fired not at Cole who hadn't moved, but at Blocker who was racing in now to assist Ewing. The shot took him in the chest and he flew from the saddle, landing, bouncing and dying against the wall of the shed.

She was aware Ewing was still behind her, saw Frank glance at her and as she turned, saw Ewing raise the shotgun, but with no hurry. He moved like he was shooting targets, taking his aim, and all she could do was watch.

Dell Bestsellers

- ☐ **THE ENDS OF POWER** by H.R. Haldeman
  with Joseph DiMona $2.75 (12239-2)
- ☐ **MY MOTHER/MY SELF** by Nancy Friday $2.50 (15663-7)
- ☐ **THE IMMIGRANTS** by Howard Fast $2.75 (14175-3)
- ☐ **SLAPSTICK** by Kurt Vonnegut $2.25 (18009-0)
- ☐ **BEGGARMAN, THIEF** by Irwin Shaw $2.75 (10701-6)
- ☐ **ASYA** by Allison Baker $2.25 (10696-6)
- ☐ **THE BENEDICT ARNOLD CONNECTION**
  by Joseph DiMona $2.25 (10935-3)
- ☐ **BED OF STRANGERS**
  by Lee Raintree & Anthony Wilson $2.25 (10892-6)
- ☐ **STORMY SURRENDER**
  by Janette Radcliffe $2.25 (16941-0)
- ☐ **THE ODDS** by Eddie Constantine $2.25 (16602-0)
- ☐ **PUNISH THE SINNERS** by John Saul $2.25 (17084-2)
- ☐ **CRY WOLF** by Wilbur Smith $2.25 (11495-0)
- ☐ **THE BLACK SWAN** by Day Taylor $2.25 (10611-7)
- ☐ **PEARL** by Stirling Silliphant $2.50 (16987-9)
- ☐ **TILT** by James Creech III $1.95 (18534-3)
- ☐ **TARIFA** by Elizabeth Tebbetts Taylor............$2.25 (18546-7)
- ☐ **THE PROMISE** by Danielle Steel based on
  a screenplay by Garry Michael White $1.95 (17079-6)
- ☐ **MR. HORN** by D.R. Bensen $2.25 (15194-5)
- ☐ **DALLAS** by Lee Raintree $2.25 (11752-6)

At your local bookstore or use this handy coupon for ordering:

DELL BOOKS
P.O. BOX 1000, PINEBROOK, N.J. 07058

Please send me the books I have checked above. I am enclosing $_____
(please add 35¢ per copy to cover postage and handling). Send check or money
order—no cash or C.O.D.'s. Please allow up to 8 weeks for shipment.

Mr/Mrs/Miss_____

Address_____

City_____State/Zip_____

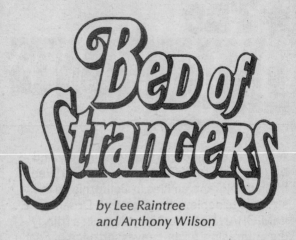